ATLANTIS
DYING

ATLANTIS DYING

RICHARD GARTEE

Lake & Emerald Publications

Books by Richard Gartee
—Fiction—
Orgone Gizmo
Atlantis Dying
Atlantis Obsession
Lancelot's Grail
Lancelot's Disciple
Ragtime Dudes at the World's Fair
Ragtime Dudes in a Thin Place
Ragtime Dudes Meet a Paris Flapper
—Poetry—
Mountain Breathing
Watching Waves
Canyon Falls
Arbor Encor
—Non-Fiction—
Skating on Skim Ice
The Hippodrome Theatre First Fifty Years

A complete list of currently available titles by the author can be found at **www.gartee.com**

Published by Lake and Emerald Publications, LLC
Gainesville, FL

ISBN 978-1-7363957-1-4

Library of Congress Control Number: 2021924679

Front cover illustration by Rocío Espín Piñar
Back cover photo by Cathy Withers-Clarke

Typesetting services by BOOKOW.COM

For Ken Elder

PART I

CHAPTER 1

Darmon, First Consul to the king of Atlantis, had never seen a mob before, but the band of men striding his way seemed to fit the description.

A change in rain patterns had caused a multi-year drought, and the crowd coming toward him looked like they wanted someone to blame. Most seemed to be farmers, but several burly-looking individuals among them might be the kind of agitators Nurlano, the leader of the Legislative Plenum, was rumored to be using. That thug in front plainly had never planted a seedling and wouldn't know the difference between a plow and a tavern bench.

Darmon glanced behind him and saw he had wandered beyond sight of the team from the techgnosia who were gathering soil samples. This did not bode well.

His heart raced as the swarm encircled him. He remembered his Mystery School training and refused to give fear a foothold. He closed his eyes and inhaled, using the incoming breath to raise his *enérgeia*—the cosmic life force within all beings. Then he exhaled, releasing all tension and fear. With his consciousness centered at a point between his eyebrows, he tried to extend a calming aura to the mob—yes, this was a mob—surrounding him.

"What are you, a child?" one loud voice said. "You can't hide by closing your eyes."

Darmon opened his eyes and offered a benign smile to the beefy man pressing in on him. He was a good head taller than Darmon and twice as husky. He also seemed immune to anything to do with peace.

Perhaps if Darmon had studied harder at school, he'd have learned how to project peace better. Too late to worry about that now. If he couldn't affect the men before him, he could at least hold on to his own serenity. "Serve the moment," one of his teachers used to say.

The man pushed out his chest, nearly touching Darmon. "What are you doing out here?"

"Searching for signs of water."

"We have no water to spare."

Darmon turned away from the man and addressed the genuine farmers in the crowd. "The king understands that, of course. He's sent some of the best minds in the techgnosia to see if they can predict how long this drought will last."

"That sounds like a job for fortune tellers. Why didn't he send us his best prognosticators instead?"

Darmon recognized the line. Nurlano often used it in his speeches. So these *were* his minions. But what was his game? Why send protesters to a mission of discovery whose only purpose was to help the farmers?

"Yes," said one of the rabble-rousers. "Send us the prognosticators. They'd be less destructive."

This brought forth a chorus of complaints from various farmers, mostly about the elephants his team had with them.

"They eat too much grass."

"They drink too much water."

Darmon didn't understand all the details, but he trusted the techgnosia knew their business. Some of the team collected different types of rocks and clods of baked earth lying on the surface, while others were collecting core samples from beneath the fields.

"What right do they have to be here?" the burly man said.

"And what are they doing to our field?" echoed a farmer.

Again, Darmon brushed the agitator aside and spoke to the farmers. "Let me explain. The elephants pound a hollow tube deep into the ground, then pull it back up. The plug of soil inside lets us study the layers of earth beneath us."

The leader obviously didn't like being ignored. He grabbed Darmon shoulder and spun him to face him. "What will that prove?"

"Perhaps whether this drought is going to last a long time."

"How?"

"I'm not an expert, but I believe they measure how much moisture the samples contain so they can tell how deep the drought has penetrated."

For as long as the Royal Archives had kept records, the capital of Atlantis had been surrounded by lush plains watered by seasonal monsoons that created agricultural abundance. However, in recent years, the monsoons no longer fell regularly. Last season, hardly any rain fell at all, and now the drought was spreading. Wells were providing some water, and some streams, rooted in the mountains, still flowed. And the king had emergency stores of grain to carry the population through hard times. But was this drought going to last beyond their resources? That's what he hoped they'd find out.

"Oh, it's not that bad," the thug in charge said.

But a farmer spoke up. "Not to you. You're not from here. It's everything to us."

Darmon sensed the crowd shifting toward approval. "I'm sorry for any trouble the techgnosists are causing. Once they're finished here, they'll move to another area, and then another. When they have samples from all the regions, they'll return to the capital and study them."

The agitator wasn't about to let him off. "Sounds to me like you plan to tear up the whole countryside."

"Only a few samples, some stones, a clod of dirt, that's all."

"That won't hurt anything," a farmer said. "We only worried about how much grass elephants eat in a day."

"And water," the agitator said. "Don't forget how much water an elephant drinks."

"He already said they're moving on," another farmer said. "If it will get us some answers, let the elephants have a drink."

The agitator liked losing control even less than being ignored. "Answers? From the techgnosia? You're kidding yourselves. They're going to claim it's a change in climate. They decided that before they ever came out here. Now, they're looking for something to back it up. It's a big waste of water, feed, and money. For what, some concocted report the king can dangle before the Plenum?"

The mob began to breakup as farmers drifted away. The lead agitator shouted after them, "You know as well as I do that Nurlano is the farmer's only friend in government."

With the farmers gone, Darmon was left alone with the burly man and his group of instigators. They began to press around him. "Speaking of friends," the leader said, "you've wandered pretty far from your herd."

Darmon was still preventing fear from overtaking him. But he *was* awfully alone.

The circle tightened around him. "Out here in the plains, outside the capital, city men sometimes don't survive long without friends. You need friends out here."

"Did Nurlano send you?"

The burly man shrugged. "It wouldn't do to name names. Let's just say I've got friends. Friends in high places."

Darmon looked around the group, now uncomfortably close. This had gone on long enough. Brutes thought their size and number give them power, but it is their very belief in power that makes them vulnerable. "Did Nurlano tell you what you were getting yourselves into, or did he just send you in unaware?"

Darmon pulled open his cloak, revealing the emblem of the royal court pinned to his vest, *First Consul to The King*. "Well, I too, have a friend. My friend commands the Atlantean navy, army, and the loyalty of all true citizens of Atlantis. So, I think you should want to be friends with *me*, not the other way around."

The men backed away.

"Nurlano has sent you on a foolish mission," Darmon said. "Ultimately it doesn't matter if he endorses the techgnosia's findings or not. What matters is what the government actually does about it. King Theop recognizes that dealing with this climate change is not a priority to Nurlano's supporters. Nurlano only cares about winning. And the reason the other half of the Plenum doesn't make it a priority is because they only want to defeat him. The king is afraid thousands of Atlanteans could die because everyone is playing politics."

CHAPTER 2

Darmon rejoined the techgnosists just as they finished packing their tools and samples onto the elephants. He approached his own elephant from the right, made sure she saw him, then patted her twice on the leg. She obediently dropped to her knees, and he took hold of her shoulder and hoisted himself onto her. He centered his weight near the neck and tapped the elephant. It rose slowly and lumbered forward. With each step, its shoulders and spine shifted, and Darmon felt the movement in his thighs and buttocks and rolled with it. The elephants carrying other members of the team had platforms strapped on their backs to hold boxes of supplies, samples, as well as the techgnosists who preferred not to sit directly on the elephants' backs. Darmon did. He found the physical contact gave him a sense of oneness with the animal.

All week, their expedition had passed the estates of the wealthy and villages of poverty. The kings of old had never intended this. King Poseidon's successor, Atlas, had divided the plain into sixty thousand lots, each of them ten by ten stadia, and gave them to families to farm. Rivers, lakes, and ample rainfall meant two crops a year. Lush meadows supplied enough food for both wild game and domestic animals.

But that was nine thousand years ago. Since then, some men intoxicated by wealth were able to get control of neighboring farms as bloodlines died out, hiring third and fourth sons from other family-owned farms to work the land for them. From those inconspicuous roots, the problems began.

The larger holdings produced more wealth, which made it possible for their owners to acquire more farms, hire more workers, and spread the contagion.

As more families lost farms, more workers came to rely on the jobs the larger farms provided. Which made it easier for the large owners to pay less, which gave them more power to take over farms. And so gradually, without anyone really noticing, what had been small ancestral farms that valued friendship more than possessions, had become a landscape of great baronies, and former farm owners were reduced to tenant farmers. By the time anyone realized what had happened, it was too late to reverse it.

Now, drought further diminished what little the tenant farmers had left. Darmon understood why they were upset.

Yet King Theop had not sent him to solve the situation—assuming it could be remedied, it wouldn't be by him.—His team was there to study the drought and report. The bountiful farming baronies fed the densely in-habited capital. Although Atlantis possessed the world's largest fleet and traded with many foreign lands, it would be unwise to end up dependent on foreigners or even her own colonies for daily bread.

The expedition had taken a week and had ranged as far as the great inland lakes. There was some hope there, for irrigation ditches brought trickling streams to thirsty fields. Elsewhere, parched crops withered, not yielding enough to feed even the farmer's children, let alone a baron's ravenous con-sumption.

The beautiful Atlas Mountains came into view. The highest peaks, white with snow, sparkled in the sunlight. He'd been there once in his youth, on a trip with Theop. The only time he'd ever experienced the cold, white, fluff.

With the mountains in sight, they could reach the capital that afternoon. But the elephants were thirsty and no doubt hungry. He spotted a small river flowing from the mountains.

"Let's water the elephants over there." He tapped his elephant to turn her, but she had scented the water and needed no guidance from him. Her gait picked up as she made for the water, and the other elephants fell in line.

While the elephants drank and grazed, he went to join Sprydion, the chief techgnosist, lying on the bank eating the pungent cheese he favored. "I'll need to report to the king as soon as we return. Can you give me a summary of your findings?"

"Oh, it'll take some time to finalize our results."

"I'm sure, but you've been muttering amongst yourselves as you collected your samples. Surely, you can provide me with a preliminary assessment. I have to tell King Theop something."

"I don't think I would want to commit to anything before—"

"I won't hold you to it."

"Well, yes, but I wouldn't want to give His Majesty a misleading impression."

"I'll give you something to report," the old astronomer, Iahms, said. "The stars have shifted position."

"What?"

Iahms had come with them because the distant plains, away from city lights, provided the clearest view of the stars that you could find, short of going to sea. At a hundred-ninety years old, he preferred not to sail.

He unrolled a large parchment, covered in labeled points, gentle arcs, and radiating lines of reference. "This is a copy of an ancient star map." He pointed to one particular point. "Look here. This star rose in this position every equinox until a hundred years ago." He pointed to a new dot, this one in red ink. "And this is where I observed her rising last week. I can say with certainty, the stars we see at night have left their seats and walked a few paces northward."

"Are you a poet or a techgnosist?" Darmon said. "And what could this possibly have to do with the weather?"

Iahms jammed a stick into the ground, straight up and down. "Ah, the answer is in why the stars have moved. If one assumes that Earth sits on an axis perpendicular to the universe like this, then the stars will never move in their positions. A star, let us say Sirius, has for as long as we've been mapping stars, sat here." He held his finger a little to the right of the top of the stick. Then he moved his finger over the tip of the stick. "Now, we see it here instead. And all its fellow stars have shifted similarly. Has the sphere of the heavens moved, do you think?"

"From your tone, I'm guessing the answer is no."

Iahms moved his finger to its previous position, then tilted the stick toward it. "You'll note the same shift occurs if the Earth's axis tilts."

"So, instead of believing the sphere of the stars has moved, I should believe the earth is wobbling like a top?"

"Which is more likely, our planet is leaning a little, or all the stars in heaven moved while we stayed in the same place?"

"I still haven't heard what this has to do with the weather."

"I think I can help there," Sprydion said. "Understand, this is not necessarily what is actually happening—that will be in my final report. But in general, hypothetical terms, we know from mariners' reports that the seasonal rains fall in a swath like a belt that girds a man's waist. If the Earth tilts, our monsoons may have slid south, like the belts on potbellied members of the Plenum."

Darmon nodded. "You might want to put it in those terms in your report. The king will appreciate that. And if that's the why of it—hypothetically

—how long will it last? What did you learn from all the tubes of dirt you extracted?"

Sprydion looked up at the sun. "Let's talk on the way home. If we want to reach Atlantis before nightfall, we'd best mount up."

It was an evasion, of course, but Darmon couldn't argue with it. He'd be glad to see his wife, Hathorah, and sleep in his own bed. Of course, first he'd have to make his own report to the king, and it had to be more than "Sprydion will let us all know in a few days". Fortunately, during the remaining few hours' ride, he managed to pry a few answers from the team's lips.

The beauty of the capital stunned him afresh as they entered the city. Buildings he passed daily without really seeing glowed with afternoon light, a vision renewed by his time away. The returning expedition crossed a bridge spanning the first of three wide canals that encircled the city. Merchant ships crowded the docks along the canals, bearing goods from all parts of the world, everything from barrels of wine from distant islands to animal pelts from the northern kingdoms.

After crossing the outmost canal, they came to the next bridge. It spanned a second wide canal, which was also dense with marine traffic, though more outbound than inbound cargo ships. On the other side of that bridge, the team left him and proceeded toward the techgnosia center, a tall white pyramid that housed the Tuaoi crystal, which provided power and light to the entire realm.

Darmon crossed the third, innermost canal to the center island, which held Theop's palace, the Legislative Plenum, and the Court of Supreme Masters. Above them all stood Poseidon's temple, its pinnacles covered with silver and gold. Its walls and pillars gleamed with orichalcum, a substance more precious that gold. Statues of every king of Atlantis since Poseidon surrounded the temple.

Some distant day, a sculpture of his friend Theop would stand among them. Hopefully a long time hence. Theop was only eighty-five years old. He still had a long life ahead of him.

Chapter 3

Darmon entered the king's antechamber and found King Theop staring out an open window at the Atlas Mountains, gorgeous in the evening light. "Your Majesty."

The king turned. "There you are, old friend."

Darmon made a slight bow—just a gesture, really. The room was absent of any servants or courtiers at the moment. Uncharacteristic, but not unheard of. "Where is your retinue?"

"I sent them on various errands. I didn't know what you would report, and couldn't chance anyone spreading rumors." He motioned Darmon forward. "Come, join me. How was your trip?"

Darmon crossed to the window and stood next to the king. "Disquieting. The farmers are worried. I'm worried."

"So am I. We should all be."

"Everyone except Nurlano and his cronies."

Theop rolled his eyes. "That tight fisted so-and-so will deny this drought until his wife is forced to make bread with sand."

Darmon snorted. "I doubt even then. Knowing Nurlano, he'll blame the miller." Nurlano was currently the loudest voice in the Plenum, louder than any other member and twice as stubborn. He had maneuvered his way into a post that held the drawstrings on the government purse.

Outside the window was a view that could only be seen from this height. Five concentric circles surrounded the capital center. Three were grand circular canals wide enough for two warships to pass each other. Separating the canals were two rings of land, dense with shops and houses, where most of Atlantis's million citizens lived. His and Hathorah's modest abode was somewhere among them on the second ring. In the distance, a channel fifty stades long connected canals surrounding the capital to the ocean. He could make out vessels laden with goods, coming and going in both directions.

Beneath the king's window, cargo ships packed the harbors made when stone was quarried to build Atlantis back in the days of the earliest kings. Elephants carried the cargo from the ships to all points of the countryside. On a quay below, a comely young woman watched two men her age, mounted atop elephants, trying to impress her.

Darmon pointed them out. "Ah, youth. Remember when winning the girl was the most important thing in the world?"

Theop smiled. "I was a mere prince, and you were an aspirant at the Mystery School."

"That didn't last long. You subverted me right out of my esoteric studies."

"Me? Subverted you? We were both young and sowing our spring wheat where we could."

"If I'd stayed my course, I might have become one of the Supreme Nine by now."

"Instead, you've humbled yourself by taking the highest position on my council, not to mention a lovely wife, Hathorah. Leave the spiritual business to her. Who knows? One day the old masters may tap her for their ranks."

"You think so?" The Court of Supreme Masters was the highest branch of Atlantean government, but it left day-to-day operation to the king and the Legislative Plenum.

The king nodded. "The Court seems to like her. And she's eminently qualified. I'd say Hathorah has a better than even chance."

With the composition of the Supreme Nine always being eight women and one man, her odds of making it were better than his would have been, even if he had stuck with his lessons. "Should I tell her?"

"If her intuition is advanced enough to be considered for a seat, she already knows. Are her students making progress?"

Darmon looked at the floor. This odd turn to the conversation made him slightly uncomfortable. He and Theop were friends beyond their respective stations, and certainly the king had the right to ask him anything. But his wife had become a leading teacher in the school he'd quit. So, commenting on her performance felt hypocritical. In their marriage they were equals, but in regard to their respective vocations, he felt unworthy to fasten her sandals.

"I believe her students are advancing admirably," Darmon said.

"Good. I fear over the next century they're going to need everything she can teach them."

One of the young elephant riders brought his mount next to a flight of stairs and extended his hand to the girl. She climbed to the top step, and he pulled her up onto the elephant's back and grinned at his rival.

"I guess we can't put it off any longer," Theop said. "What's happening to my kingdom. What did you learn?"

"Sprydion will give you his full report in a few days—"

"Of course he will."

"—but I've talked to our best weather prognosticators, and they believe this whole area will be completely desiccated in one or two generations."

The king blanched. "That soon?"

Darmon nodded. "Samples the techgnosists collected confirm it."

"And what do they say is the cause?"

"Believe it or not, according to our best astronomer, the stars have shifted several degrees away from their positions recorded on the ancient sky maps."

Theop stared at him for a moment. "The stars are not moving."

"No, that's just his manner of speaking. But apparently the planet is. The way Iahms explained it, our whole planet has tilted a little further to one side."

"Is there anything we can do to right it?"

Darmon shook his head. "If Atlas himself had a long enough lever and a place to stand on, he might nudge it, but barring that—no."

"I wonder if something might be done using the Tuaoi Stone."

"You're not serious? That crystal powers every light and pump in the land. But it's a small land and a big planet. Besides, if we remove it from service, civilization, as our people know it, collapses."

"It's not the only stone. There is a second on Tartessos, and a third on Ogygia."

"But whichever you chose, you would be sacrificing one Atlantis capital to save another."

"We don't know that," Theop said.

"We don't know if a Tuaoi crystal would help at all."

"You're right, Darmon. Talk with our techgnosists, see what they think of using the Tuaoi."

"What do the temple priests say?" Darmon said.

Theop turned back to the window. "What do they ever say? 'Let go of worldly concerns and seek higher realms.'"

"Sounds like my wife."

The doors behind them swung open. Two guards stepped through and stood on either side of them. Members of the Plenum seeking an audience, no doubt. Great.

Sure enough, the head steward stepped through. "Forgive the interruption, Your Majesty, but the leader of the Plenum, Nurlano, has requested to see you."

"As if he would take no for an answer," Theop said softly. Darmon struggled not to smile.

Nurlano strode into the room, followed by ten men and women, supporters from the Plenum, all bowing and curtseying. After Theop acknowledged them, Nurlano turned to Darmon. "I heard you were back. Have you put an end to this hoax?"

In age, Nurlano was approaching one hundred eighty, with more hairs on his liver-spotted hands than remained on his head. He had a weak, almost non-existent chin, and a voice like an old fishwife. But he had power, and many felt this qualified him as a leader.

Darmon stared into his beady, black eyes. "I'll want to check with the techgnosists, but I believe that giving a problem a derogatory label does not make it disappear."

Theop stepped between them. "Nurlano, you need to listen to what numerous techgnosists have told Darmon." He walked over and sat at the head of the conference table. "Sit down, all of you, and let's discuss this crisis. Steward, have the servants bring refreshments for everyone."

The members of the Plenum took seats around the table. Darmon pulled out the chair on the corner to the king's right. Nurlano sat across from him.

The king looked briefly at each participant. "I hope you don't have any plans. This may take all night. Darmon has a preliminary report concerning the future of Atlantis. You'll each have a turn to give your suggestions and ideas, but we're not going to leave here without a plan, even if it's nothing better than a resolution to defer the question to the Supreme Nine."

* * *

It was well past the darkest hour of night before the meeting adjourned and Darmon finally reached home. On returning from his mission to the outlands, he'd gone straight to the palace. Now, he quietly set his travel bag in the foyer, slipped off his sandals, and tiptoed into the main house, trying not to wake Hathorah.

She was sitting calmly on an upholstered chair in the front room. "Hello, husband."

He rushed to her and kissed her fully, taking in her fragrance.

She responded in kind, completely immersing him in her emotions, but seeming to do so without hurry, always in tune with the natural order. Gentle, the way a lotus opens slowly in the dawn light. The gossamer tunic she was wearing reminded him of a white lotus, too.

Hathorah ran her fingers through his thick mane of dark, curly hair. She had convinced him to grow it long. He didn't think he would like it at first, but now he couldn't imagine it being any other way.

"Nurlano give you a hard time?"

Darmon grimaced. "I've dealt with him enough for one day. Can we just forget him and go to bed?"

"Yes, but let's go to the meditation room first. I would like to raise your enérgeia up into your higher centers and cleanse the effects worrying has had on them."

"You mean the footprints Nurlano left when he walked all over me."

Hathorah kissed him gently on the forehead. "Nothing he said can stick to you unless you hold on to it."

"I know that." And he did, now that she'd reminded him.

"Then go back outside, wipe your feet on the mat, and leave him there. I'll light the meditation candle."

CHAPTER 4

The next morning, Darmon had hardly sat down in his office before Nurlano was upon him. Whatever Hathorah's enérgeia had done the previous night to repair his spirit was gone the moment Nurlano opened his door. He knew Hathorah would say Nurlano wasn't the problem, he was. But . . .

No, there were no buts. She was right. He shouldn't let Nurlano get under his skin.

"Good morning, Nurlano," he said as evenly as he could. "Did you think of something you forgot to say last night?"

He knew he hadn't. Nurlano had a trap-door mind.

Nurlano waved a papyrus like a fan he was trying to cool himself with. "You didn't mention *this* plan at yesterday's meeting."

"That? It's only a hypothesis. We draw those up all the time."

"This looks like the king intends to carve channels across vast tracts, sacrificing good farmland. The barons will never go along with that. The work will disrupt an entire season of crops, not to mention what it will cost our treasury."

Darmon patted the air like a baker smoothing out dough. "Calm yourself. It's only theoretical. The techgnosists haven't even—"

"More like a meddlesome, expensive proposition."

"We're a seafaring nation. What if the water level in our canals became too low for ships? Trade would stop. Naval forces would be stranded. The techgnosists were looking at ways to maintain canal depths if it ever came to that."

Nurlano crossed his arms. "Yes, but these plans draw water from the lakes. Why can't they refill the canals with seawater? There's a whole ocean of it just fifty stades away."

"If you'd studied techgnosia a little more, you'd understand how much power it would require to pump water uphill for that distance."

"So what? Isn't the Tuaoi crystal limitless?"

"I don't know if that's true. Perhaps we just haven't found its limit, nor should we try. Besides, the point you're missing is that water flows downhill. Lake waters eventually reach the sea naturally, anyway. The plan you're waving in my face would merely direct the water through our canals first."

"At too high a price."

"I agree. That's why it's not a plan we'd ever use. The king instructed our techgnosists to research every alternative to preserve our people and way of life. His mandate is to save Atlantis."

"From a little dry spell? Pshaw. We've weathered them in the past, and previous kings didn't bankrupt the treasury to do it. The trouble with King Theop is he's had all the money he ever needed since he was born. He has no concept of thrift."

"My apologies. I hadn't realized you'd started out poor."

Nurlano sputtered, "Well . . . well, I pay taxes. He doesn't."

Darmon was getting a headache. "Look, I answered your question about a plan for canals. I told you, it's not something we're even seriously considering. You shouldn't even have that. Where and how did you get it?"

"The Plenum has every right to know what plans the king is making." Nurlano shuffled around in his satchel and brought out a different set of plans. "Now, here is a better use for our money. My committee has been working on an act which will authorize funds to construct a wall around Atlantis."

"A wall? For what? Atlantis has the most powerful navy in the world."

"A navy won't stop the immigrants."

"What immigrants?"

"The farm workers. With this drought, the barons had to let a lot of their workers go. They're pouring into the city from the eastern plains like locusts."

"Why shouldn't they? These 'immigrants' are as much Atlanteans as we are."

"Well, be that as it may, they've still become a real problem, a burden on society. This wall will stem that influx."

"I thought you didn't believe this climate change was real."

"I accept that we're experiencing a severe drought. The question is how to address it. Let our agriculture workers crowd into the city now, and who will work the fields once the weather returns to normal? Don't you see? A wall will keep them where we'll need them when the rains return."

Before Darmon could respond, a page came in and bowed. "King Theop wishes to see you."

Darmon and Nurlano both rose and headed for the door. The page held up his hand. "Just Darmon."

Nurlano's face turned scarlet, and he stormed past the page and out of the palace.

CHAPTER 5

Late that afternoon, after a day of political haggling, Darmon sat on the floor against the cool wall of the Mystery School, watching his wife teach a class of advanced students. He was still as a mountain, waiting without hurry, just as he'd been taught when he was a student here. Somehow, the old familiar surroundings made the discipline easier.

Hathorah spoke to the class in a slow, even tone. "As you inhale, move the enérgeia up your spine to the point between your eyebrows. Hold your attention there, and at the exhalation release the enérgeia out through the crown of your head and let it hover there. With the next breath, direct the enérgeia to rise into the space above you and express in six directions, like a vertical line with an X across it. Allow your body to cease breathing and focus your consciousness on the expression above you." She paused to let her students complete the step, including a few stragglers who took several breaths to get it right.

"Next, generate lines of enérgeia connecting the four points of the X into a rectangle, then diagonal lines to connect the corners of the rectangle to the top and bottom points of the vertical line."

The octahedron. Darmon couldn't create even this elementary figure, nor see them floating above the students' heads. But he could sense a flux in the room's ether, like the shimmer of heat on a hot day. That awareness itself only came with extensive training. Maybe if he'd studied here longer . . .

"You now see the outline of an octahedron consisting of two pyramids, one pointing up and the other down."

He wondered, not only that the students could actually do what he couldn't, but that his wife could simultaneously keep the whole class elevated to the higher overtone required to perform the feat.

"Gently, resume breathing," she said.

Had he stopped? Her students apparently had.

"As the enérgeia continues to flow up and out your crown, rotate the octahedron rapidly on its three axes, creating a sphere."

The shimmer in the room intensified. He heard Hathorah speak to him mentally, softer than a whisper inside his head. "Darmon, my love, keep your mind very still for this next part, so as not to disturb them. They are only third-years."

She projected her next words to the class in the manner one might guide a child toddling on a ledge to safety. "Without causing the sphere above you to dissipate, carefully raise your arms over your head, palms facing inward. You can feel the aura of the sphere pulsing against your hands."

Darmon kept his thoughts as still as he could, but he wasn't the master she was.

"Be patient for a moment until everyone has found their place," she said wordlessly.

He waited for a couple of breaths.

"We're ready," she projected. "Together now, touch your creation and throw your arms up and out, expanding the sphere to surround Atlantis and outlying lands with peace and blessings."

Darmon dissolved in a flood of tranquility. It reminded him of the effect of the hot springs he and Hathorah liked to visit. They hadn't done that in, how long? And he knew that the feeling would spread throughout the kingdom. Even though most citizens wouldn't be adept enough to recognize it consciously, nearly the entire population of Atlantis was about to have a good evening.

While she resumed teaching, reiterating the basic steps of the day's lesson, he drifted back into memories of their youth.

He'd known Hathorah since they were children, but then, like most schoolboys, he thought girls were dumb. Well, most girls. She was clearly gifted, even then. But her gift wasn't her friend at that age. It made her different, and children did not tolerate difference well. They teased her mercilessly. One day, as his classmates tormented Hathorah, Darmon suddenly saw the wrongness of it, and stepped in. They'd been friends ever since.

Throughout their school years, it was just friendship. They were both too young for it to be anything else. Later, when girls began to have a new attraction, he and Prince Theop were too busy pursuing their options for him to focus on Hathorah that way. She remained merely a confidant to whom he could confess his follies.

It wasn't until they were both attending the Mystery School that he'd realized they could be more than friends. During their second year, she was excelling, and he was stalled. One afternoon, they were soaking in the hot springs, idling away a couple of hours with unimportant chitchat. He suddenly felt the rightness of their relationship as certainly as he had felt the wrongness of her tormentors when they were children.

A small smile played at the corners of her mouth, as if she'd known it was coming. And maybe she had. Her face leaned toward him through the steamy mist. To this day, he would swear a spark, a tiny lightning flash, jumped between their lips. He'd never been with, or wanted, another woman since.

Her voice pulled him back into the present. Hathorah's bare feet were standing in front of him. His gaze moved up her body until her eyes captured it. "Class is over," she said. "You can wake up, now."

He stood, and they walked arm in arm outside into a warm, fragrant breeze. He was going to miss this scent of spring flowers. He was going to miss her.

"There's something I need to tell you," he said. "The techgnosists have produced their report. The water beneath the fertile land has fallen deeper than ever before. The drought is going to get worse, and it may not get better for millennia. Atlantis will lose its ability to sustain its people."

"Oh, no! How soon?"

"Within a century or two. Theop thinks we need to prepare now, to find someplace to move the majority of the population, to keep the culture alive. That means the colonies. And he can't let the news of this leak out, so . . . he needs someone he trusts to survey the colonies to see if they can handle floods of refugees. Someone who already knows about the problem."

She glared at him. "Someone who is you."

"I'm sorry," he said. "I know I scarcely got home, but the king needs me for this."

He watched her finding her peace again. When she had it, she said, "When are you leaving?"

"With the evening tide; one of the royal fleet is waiting in the harbor."

She pulled him into her arms and kissed him. "I understand. Do you have time for a last meal?"

He glanced at the sun. "Barely."

They chose a harbor restaurant near the ship. A trip to both colonies would keep them apart for a long while. He wanted to be with her until the last second.

"Don't you have to go home and pack?" Hathorah said.

"I did that before I came to meet you. My bags are already onboard."

They found a quiet table.

"Let's have the flounder stew with dumplings," Hathorah said.

He nodded and ordered it. A minute later, their server set a large earthenware tureen on the table between them and ladled generous portions into each of their bowls. Chunks of white fish floated between soft dumplings in a buttery broth. Bits of carrots, onions, and clams drifted, submerged. Darmon brought a spoonful to his lips, blew to cool it, then sipped it. The soup lacked something. He took a pinch from a salt cellar on the table and sprinkled it over his bowl, stirred, and tasted it again. That was better.

He slid the cellar to Hathorah. "This stew wants for salt."

"I think so, too."

They ate, enjoying each other's company, largely in silence, exchanging affectionate glances.

Darmon stirred the pot with the ladle and refilled their bowls. "I had another encounter with Nurlano this morning."

"Oh? How was that?"

"I don't want to talk about it."

"Yes, you do. That's why you brought it up."

He hated to let Nurlano intrude on their time together, but he realized he had wanted to talk about it. "I started wondering why his short-sighted, self-centered, message appeals to so many Atlanteans. Has education failed to impart sufficient respect for the good of all of Atlantis?"

Hathorah placed a finger to her lip.

"I understand that not everyone is qualified for the Mystery School," he said, "and some of those admitted don't stay with it. But shouldn't the fundamentals that every Atlantean pupil learns make them aware of our techgnosic and mystic traditions, no matter what their eventual vocation is?"

She nodded. "It does. So, it would follow that Nurlano's followers are deliberately choosing to ignore the ideals that brought Atlantis to its pinnacle."

"Not all of them. The poorest attend school, but I don't think it gives them a real understanding of the mysteries and what they mean. So a lot of them are simply fooled into thinking that Nurlano is acting for the good of Atlantis. But the barons? They're highly educated, yet they seem sympathetic only to themselves."

Hathorah laid aside her spoon and blotted her mouth with her napkin. "The Mystery School doesn't recognize economic distinctions."

Darmon softened his tone. "I know it doesn't. But once it culls the most talented, what of the rest? For every student who makes the cut, fifty or a hundred highly developed, almost good enough individuals are left out. The wealthy can take the path to business or politics. The less fortunate finish school and find themselves stuck in menial labor with a heightened awareness of their surroundings. The disgruntled among them are easy pickings for Nurlano's party, who pretend to be their only friends in the Plenum."

The ship's bell rang.

"I'm sorry to end our dinner with such unpleasant thoughts."

Hathorah stood. "Don't be. Your concern for Atlantis is what makes you a good First Consul." She held him close. "It's also one reason I love you."

They walked together to the gangplank, dragging their heels even when the harbormaster spotted them from the quarterdeck and gave them dirty looks.

"I'll miss you," she said, "even knowing we're always conjoined in the higher realms."

He embraced her and whispered in her ear, "I love you, heart and soul."

"And I, you. Travel safe."

CHAPTER 6

Hathorah's eyelids fluttered open. Out of habit, she reached for Darmon and touched his empty side of the bed. She rolled onto his pillow and took comfort in the smell of him that lingered there. She sent waves of love toward—where? Somewhere at sea. He hadn't been gone long enough to be in Tartessos yet.

She could probe the ethers, locate him, and send him her thoughts. It would leave her a little tired, but not enough to disrupt her teaching. But she brushed off the notion. The ancient skills of which she was teacher and keeper hadn't been preserved for thousands of years so she could satisfy personal whims. She rose, washed, put on a clean tunic, entered their meditation room, and lit a candle.

She bowed to the images of Ascended Masters hanging on the wall and sat on her cushion. Although no longer in their bodies, they watched over the Mystery School they had established millenniums ago. Members of the board of governors, masters in their own right, were her immediate superiors and ran the school. But even they revered the Ascended.

Atlantis provided basic education to all citizens—literacy, the ability to manipulate numbers, at least the outline of history and basic principles of techgnosia—followed by at least one year of instruction in supernal studies at branches of the Mystery School throughout the kingdom. From these classes, they selected students whose potential could develop further at the main school where she taught. Many would be released with just enough knowledge to teach first years at branch schools. Some would leave the Mystery School to become temple priests, knowing a little more, but not everything. A few would become masters, instructors like her, and would be introduced to the true mysteries.

She stilled her thoughts and entered meditation, rising through the higher overtones.

When her meditation ended, she went to the kitchen, diced three black plums, and stirred the pieces into a dish of clotted cream sweetened with a bit of honey. She sprinkled it with a spoonful of crushed, roasted grain.

Vestiges of her parting conversation with Darmon nagged at the edge of her consciousness as she carried her breakfast to the table. To what extent had the practice of holding back ancient secrets for everyone but a chosen few contributed to the unsympathetic turn the Plenum was now taking toward its own citizens? Anyone who even briefly touched the higher realms during their year at a branch school should have gained compassion from experiencing the oneness of all. Why, then, would leaders turn gluttonous and the common folk turn blind?

Whatever had happened couldn't have happened overnight. Things must have been slipping in that direction for centuries. Then the climate crisis had split open society's complacent veneer as surely as dried mud fields cracked from drought. It would be too easy to blame techgnosia, though with each new application of the Tuaoi's immense power, less effort was required. Had that invited ever increasing inattention and idleness?

She knew Darmon was mistaken about one thing. The Mystery School did not harvest its members from the best of society. They looked for students naturally adapted toward study and lengthy meditation wherever they could find them. One did not attain the higher realms because a master infused you with enérgeia. It required hard work and consistent practice. The ancient mysteries were secret for a reason. You had to master them one step at a time, rise through each of the overtones as you gained ability. For a student to leap from ordinary waking consciousness to the highest realms without years of preparation would burn the student out and make them useless. Even the Ascended Masters weren't gods born with world-changing mystical powers. They were masters who attained the highest states of consciousness, then chose to retain their connection on this plane after they dropped their physical body. And that was rare. Over the last nine thousand years, fewer than twenty masters had made that choice.

She finished eating, rinsed out her bowl, and left for work. The stroll across the bridge over the inmost canal and along the wide boulevard toward the school took her past beautiful gardens, rich with a mixture of exotic scents. Whatever havoc drought was wrecking on the agricultural plains, city dwellers knew of only by word of mouth.

On the opposite side of the street, Nurlano and several members of the Plenum came her way. He paused and gave her a friendly mock salute. She nodded politely to him and his companions, but continued walking.

Nurlano wasn't her enemy. Not really her husband's either. But he frequently opposed King Theop and aggravated Darmon, who, with Theop, served Atlantis selflessly. Unlike Nurlano, who served the barons, or they, him—it was difficult to distinguish who was commanding whom.

She'd never told Darmon about the time she'd seen Nurlano at her great-grandfather's house. It was before they wed, while she was in her first year at the Mystery School. There was a large family gathering—her parents, grandparents, great-grandparents, numerous aunts, uncles, and cousins. Nurlano had brought a slate of candidates, hoping to elicit her family's support. She was a quiet girl, a fly on the wall, but already sensitive enough to detect duplicity.

So was her great-grandfather. "Nurlano, I fear these men you've brought into my home are too much on the side of merchants and barons."

"I think that's short-sighted," Nurlano said. "We are a great seafaring nation. Imports and exports are the blood of Atlantis. And merchants are the heart."

"That may be, but the Plenum's job is to enact justly for all Atlanteans."

Nurlano slapped himself on the forehead. "Oh, don't bring up justice or we'll be here all day."

Her great-grandfather folded his arms across his chest. "It's quite simple, really. Justice acts in the interest not of the king, or the Plenum, or the court, but of those who are its citizens—*all* citizens."

"Nothing in governing is so simple," Nurlano said. "But I'm here not for myself. My position is already secured. We've come so you can meet honest fellows who are standing for election purely out of love for the office."

Great-grandfather turned toward the candidates. "Is Nurlano saying you will forego your pay for the honor of serving?"

"Our families still have to eat," one of the men said. "But we expect only our just measure, as befits a nation's rulers."

From her meek position in the corner of the room, Hathorah perceived that Nurlano's men intended to fill their own treasuries by serving the barons, so of course they could honestly claim their motive wasn't a government salary. If she wasn't fooled, neither was her family, which soon sent Nurlano's party away.

She reached the white edifice of the Mystery School, entered, and put her mind on her classes. Time to begin her own service.

At the end of the day, she caught up with Xander, one of the school's governors, on the steps outside. "Good afternoon, sir."

"Hello, Hathorah," he said. "How are your students doing?"

"Coming along nicely. I wonder if I might ask you about something else— if you have time."

"Of course. Why don't we sit on that bench in the shade?"

They sat, and she made a quarter turn to better see him. Xander, she knew, was the son of a tenant farmer from out at the base of the mountains who had risen through the ranks. He might have the perspective she needed.

But before she could ask, he said, "How is your husband?"

"He's on a ship bound for Tartessos."

"Oh, yes. I heard that."

He had? Darmon had barely left.

"Well, then you may also know that he recently returned from studying the drought in the eastern plains."

He nodded and waited for her to go on.

"Darmon asked me whether all strata of Atlantean society are receiving equal education."

"And this concerns the drought, how?"

"It doesn't, not directly. But his expedition brought him closer contact with the country folk than most of us have had. Our conversation about his journey led me to wonder if we ought to do more to ensure that every Atlantean touches the higher realms, at least enough to know that higher states of consciousness exist and are attainable by everyone. It's not enough for priests to just tell them to believe. They need a clear memory of having experienced it themselves, and the knowledge that they can do so again."

"Isn't that what the year in a branch school is for?"

Hathorah sighed. "Yes, but do we know that the poor stay in school for that final year?"

Xander shrugged. "I hope so. I know I did."

"I'm aware, sir. But you are the first master to come out of a farmer's family in at least a century. You are extraordinary."

"Well, I had an extraordinary teacher. She just barely failed to qualify for further studies, but that gave her about the best abilities a branch school teacher could possibly have. She loved her subject and inspired us to love it as well."

"Fortunate for all of us, but Darmon suspects many rural children are pressured into dropping their branch school year to help on the farm. You didn't?"

"I don't remember that being true in my day, but we didn't have the drought then. It could be happening in the schools far removed from the life and culture of the city." He shook his head. "I certainly hope not."

"If an ever increasing portion of our society misses out or is squeezed out of our courses by economics, then eventually the ancient teachings could be lost."

"Oh, I'm sure the Ascended Masters won't let that happen."

"According to my husband, it seems to be happening already. Why don't the Ascended Masters step in?"

"Whenever Atlantis has faced grave matters, that is the first question that is asked. Their answer is that they are concerned with the broader scope of human development thousands of years in the future."

"But if they let what's happening now continue unabated, it could alter the future."

"One advantage the Ascended Masters have over us is the ability to recognize gradual changes that come at a glacial pace. Either our now won't affect the future or it doesn't matter."

Hathorah's eyes widened. "Doesn't matter!"

"What's happening right now may not have the dire consequences we think it will. The Ascended see from a different perspective. Honestly, if some farm children never get introduced to the deeper mysteries, are their lives worse off?"

"But that sense of oneness, of the connectedness of the world, must be enriching even if you spend your life milking cows." She bit her lip. Should she say more, reveal what Darmon was really doing? She decided if Xander knew that Darmon had gone to Tartessos, he probably also knew the reason. "If we hope to persevere after migration, every citizen—farmer or not—will need that year of Mystery school."

He stood. "I'm sorry. I have to go. Given what your husband has seen, I may have underestimated the problem. Thank you for bringing me your concern. I'll look into it further, and perhaps you should too. If the school is failing our mission to all Atlanteans, we need to know. Report your findings to the Board of Governors."

"Me?"

He nodded. "This matter has come to your attention for a reason. Good luck."

The governor departed, leaving Hathorah staring. She had been looking for possible insights she could pass on to Darmon. Instead, she had a new task.

Chapter 7

It was Darmon's first visit to Tartessos, Atlantis's oldest, most established colony. After being shown to a sleeping chamber larger than the king's back in Atlantis, and allowed time to wash away the dirt of travel, he was led into a ballroom, where the king's regents had prepared a reception they felt was befitting a king's emissary. A bounty of seafood had been set out on small tables throughout the hall—some served cold, some kept hot on braziers, with servants tending the coals. Instead of sitting down at a proper banquet table, the guests milled about holding plates heaped with shrimp, oysters, and squid in one hand and a goblet of wine in the other. Darmon found himself similarly laden and staring at his plate. A person would require a third hand to actually eat any of it.

He balanced his plate on top of his goblet so he could eat a shrimp or two with his free hand. But then he had to lift the plate off his cup to take a drink of wine. The wine was not bad, almost up to that in the king's cellars, and the shrimp was cooked just to tenderness and treated simply, with lemon and salt. But it was a tiresome way of eating. One should probably either carry a drink or a plate, but not both at the same time.

He was approached by one of the regents, a bald, rotund fellow with a broad, possibly inebriated, smile. "There you are!" He attempted to embrace Darmon in greeting, but saw his hands were full. "Oh, you poor man." He snapped his fingers, and a servant came. He waved the back of his hand toward Darmon's food and drink. "Take that."

The servant took the plate and cup from Darmon.

Once his hands were free, the regent embraced him briefly, and then pulled him toward the middle of the crowd. "Come, many here are anxious to make your acquaintance."

He fought the urge to glance back at the servant holding his dinner. He guessed that was it for dinner. He should have eaten more quickly.

The regent took a goblet from a man walking beside them, drank from it, and handed it back. *How rude.* Then the servant holding Darmon's wine offered it to him. He took a sip, and the man held out his hand, waiting for him to give it back.

Darmon saw the room with fresh eyes. Only half the milling crowd were guests. The rest were servants carrying their plates. Essentially, living side tables. *Excessive.*

Tartessos was once ruled by a king, Poseidon's second son. But as the colony grew, it was subdivided. Now it had ten districts, each with its own regent king. In theory, they were subservient to Theop and the Plenum, but given their distance from the capital, they pretty much did what they thought best for Tartessos. Resettling a sizable portion of the Atlantis population here was going to require separate negotiations with each district. And feeding and housing a whole new population was going to be daunting. The king was right to get the process started now.

Darmon and the regent, accompanied by the bearers of their victuals, approached a group with a trio of old men at its center. Gathered around them were their three servants, and three coifed, powdered elderly women —probably their wives, since none of the regents were women—and the wives' servants—a dozen people in total. *Definitely excessive.*

Introductions were made all around. A servant held an oyster shell to one man's mouth without being asked. The old man slurped the raw mollusk. The other servants held oysters to their patrons' lips. Darmon accepted his and swallowed it. Apparently, the servants also decided what you should be fed and when. He wondered if the man would wipe his chin and burp him afterwards.

He reached for his wine, and all the surrounding servants handed goblets to their charges. If everyone had to eat or drink whenever anyone ate or drank, he wasn't going to get time for much conversation.

"We're honored by your visit," said the oldest man. "But . . ."

He waited for it.

"It's introduced a disruption to our schedule." The old man coughed, and his servant gave him wine.

Everyone was handed their goblet and took the required drink.

If this continued all night, Darmon would be hard pressed to keep his wits. He took a tiny sip, and the servant took the cup back. "Sorry, if my visit was unexpected."

"No, we are pleased to have you. The question we were pondering is this: in ancient days, the kings met at alternating intervals of five years, then six, then five, and so forth. The districts have maintained that tradition until now. This is the first time in memory that we have all gathered when it was not a fifth or sixth year interval. So the question is, does this meeting represent a change to our cycle, or do we simply pretend it never happened?"

Great. He arrived, and they were concerned that he was throwing off their meeting schedule. How was he going to prepare them for the disruption when he flooded the place with a half-million Atlantean refugees? He took the approach he most often did when he didn't have a good answer. He said nothing.

His effort was aided by the decision of his servant to stuff a piece of squid into his mouth. The other servants did likewise. The squid was tough, gristle-like, and took forever to chew, which ground conversation to a halt. It resumed after another round of wine, when the third old man pointed out that if this meeting counted, they would have to redefine what interval to meet in the future. This sparked a heated discussion among the others, and Darmon took the opportunity to slip away. His servant followed.

A frail woman, older than the moon, pulled Darmon aside. Age had shrunk her to the height of a child. Her face, wrinkled as an unmade bed, possessed a gentle mouth and two large obsidian eyes that looked like they belonged on a newborn. A white pinpoint in the pupil of her left eye reminded him of the star Sirius. Although they had never been formally introduced, he recognized her as the ninth member of Atlantis's Court of Supreme Masters. He bowed.

"Don't," she said. "The Supreme Nine aren't royalty. Call me Aigna."

"Sorry. I thought the Court met in Atlantis. I'm surprised to find you on Tartessos."

"Distance is not a factor. When necessary, we can meet from wherever we are."

Her servant attempted to stuff a triangle of fried fish into her mouth. She slapped his hand away.

So he could do that? Good to know.

"Go fetch me a piece of bread and some of those little round puffs," she said.

Her servant left, and Darmon's servant went with him.

"The Plenum has funded the wall," she said. "Nurlano had workers start building it the next day."

"Already?"

She nodded. "As soon as you left. That's probably not a coincidence."

"How do you know this?"

"One of the Court's functions is to watch what goes on. We don't necessarily interfere, but we observe."

"But you're here?"

"I thought I explained, proximity is not a requirement."

"I'm amazed Nurlano found enough labor so quickly."

"He's hired the unemployed farm workers who migrated to the city."

"That's diabolical. Building a wall with the labor of the very people it's intended to keep out." Darmon shook his head. "Pointless expense, too. Since you observe things, I assume you know, if the prognosticators are correct, none of us will be living there in another generation or two."

She made a noncommittal grunt.

The servants returned and shoved a warm, airy ball of something into each of their mouths. It vaporized into a bit of sweetness he couldn't identify.

"If you think the regents of Tartessos will welcome the idea of relocating a large portion of our populace here, you have your work cut out for you."

"Well, not the whole of Atlantis. The king wants me to visit our colony on Ogygia, too."

"Regents in both colonies are going to claim they don't have the resources to support a sudden population surge."

"They may not have an option."

"I agree with the king about that," she said, "but the regents aren't wrong, either. Theop can't cram a whole continent of people into two colonies."

"We may need a third location."

"The Masters agree. In the meantime, if you can't convince the regents while you have them in one room, you'll have to traipse out to their home districts."

"Would that be easier, tackle them individually rather than collectively?"

She patted his hand. "Neither approach is going to be easy, but you have no choice. The king has sent you to succeed where a thousand warships would not. At home or abroad, all of us are Atlantean."

Exactly what he'd tried to tell Nurlano. Oh, well, he'd do what he had to here, and maybe learn from it what to do when he met the regents who governed Ogygia.

CHAPTER 8

In the morning, Darmon packed his bags. The fancy reception on Tartessos had turned chilly as soon as he revealed that the Atlantean leadership planned to relocate a large portion of their population here. Just as Aigna had predicted, the regents immediately declined. "We don't have the resources to support so large an influx."

"But Tartessos is on a peninsula," he'd said. "You can expand farther inland if necessary."

"So can Atlantis. You have an entire continent to your east."

"Our best techgnosists say the eastern territories are also going dry. Atlanteans are seafarers. We must relocate to someplace on the ocean."

"When men of techgnosia speak of the future," one older regent said, "I distrust their motives. Isn't the future the job of the prognosticators? Let the techgnosists stick to their geometry and astrolabes."

Others around him nodded.

Darmon saw the wisdom of Aigna's hint that he meet with them individually. So he changed the subject and let them brag about their districts until he wangled an invitation to visit one. The others jealously jumped in and insisted he honor them with a visit as well. By the end of the evening, a tour had been planned that required him to spend a week or more in each of the ten districts. This morning he was departing for the first and farthest.

He didn't understand what it was about bureaucrats that they seemed unable to sense the needs of people in the real world, but while staying in their homes, he intended to convince them to share. He had to succeed. If he failed, what would that mean for Atlanteans? No. Theop had chosen him for this mission because the king trusted he could manage it. There was too much at stake if he fell short.

A knock on the door turned out to be a servant who took his bags. He followed the man to the wharf, where they boarded a well-appointed galley. The regent was already aboard, sitting on the elevated rear deck in a cushioned chair. Two servant girls were cleaning and trimming his toenails.

"Welcome, Darmon."

Darmon handed the servant a letter and a coin. "Please give this to the captain of the next ship bound for Atlantis."

"Reporting to Theop already?" the regent said. "I trust you praised last night's grand reception."

"That letter? No, it's just a missive to let my wife know I'm thinking of her."

"Ah, wives do appreciate the romantic gesture. Have a seat." He motioned toward a nearby chair.

Darmon sat, and the regent nudged one of the girls with his foot. She moved next to Darmon and began unfastening his sandals.

He touched the top of her head. "You don't have to do that."

"Oh, it's wonderful," the regent said. "She has terrific hands and gives a delightful foot massage. Passes the time. We're going to be stuck on this boat all morning. May as well enjoy it."

Darmon enjoyed sailing for its own pleasure, the interplay of wind and water. He'd even managed to sail a skimmer the length of the passage to the sea, dodging around the great warships and barrel-hulled cargo vessels, tacking in tight quarters almost intuitively. Part of his misspent youth. But there was no interplay with the wind here, just twenty beefy, half-naked oarsmen in the well, plying oars. Well, at least, the trip would keep the regent in his seat—a captive audience.

Once his sandals were off, the woman placed his feet in a basin of water.

He leaned back and closed his eyes. "A significant portion of the Nurlano's followers continue to deny the basic facts of what is happening."

"Oh, are we going to get into all that first thing?"

"You said it would pass the time."

"I did, but can't we edge up to the topic gradually?"

Perhaps he *had* rushed into it. Things in the colonies might move slower than in the capital.

Waves slapped the side of the ship. Darmon realized he had put himself in the power of the regents. He had no choice. His mission was important for the future of the Atlantean people.

* * *

Two weeks later, Darmon had finally won his first regent over. It had required ten days of touring the district, with feasts at every estate, and letting the regent show him off to the locals like a prize hog. A fatted one. If he had to eat like this to satisfy every district regent, Hathorah wouldn't recognize him when he got home. Still, all the feasting had been worth it. He was leaving with plans for new settlements and figures for how many Atlanteans each would accommodate. The regent had also given him friendly insights into how to win over the regent in the adjacent district.

With courteous farewells, Darmon departed, a week behind schedule, but wiser in his approach. He no longer doubted his mission would succeed.

It would just take longer than he'd expected. He sent Hathorah another letter.

Darmon continued his visits, making his way through all ten districts. Along the way he wrote Theop innocuous reports praising his hosts, certain that his letters were being intercepted in transit and read by the regents. He also wrote regularly to Hathorah, telling her how much he missed her. If he'd known it was going to take him so long, he would have brought her along. Well, no, he couldn't. She would not forsake her students any more than he would shirk his mission.

His letters received sporadic replies—not the same as talking with her in person. When he didn't hear from her, he assumed it was because he'd moved about too frequently. Her letters were probably just in the wrong district or accumulating at the main port, and he'd get them when he left Tartessos.

CHAPTER 9

Darmon and Hathorah had been apart far longer than he ever intended, going on twenty weeks by the time he was ready to leave for the next colony. After he'd spent a fortnight in the first district, each regent insisted he spend the same amount of time with them. Such were the intricacies of diplomacy.

He wished to be sailing home, but Tartessos wasn't his sole destination. He still had Ogygia, Atlantis's second colony.

Hathorah, my love, can you feel how I thirst to be with you?

Well, if he stopped mooning and finished his report to the king, he'd be one step closer to home. Darmon had done his task well, convincing each regent that resettling Atlanteans in his territory would be a boon to all. More workers, who could open new farming territory. More craftspeople, more goods, a more robust market. In a western district, he'd met Milos, a young prince loyal to the king, and decided to have Milos carry his letter to Atlantis while he went on to Ogygia.

Darmon studied his notes and crafted a detailed list of how many additional people each district could accommodate. He wrote that the king could begin sending people to Tartessos immediately—the first groups would help build the residences for future groups. Of the regents he wrote: "Their words are slippery, even more so than members of the Plenum, if you can imagine. When they're together, they say one thing and mean another. Only by separating them and meeting each in their own district was I able to make contact with the real regents. Even then, they are fond of pompous language. Yet they have sharp wits and are not without cleverness. Fortunately for Your Majesty, they only assemble officially every fifth or sixth year. So, if we are expedient in relocating our people here, they should be well entrenched by the time the regents next convene. I urge you, don't dawdle."

Darmon reread what he had written, then sealed it. He located Milos in the courtyard, drinking wine. A servant approached Darmon and tried to press a goblet into his hand, but he waved him off and took the prince aside. "How soon can you be ready to leave for Atlantis?"

"Quick as a gnat flies."

"Good. Have your man bring your bags out while we say farewell to our host. We'll want to get to the port early."

Once they said goodbye to the regent and were on their way, he handed the prince the sealed report. "Keep this on your person and don't let anyone know you have it. When you reach Atlantis, go directly to the palace and seek a private audience with the king. You can tell his guards that Darmon sends his finest regards—that will get you in. But don't show anyone my letter or let them take it from you." He tapped the parcel with his finger. "This is for the king's eyes only."

Darmon was sufficiently confident that the prince would not accept a bribe, but Milos was young, and perhaps pliable. "Should you run into a minister of the Plenum named Nurlano, say only that you are in the capital on holiday and hoped to meet the king. Although it will be better if you can avoid him altogether."

The prince tucked the packet deep in his tunic. "You can trust me."

Darmon clapped him on the shoulder. "I'm certain of it."

He saw the prince safely aboard his ship and then inquired if there were letters from Hathorah being held for him. As he expected, there were two.

Elated, he next inquired about ships bound for Ogygia, and found one leaving tomorrow. He rented a room for the night and ate a light supper. The regent would have welcomed him back, but he'd had enough fawning. He only wanted a quiet night and retired to read Hathorah's letters and dream about her.

CHAPTER 10

With Darmon still away, King Theop was in his private chamber, girding himself for another day of arguments between the techgnosists and the Plenum's baronial faction. How had he allowed Nurlano to become so powerful? Not something his father would have let happen.

He pulled on a tunic and settled his beaded collar in place. He always dressed himself, a habit that had sometimes mystified his father. But Darmon had convinced him that having a servant whose only job was to tie his sandals was a little ridiculous.

He missed Darmon and his steadying counsel. His friend had been gone . . . it must be nearly five months now. And still no decisive report, something he could act on. Theop often regretted having sent him. Would a lesser envoy have been able to manage? No way to know for sure, but at least he'd have his trusted counselor here when he felt outnumbered —which happened regularly.

Theop took comfort in knowing Darmon had arrived on Tartessos safely and the only peril he faced was too much rich food. After his initial message explaining the necessity of visiting each regent individually, Darmon sent only occasional missives containing nothing tangible he could lay before the Plenum. He needed something substantial to shut Nurlano up. How that old man's voice irritated him. What good was being king if he had to put up with people like that?

A page appeared at his doorway and exchanged a few words with the guard, who let him in. The page stepped before him and bowed. "Your Majesty."

"Yes, what is it?"

"There is a prince in your antechamber requesting an audience. He's been informed that you're not available today, but he insists."

The king shrugged. "Who is he?"

"He says Darmon sends his finest regards."

Theop broke into a wide grin. The happiest words he'd heard all week. "Tell the guards to let him pass."

The page dipped his head. "With respect, sire, I lack the authority to command the king's guards."

"Guard!" Theop called out. "Go with this page to find this prince and bring him here at once."

Theop paced the floor. He'd rather it had been Darmon, but perhaps this prince—

The guard came in and rapped his spear butt on the floor. "Your Majesty, Milos, a Prince of Tartessos."

A young man in his early thirties entered the room and bowed.

The king waved him over. "Yes, yes, come."

The prince wore the brilliant indigo vestments of royalty. He walked with a regal bearing, betrayed only by his boyish face. Theop studied it, trying to puzzle out from which of his uncles the prince might be descended.

"Tell me, how is my old friend, Darmon?"

"He is well, Your Majesty. When we parted ways, he was headed to Ogygia."

Theop frowned. "I'd hoped he'd be there by now and ready to return home. I need him here."

"I'm sure he's reached Ogygia by now. We left the same day, as far as I know. But he sent me to give you this." The prince reached under his vestments and pulled a wrapped, sealed packet from his inner tunic.

The king snatched it from him, broke the seals and began reading at once. Then he remembered his manners. "Oh, help yourself to eggs, juice, fruit, whatever you like."

Theop smiled as he continued to study the report. When Darmon said he would do something, he kept his word, no matter what.

"This is exactly what I needed today. Exactly." The king strode out the door, then doubled back. "Thank you. You'll stay at the palace, of course." He turned to a pair of servants. To the first he said, "Run ahead, tell the Plenum I'm coming," and to the second, "Prepare a royal apartment for the prince." Theop was down the steps and out the door before he realized he'd forgotten to ask the prince his father's name.

Fanfare heralded the king's entrance to the Plenum. He seldom came here —it was their place to come to him—but this day he hadn't the patience to wait. The room was crowded with Plenum members, servants, clerks, and techgnosists being grilled by Nurlano's people. Sprydion looked like he was ready to start throwing punches. Everyone stopped while Theop made his way to the throne. It wasn't a throne he used often, principally ceremonial in nature, representing the king's presence in his absence. But he lowered himself onto it gracefully today.

The king turned to Sprydion. "Have you found a solution?"

"No, Your Majesty," he said. "If the Plenum stays the course we're on, we'll become a land of dunes. Ships can't sail the desert, sheep can't graze on sand, and crops won't grow in dust. Atlanteans are people of water, and the water is abandoning us."

Nurlano sneered. "Keep fear mongering and you'll have everyone walking around with scarfs wrapped over their noses."

The king held up his hand for silence. "Yet, members of the Plenum only need walk outside to see the canals are dangerously low, and our store of grain from previous seasons is not being replenished."

"We do not deny that we badly need rain," Nurlano said. "We only disagree with doomsayers who say this drought will last forever."

Theop shook his head. "I don't know that anyone said forever, but you have at hand the best minds in Atlantis. We should at least listen to them."

"Thank you, Your Majesty," Sprydion said. "The government must take us seriously. We estimate that we have less than two hundred years to emigrate everybody away."

"That won't be necessary," Nurlano said. "It won't be dry anywhere near that long. Besides, once the wall is complete, it will effectively stop immigration and thereby reduce the strain on our resources."

"By putting more strain on the abandoned farm workers?" Theop said.

But the old crow continued as if the king had said nothing. "I accept that this drought is real."

"That's a surprise."

"It shouldn't be. Drought is a concern we all share. Isn't it better to tackle it through innovation instead of running away? The barons have endorsed a plan we rejected earlier that channels water from the lakes. The barons believe the same aqueducts could be tapped along the way to irrigate their lands. That would solve our food shortage and keep the immigrants out on the farms where they belong."

A chorus of Nurlano's cronies shouted, "Here, here."

"I am prepared to bring such a measure for a vote as soon as details can be worked out."

That was met with a chorus of objections from the techgnosists.

The king turned to them. "You think it's a bad idea?"

Sprydion spoke for the group. "Draining the lakes will greatly exacerbate the situation and likely shorten the time we have left by several decades."

"Six months ago I saw the techgnosia's plans to build aqueducts," Nurlano said. "Now you oppose it?"

"It was drafted before we knew the situation and rejected for good reason. Darmon asked us to prepare various contingencies. We do it all the time. They are not intended for implementation."

"Darmon!" Nurlano said. "Where is that laggard?"

"On assignment for me," the king said. "In fact, his report has just arrived." He handed it to Sprydion. "Here are his calculations of how many Atlanteans we can place on Tartessos, broken down by district. He's even worked out how many ships will be required, how many trips, and the number of years it will take to complete." The king knew he had sent the right man. His friend had not failed him and had even won the cooperation of all ten regents.

Nurlano leaped to his feet. Quite an accomplishment for the old codger.

"Move half the people to Tartessos! The Plenum will not approve money for any such foolishness. Never!" A line of spittle formed on Nurlano's lip. "Atlanteans are not cowards who will leave their homeland over a little dry weather."

The techgnosists started to reply, but the king stopped them and answered instead. "It is not cowardice but wisdom to see the future and act in time to save everyone."

Sprydion held up the report the king had given him. "If we began transporting our citizens tomorrow, it would not be too soon. We have a lot of ships, but only so many passengers and their baggage will fit on each boat."

"Atlantis has the mightiest navy in the world, but who will defend us if you divert our navy to transport people? And don't even think about the merchant ships. That would completely disrupt trade and ruin our economy."

"Given a choice between risking the economy or saving our citizens, I choose my people every time," Theop said.

Nurlano turned a shade of red Theop thought looked particularly unhealthy. "I forbid it."

The king stood. Protocol required the assembly to stand. "It is not your place to forbid anything. That privilege is exclusively mine."

"Then I—I mean the Plenum—will refuse to fund it."

The king sighed. "We have been in a stalemate for some time, but now that we see Darmon's figures and understand how long it will take, we can delay no more. Your persistent resistance has kept us at an impasse. You leave me no choice but to refer the matter to the Supreme Nine."

"The Court doesn't scare me," Nurlano said.

"I didn't say it to frighten you. It is precisely their role to advise our course in matters of grave importance on which we cannot agree." He turned to the Plenum scribe. "By order of the king, this matter is referred this day to the Court of Supreme Masters. Prepare the document for my signature and seal."

CHAPTER 11

Hathorah was teaching her sacred geometry class how to form a twelve-sided dodecahedron in the ether when she sensed the presence of a second-year student standing quietly outside her door. Even a first-year knew better than to interrupt her class, but the girl wasn't advanced enough to keep her impatient thoughts still.

When Hathorah reached a stopping point, she walked over to the girl. "Yes, how can I help you?"

The girl looked at her with eyes as large as muskmelons. "I have a message."

Hathorah nodded. "Go ahead. What is it?"

"The Supreme Nine has asked to see you." The girl was practically dancing with effervescent excitement. "Imagine being invited to the Court of Supreme Masters!"

Hathorah put her hand to her mouth. No wonder the girl was excited. She was excited. She'd never actually met one, let alone all nine.

"What do you think they want?" the girl said.

"I have no idea." Why would they send for her? She was a mere teacher. Her husband was First Consul to the king, yes, but nothing in his job involved her. And in her areas of expertise, every member of the Court was more advanced than she.

Hathorah dismissed her class and went home to change. She selected a long, dark tunic suitable to the seriousness of the occasion, but still couldn't fathom what use she'd be to the high court. The Mystery School didn't involve itself in politics.

As she crossed the threshold of the great white edifice that housed the Court, a woman in a flowing robe met her in the hallway and led her into a cool, dimly lit room. Nine upholstered chairs with leather armrests were set in a circle. Sconces on the stone walls cast pinkish-lavender light, drawn from the Tuaoi Crystal through sympathetic vibration. The woman placed a straight-back chair on a circular platform in the center of the room. "Please sit here."

Hathorah did as she was instructed, but grew uneasy. This was all very strange. Still, it wouldn't do to meet these masters in any state of disquiet. They'd sense it in a heartbeat. She closed her eyes and used her breath to dispel her fears, telling herself that sitting at the focal point of nine magnifying lenses was perfectly safe. She deepened her meditation until she waited without concept of time.

After—she didn't know how long—she gradually returned to this plane. When she opened her eyes, she saw the surrounding chairs had been filled. Ancient eyes looked back at her with kindness, some from faces wrinkled as raisins, others had the faces of babies, but all of them were centuries older than she.

The woman across from her appeared no taller than a child, her head barely reaching the top of her chair back. The pupil of her left eye had a white star in it. Her wrinkled face smoothed slightly as she spoke. "Welcome, Hathorah. Thank you for coming."

"I am honored. And also puzzled as to how I can be of service."

The platform holding Hathorah's chair rotated slightly as the only man in the group spoke. "It is a time of unease. Changes in the planet's rotational axis have disturbed many Atlanteans and raised questions of how long this drought will go on."

It turned again when one of the other women spoke. She found herself gripping the armrests. "There are opportunists who seek to profit off their fellow citizens. This is easily done when fear mongers alarm the people."

"I'm sure that's not the techgnosists' intention," Hathorah said.

"I'm not speaking of the techgnosists, or the prognosticators, either. There are others who, whether from malice or ignorance, precipitate evil."

"You mean Nurlano?" Hathorah said. "He doesn't love doing evil, he loves power."

The woman nodded. "He deceives himself and others by convincing them he is acting in the best interest of Atlantis. That is his evil."

The man cleared his throat, causing Hathorah's chair to turn again. "We feel it's necessary that all nine of us remain available in case we're needed. . . For balance, you understand?"

She didn't.

"Yet, someone has to, and Aigna–" He gestured toward the woman with the star in her pupil. "– believes you've reached the necessary dimensional overtones to be capable—"

"Oh, stop," said another woman. "You're only confusing Hathorah. Let Aigna explain."

She was growing used to the rotations of her platform and stopped paying them any mind. Whatever this was about was important.

Aigna sat up straighter. "Whales possess the longest-term collective memory on the planet. Within their tremendous brains, they have archived the history of every climate change since they first entered the ocean. Maybe even before that, we aren't sure. Lacking written language, they have passed these memories from generation to generation and species to species as they evolved."

Interesting, but what did that have to do with her? Or them, for that matter?

"The king left it to us to decide a matter that requires more information than anyone alive today possesses. We are certain that the whales preserved this knowledge. But they do not organize their thoughts like we do. The only way to understand them fully is for one of us to enter the mind of a willing whale, swim with their pod, and remain with them until we ascertain the answer."

The man fixed her with his stare. "It has to be someone evolved, but we can't spare any of us during this crisis. Don't you see?"

She thought she saw where this was headed, but . . . no. That wasn't possible.

Aigna took over. "Hathorah, it's a lot we're asking. You could be gone for years. But of the entire faculty at your school, we think you are the only one who could succeed."

Flattery. And what of her students?

Aigna read her mind, of course. "Others, fine teachers, can take over your classes, but they are not able to take on this task. You can."

"I don't know how to do what you're asking."

"No, but you are already at the next level. Everything you need to know will come to you as you need it."

The assemblage was silent.

Awaiting her decision, she supposed. Of all the things she could have imagined the Court wanting from her when she was summoned, this was farthest from her mind. She looked around the circle. "I will. What do I do?"

The woman next to Aigna answered, "You will enter a chamber in the Temple of Poseidon. We will help you find a willing host. Once you have merged, a priest or priestess will lock the chamber. You will unlock it when you emerge."

"What about Darmon?"

"I'm afraid you'll be out of contact," Aigna said. "While you are quite advanced, don't expect that you can swim in a whale's mind and communicate as a human at the same time. However, we Nine will take turns constantly monitoring your situation. Should you get in trouble, you will be able to reach out to one of us."

There wasn't really a choice. Atlantis needed her. If Darmon were here, he'd understand.

CHAPTER 12

Theop stood at the window overlooking the Atlas mountains. It was hard to believe this land, with all of its beauties, would have to be abandoned.

But not quickly. With the fate of Atlantis now handed over to the Court, Theop expected things to slow to a glacial pace. The Supreme Nine rarely rushed. Tension over the whole affair had his muscles in knots. He could use a good soak in Atlantis's hot and cold springs.

He remembered young prince Milos who had conveyed Darmon's report and whom he had offhandedly dismissed in his rush to the Plenum. Perhaps Milos was due more than a cursory wave of the royal hand.

Theop pointed to a page. "Find the Prince who arrived from Tartessos two days ago. We gave him an apartment somewhere in the palace."

"Yes, Your Majesty. I know the man you mean."

"Invite him to take the waters with me."

"Yes, Your Majesty. What time shall I say you are going?"

Theop shifted his spine and heard it crack, yielding momentary release. "As soon as you locate him."

The page returned in short order, with Milos in tow. The prince bowed. "I am honored, Your Majesty."

"I apologize for not giving you a more gracious welcome when you arrived. Matters of state took precedence."

"I am just a messenger. I did my duty without expectations."

"That wasn't exactly the reception Darmon received on Tartessos, though."

The tips of Milos's ears turned red. "Certainly not. Every district hosted him. Every regent threw him lavish banquets."

Theop smiled to himself, knowing how little his First Consul cared for fawning pretense.

"So shall we." Theop turned to his major-domo. "Organize a welcome reception and feast for the prince at the end of this week." To Milos, he said, "If you have family or friends in Atlantis, provide my staff their names so they may be invited."

Milos put his palms together and made a slight bow. "Your Majesty is too kind. But the only soul I know in the capital is you."

"Then we should get better acquainted. Let's be on our way."

The king, the prince, two servants and two guards left the palace and made their way to a grotto, where natural spring-fed pools spilled over rock ledges, creating waterfalls into additional pools below. The water was hottest in the pool at the source, where the hot springs gushed to the surface, then tempered as it flowed into the lower pools. This natural arrangement allowed bathers to choose a temperature that suited them.

At the base of the hottest waterfall, servants unfastened their sandals. Theop slipped off his tunic and eased into the springs. Milos doffed his tunic and tested the water with his toe. "Oh, very hot!"

"Enter gradually," the king said. "You'll get used to it."

Milos sat on the rock edge and dangled his feet in. His pale skin turned pink all the way up his calves.

Theop's muscles began to unknot. He walked through the shoulder-deep water and stood beneath the waterfall, letting it pound his shoulders and back. He leaned into it and let it cascade over his scalp and face. After the falls had thoroughly beaten the kinks out of his muscles, he made his way back to Milos, now immersed to his waist.

"Duck all the way under," Theop said. "Then we'll cool off."

Milos submerged for a split-second, then leaped up and crawled onto the ledge like a lobster escaping from a pot. The hottest spring did take some getting used to. Theop climbed out and led Milos to a second waterfall some distance away. "This one's from the cold spring."

Theop stepped beneath the falls and relished the sudden icy shower. If a person were hot enough, the first moments weren't that cold. Refreshed, he stepped out of the flow. "Bracing! Try it."

Milos tested the water with his hand and looked at the king. He hesitated, then dashed through the falling water and stopped beside Theop, shaking off water like a dog.

The king laughed. "Each of these pools is a different temperature. Let us find one where you can be comfortable."

They tested several, and true to his word, Theop let the prince pick, refusing to even hint at his own preference. Once Milos had chosen a pool the temperature of warm soup, and they were immersed up to their necks, the servants brought goblets filled with lemon water.

Theop took a sip, then said, "Is your apartment in the palace acceptable?"

"Very comfortable, Your Majesty. More than I could have asked for."

"You said earlier that you have no acquaintances in Atlantis. No one in the Plenum, none of the barons?"

"That's right. This is my first time in the capital."

"What about your education? Didn't your family send you here for your year of Mystery School?"

"My father took ill in what was to be my first year, so rather than send me here, one of the Mystery School governors came to Tartessos to tutor me."

That fact bespoke a family of significant influence. Even Theop wasn't offered a private tutor, not that he'd minded. Attending the school had been a way to get out of the palace and make friends with students like Darmon and Hathorah.

"So, are you destined to take your father's place?"

"Hardly. I am fourth-born and will never reach the head of the line. My eldest brother and his heirs will carry the family forward."

Heir apparent since birth, Theop had never considered how a prince in a lesser position would occupy his time. "What are your duties on Tartessos?"

Milos moved the water with his hand. "I have none. I've longed for some way I could be of service. When Darmon charged me to carry his letter to you in secret, I jumped at the chance."

"Secret?"

"Yes. He told me to hide it on my person, not let anyone know I had it, and give it only to you."

Theop nodded. "That you did. And you never said a word to anyone?"

"Oh, no one, Your Majesty. Darmon also told me not to reveal the purpose of my trip to a certain minister of the Plenum. But I never ran into him."

"Nurlano?"

"Yes, that's the name."

"He'll be at your banquet. Inviting him is unavoidable."

"What should I say to him?"

"Well, at this point, he and all of the Plenum know the contents of the letter, although not who brought it. So I don't think you need to worry about keeping secrets. What were Darmon's instructions?"

"He told me to say only that I was here on holiday and hoped to meet the king. But he thought it better for me to avoid the man all together."

"That won't be possible at your banquet. Still, being a prince on holiday may prove useful."

Milos paled. "Is it right to lie to a member of the Plenum?"

"Where is the lie? You are a visiting prince. You have met the king. Since you have no pressing duties at home, extend your stay in Atlantis, and it becomes a holiday."

Milos bowed his head. "If Your Majesty wishes."

"His Majesty does. You may keep your apartment at the palace until you are recalled home."

"That's unlikely to ever happen. I've told you, I have no responsibilities on Tartessos, but I am eager to make some contribution. If, while I'm here, I could be of any service to Your Majesty in any way, you need only command me."

The king patted Milos's shoulder. "I prefer to ask rather than command. My father used to say, 'A willing subject is more faithful.'"

"Oh, I am your most faithful subject."

Theop sensed no guile in the prince. His words were those of a man whose naivety had never been pierced by thorny politics. Darmon was the king's most reliable judge of character. If he deemed Milos trustworthy, the man must be.

A stranger to intrigue, yet of a rank to move freely through all strata of Atlantean society, he could pick up useful conversations. With his First Consul absent, it would be good to have a confidant loyal only to the throne. He need only teach Milos to listen more than he spoke. Not difficult around courtiers and politicians who preferred the sound of their own voices.

Tensions in the king's back and neck had eased. He looked at his hands. The skin on his fingers puckered like wrinkled prunes. "Let's return to the palace and hear the plans for your welcome banquet."

CHAPTER 13

In many respects, the buildings in Ogygia colony resembled Atlantis, as well they should. The tallest peak on the island was named Mount Atlantis, a friendly reminder whose land this was. The island offered good ports that could handle many ships and would allow Atlantean merchants to continue their brisk trade. It was not as large as the capital, but Darmon could see residents would feel at home here.

The farms he visited further inland raised fava beans, barley, artichokes, cauliflower, endives, fennel, garlic, and onions. Orchards yielded olives, figs, loquats, apricots, peaches, plums, grapes, and tiny sweet pears. Despite this agricultural abundance, it was becoming clear two colonies would not hold all the Atlanteans. The fundamental problem was water. Being an island, Ogygia had limited fresh water—enough for now, but not if he doubled the population.

He needed to find a third location, a task he didn't relish. Dividing the Atlanteans among several lands would ensure adequate resources for all, but bring with it the risk of their society growing apart into three or more cultures, without the esteem of the ancient capital to hold them together. There was also the pain of separation, a feeling he was experiencing fully at the moment. He missed Hathorah.

Darmon worried. He'd been sending her letters with departing ships just as he'd done on Tartessos but had yet to receive a reply. If she'd received even one letter from Ogygia, she'd have his new address. He went to the port and asked, again. No letter.

If the salvation of Atlantis didn't depend on him, he'd board the next ship home. But he couldn't. When you're the only man who can do the task put before you, then it's up to you to do that task. But could he? His absence from Hathorah caused an ache in his heart more painful than a wound. The same anguish he would bring upon his people by separating thousands of them across three colonies.

It wasn't like her not to have written back. What if . . . ?

A sharp pain struck his chest, and he couldn't breathe. Darmon fell into a seat at a small table outside a tavern near the wharf and rubbed his sternum with his knuckles. When the agony abated, he asked a server to bring him wine. Mediterranean breezes carried the smell of salt air and drying fishing nets. His skin felt clammy.

The server returned, set two goblets and a flagon of wine on his table, and filled his cup.

"Thank you, but I'm drinking alone." Darmon took a sip. Sweet, with a hint of mulberry. Well, why not?

"Why not, indeed," said the old woman now sitting across from him, gazing out to sea.

He studied her wrinkled profile. It seemed vaguely familiar. She turned to face him, and he recognized those eyes. "Aigna?"

"Aren't you going to pour me some?"

"Of course, forgive my manners." He poured. "You're here. But how?"

She fixed him with the stare of a strict school teacher. "How did you get here?"

"By ship, of course."

"Then why ask such an obvious question?"

This was the part of school he never liked. Having questions answered with more questions.

"Far better to ask me, 'What news from Atlantis?'"

"You've been there since I last saw you?"

She sniffed, as though he'd again asked the wrong question.

"Sorry. What news from Atlantis?"

"Aside from the Plenum being selfish, self-centered, and wasting time? Of course, that's just one opinion—others are free to form their own."

That didn't sound good. Now he started to worry, not only for Hathorah but also for the king. Oh, well, with such a mass emigration, a certain level of chaos could be expected.

Aigna frowned. "It would be if anyone were leaving."

Had he said that out loud? And . . . what? "You mean the people haven't left for Tartessos yet?"

She shook her head. "Nurlano is telling the populace they are in no danger and Atlantis is perfectly safe."

"Didn't the king receive my report?"

"Oh, yes. And the techgnosists agree that time is short and water is disappearing. But the Plenum refused him the funds. They're currently at a stalemate. The king has sent the matter to the Supreme Nine."

"Then why are you here instead of meeting with the court? This is literally the most important decision the court will ever make."

"I told you when we met on Tartessos, the Court does not have to be in the same place to meet. Thought is instantaneous. Besides, we have the best person for the job working on it as we speak."

Who was he to tell one of the Nine how to do her job? Best to shut up and do his.

"However, you will be interested to know that Nurlano reversed his position on the aqueducts and had the Plenum pass an act authorizing their construction."

It wasn't like Nurlano to change his mind about anything. He wondered what caused that.

"His supporters, the barons, realize if the government builds aqueducts, they can siphon water from them to irrigate their fields."

He was beginning to take it for granted that he didn't have to speak out loud. Darmon made a quick calculation. "Well, so long as they don't divert too much, it might buy us more time."

"I wouldn't count on it."

That seemed foreboding. Did she mean the aqueducts wouldn't buy them time, or the barons couldn't be trusted? In either case, there was nothing he could do about it until he got back home, where he could advise the king in person. Obviously, letters weren't enough. He wouldn't have known Nurlano thwarted his plan to send people to Tartessos or started building aqueducts if Aigna hadn't shown up. He needed to quit this journey and return to Hathorah as soon as possible.

He poured a little more wine in her glass, although she'd barely taken two sips. "It's the strangest thing. I haven't heard from my wife since I left Tartessos. I'm frightened something has happened. Do you know a teacher at the Mystery School named Hathorah?"

Aigna made a slight nod.

"You're the first person to bring me word of what's going on in Atlantis. Have you heard of anything befalling her?"

Aigna's eyes flicked away for a microsecond.

"You do know something."

"I know nothing bad has happened to her."

"Tell me!"

"If she were here with us now, she would advise you not to give into fear. Fear is the great obstructer. It blocks the natural flow of enérgeia."

He jumped up from his chair. "Telling me to stop feeling fear is only making the fear worse."

"Sit down."

"No." But he sat anyway. "I need to speak to Hathorah. Right now. To know she's all right. You say thought is instant, and you masters are able to meet on matters of the Court from anywhere."

She nodded.

"Well, my wife is pretty advanced, possibly the top instructor in her school. I want you to reach her and connect her thoughts to mine. I need her reassurance, or I can't go on."

Aigna bit her lip, as if considering it.

And as she did, he realized just how much he'd overstepped. He was ordering a Master of the Court around like she was a recalcitrant servant. It was wrong in so many ways.

Aigna spoke as if to a child, "I'm sure your supposition of your wife's evolution is correct. But what of your own? Perhaps if you'd stayed in school, you might be capable of such a thing as you ask, but . . ."

Despondency overtook him. Darmon put his head on the table. "I can't go on."

"Listen to me. It is times like these that all your years of meditation are for. It doesn't matter that you dropped out of the Mystery School. What matters is that you remained steadfast in your practices. Now, apply the fruit of them."

He raised his head and looked into her eyes.

"We do not live in the future or the past. The moment we are in is the only one we have. Then it is gone, and we are in the next. To serve your wife, your king, our people, do what is presented to you in this place at this second. Take the opportunity to raise the situation by interacting with it from your highest state. That is what your wife would do. That is what she *is* doing."

Now he felt worse. "I'm sorry. I should never have spoken to you the way I did."

"Don't be. That moment is over. Get on with your work."

"I will. I can ignore the pain. I've done it for this long."

"Pain?"

"Hathorah. It feels . . . physical, like a tear, right in here." He pointed to his heart.

"Oh, my."

"Don't worry about it. I'm sorry I troubled you."

Aigna's eyes glazed over and she went silent for no more than a few seconds.

"Darmon, in nine days the moon will be full."

"That sounds about right." He hadn't been tracking it.

"It will be." She pointed to the dominant feature on the island. "There is a temple at the top of Mount Atlantis. Meet me there in nine days, after the sun has set and the full moon has risen."

He nodded. "All right, I will."

"Until then, don't do something foolish like giving up." She stood abruptly and disappeared into a crowd of fishmongers.

CHAPTER 14

Hathorah's awareness nestled unobtrusively in a ganglion of this leviathan's vast brain. Her host gave no indication of being aware of her presence, though the Supreme Nine assured her they'd received permission for her to be here. She hoped that was true. To intrude on another sentient being's conscious self uninvited would violate the fundamental ethics of the Mystery School.

She sometimes wondered why, if the Masters could communicate well enough to ask permission, they hadn't just asked for the answers they wanted? For Hathorah had yet to understand the whale's thoughts. Concepts in here were a disorganized jumble. So, she concentrated on physical and emotional sensations that did not require words.

Above her, light jittered in refraction—they were about to surface. Then brilliant sunlight and the roar of water and air spouting from her blowhole. They would remain up here, inhaling and blowing about forty times before diving again.

The whale had good eyesight, and Hathorah had been able to observe that she was traveling in a pod of females, juveniles, and two babies. Comparing her companions to the only large animals she was familiar with gave Hathorah a sense of their enormity—three times the length of an elephant and twenty times its weight.

The first emotion she connected with was their nurturing social structure and the lack of an adult male presence. Males, she intuited, only came around at breeding season. In the afternoons, the pod socialized, carrying on what were apparently conversations with clicks and codas beyond her comprehension. During afternoon socials, her pod spent much of the time rubbing against each other as well. She sensed their emotions, although she couldn't label them with any confidence.

Hathorah taught her students that when we think, we think in words, as though we are talking to our self silently inside our mind. If that were true for other species, she'd never grasp the whales' thoughts until she decoded their sounds.

Her whale lifted its flukes high out of the water as she closed her blowhole and began a feeding dive. While submerged, air passed through her phonic lips and recirculated back to the lungs. Hathorah had no precise means to measure time but her own sense of it. She judged these forays to the depths lasted half an hour or more.

She'd been amazed to watch her host slow its heart to a stop and access oxygen saturated in blood and muscles. Besides gender, this was the first point they had in common—it was similar to one of the meditation techniques she taught. The difference was, she used it to raise enérgeia and still the body. Her host used it to survive incredible depths.

The pressure squeezed the whale on all sides, but her flexible ribcage bent rather than snap. She intentionally collapsed her lungs. The darkness increased, and she rolled over, scanning the ocean bottom for silhouettes of giant squid.

Oh! Delicious squid!

This body required a lot of food. Nearly three quarters of her waking hours were spent feeding. She swam, emitting sharply focused clicking sounds, which echoed back to the concave surface of her cranium and were instantly interpreted as distance, object, location.

A giant squid, nearly as long as she was! In an instant, her powerful jaws had it. She swallowed it whole. Though its suckers and razor-sharp claws fought, the thick muscular walls of her first stomach were unharmed as it crushed the squid. She surfaced and breathed again.

Hathorah realized her host lived entirely without fear. She and other members of their pod were the largest predators in the seas. Nothing could harm them once they were adults. A nasty group of killer whales had tried to get one of the babies the first week she came here, but the adults encircled the calves, facing inward with their tails out. Powerful tails that landed blows on two of the aggressors, making the villains speed away. Hathorah was glad when they left. She had never killed anything in a fight, and even though it wouldn't be her doing, she would experience it. She was relieved it hadn't come to that.

The pod slept only briefly, assuming a vertical position with their heads just below or at the surface. From glimpses of the sky, Hathorah figured this occurred sometime after sunset. Since Hathorah was not in her body, she did not require sleep. She used these hours to explore her whale's brain, trying to fathom its syntax. To have a memory of something, you had to have a framework in which you stored it. Hathorah needed only to puzzle that framework out.

Atlantean techgnosists oft claimed elephants never forgot. Hathorah believed them—although she'd never been inside one's mind, she had seen elephants greet the people who raised them decades later. The Supreme Nine asserted that whales had an even more extensive repository because they were able to pass memories from one generation to the next. There were juveniles in her pod. They must be approaching the age when a teacher would begin to transmit deeper secrets. At least, that's the way it worked at her school in Atlantis.

If she was going to have a chance of understanding what the adults were telling the youngsters, she had to crack this language barrier.

One day while they were socializing, she vomited out the indigestible beaks of squid she had eaten. She felt embarrassed by it. The others ignored it, of course—this was a normal thing, and they all did it. But . . . Hathorah felt she had done it. She'd identified with the body she was in. This was the opposite of what she taught her students—to separate yourself from identification with body and mind. Instead, she was identifying with the body. Would that eventually lead to understanding the mind?

The chatter of clicks and clacks of the pod continued. Although Hathorah still didn't recognize their meaning, she sensed a hint of contention. She affectionately rubbed alongside the others without knowing why. Eventually, the present disharmony melted. The pod resumed swimming, and Hathorah sensed an irresistible draw on a new course toward a part of the sea they hadn't seen since she'd joined them.

She took forty deep breaths and plunged to the depths with her pod mates, looking for a good, big squid. It was going to be a nine-day journey, and they needed to eat well.

Hathorah didn't even pause to question how she knew that.

CHAPTER 15

It was a good thing Aigna chose the night of a full moon because the narrow path up Mount Atlantis would have been impossible to navigate with any less light. Fortunately, the temple was lit and served as his polestar. But the gravel on the footpath was loose, and Darmon couldn't move as quickly as his emotions were pressing him.

He wasn't certain what was going to happen once he got there, but he'd try anything at this point.

Darmon mentally revisited his conversation with Aigna. She definitely said she would meet him in the temple. He was fit and climbed without breathing hard, so how was a frail old lady going to make it? He kept constant watch, expecting to stumble over her fallen body.

The closer he got to the temple, the more impatient he grew. He was sprinting when he reached the portico but stopped as he entered the sanctuary. It wasn't much. Just an empty vault bounded by columns built from mud bricks and open to the sky. Torches set in the columns blazed, giving the room a yellow glow—the light he'd seen from below. Aigna apparently hadn't made it yet. He wondered if he should go back and look for her along the path.

"Darmon, still your mind."

Startled by her voice, he whirled around, but saw no one.

"Walk to the center of the room and sit down."

He did as he was told. After he was seated, he looked around. No altar, no statues. The building wouldn't even be considered a proper temple on Atlantis.

Aigna stepped out of the shadows, came over, and sat on the floor in front of him.

He felt bad there wasn't a chair for her. He took off his cloak and folded it like a cushion. "Here, sit on this."

She waved it away and put her finger over her lips, signaling him to be silent. He guessed they were supposed to meditate. He inhaled, drawing the enérgeia upward as he did so, until it felt centered at the point between his eyebrows. There, he waited. For how long he didn't know. Eventually, he caught himself thinking of Hathorah, wondering what Aigna had in mind.

"Hathorah is busy at the moment. She'll be in touch as soon as everyone is asleep," Aigna whispered.

That puzzled him. Who had to be asleep? And what did Hathorah have to do with it? They had no children.

"You seem to have a habit of musing. I wish your teachers hadn't let you drop out of school. Who knows what you would have achieved."

He swallowed a lump in his throat. Guilt? What did he have to feel guilty about? He was right hand to the king. Wasn't that achievement enough?

"Be still. Focus on your breath if you have to."

The beginner's technique. Darmon did as he was told and resumed his meditation.

After a time, he opened his eyes. The moon was higher overhead and lit the temple more brightly than the torches. He had the impression that Aigna was talking to herself, but her lips weren't moving. It was probably his imagination. He wondered what time it was and glanced up at the moon, but that didn't help. Who could judge time by the moon?

He told himself to relax and trust Hathorah. If she could come at all, it would be in her own time. Darmon tried a technique he'd learned as a youth, tensing and relaxing each muscle group, starting with his toes and working his way up to his brow. With each release he withdrew the enérgeia, leaving only enough to remain sitting. As he tightened, then released the muscles in his neck, he heard Aigna saying something, but still her mouth didn't move. Was he suddenly privy to her thoughts?

When she didn't respond, he concluded, probably not.

Then her voice came again, this time more clearly. *So they're asleep now? Are they upset by the inconvenience?*

A moment later, *I wouldn't have, but he seemed ready to flee his responsibilities.* She paused. For a response? *Yes, he's here with me now.*

Who? Was she in contact with Hathorah? Oh! Hathorah! His heart flooded with love. And confusion. Was she home? No. There wouldn't be anyone sleeping there. Maybe at school, some overnight exercise for advanced students?

Aigna opened one eye and caught him studying her. "Darmon! Discipline yourself. You are nearly blowing me out of the ether."

"I'm sorry, master."

"This is a sensitive endeavor. Years of meditation are required. We're both doing our best, but you must do your part, too. Remember your training and practice it. Now."

Aigna closed her eye, and again he could hear her thoughts. *He wants to know where you are. I suggest we tell him you're in repose in Poseidon's temple.*

Well, in a sense, that is truth, though my consciousness is—

Hathorah! His thought nearly knocked old Aigna over.

Yes, Darmon, I am joined with you through Aigna.

Oh, what joy! But . . . "Am I really hearing you or is this only my imagination?"

You don't have to talk out loud, Darmon. It was Aigna, that time. Then she too spoke, "But if verbalizing helps you keep focus, you may continue to do so, quietly."

Hathorah answered him, *You're receiving my thoughts. It's your memory of me that makes them sound to you like my voice, so you are contributing something.*

What about your host? Aigna asked.

She obviously knows I'm here. Always has. But recently our connection has deepened, and I'm gaining a better understanding of how her mind works.

"My love, I've been so worried," Darmon said. "You haven't replied to my letters since I got here."

I'm sorry if I worried you. I didn't know about the letters because I haven't been home.

"Where have you been?"

I sequestered myself in Poseidon's temple to assist the Supreme Nine with—

"Your wife's helping us research historical information for the king," Aigna said.

"Theop? He and I have been communicating regularly. He never mentioned he'd given you an assignment." Of course, he'd never presume to bother the king about not receiving letters from Hathorah, so maybe he didn't know.

"Don't forget we can hear your thoughts even when you stop speaking aloud," Aigna said. "The king doesn't know."

"That I haven't been getting letters?"

That the Court tapped Hathorah for this task.

"Hathorah? Can you still hear me?"

Yes.

"I miss you so, but I don't know how much longer I'll have to be away. It's becoming clear that two colonies won't be sufficient. I fear I will have to find us additional locations."

Do not give into fear. It is the opposite of love.

"I know, I know. That's just an expression people use. I do fear for our people, though. That is real fear, born out of love. Aigna shared with me distressing news about what Nurlano and his minions are up to back home. I urged the king to begin emigration, but apparently—"

A cloud moved across the moon. The temple visibly darkened, leaving only the flickering torchlight splaying ragged patterns over the floor.

Hathorah? Then aloud, "Hathorah!"

The connection was gone. Darmon clutched his chest, feeling the pain of her absence. He grabbed Aigna's shoulder and shook her. "Bring her back. Bring her back!"

Aigna pried his fingers loose. "That's it for tonight."

"No!"

"Get hold of your emotions. Be grateful for the time we had with her. I know I am."

What was he doing? He hid his face in his hands and bowed before her. "I am so sorry for my outburst. Thank you for what you have done."

She raised him upright. "Sit here a while."

CHAPTER 16

Eventually, the cloud drifted past the moon, and once again the temple was bathed in lunar light. Aigna had been silent a long time, but now she spoke. "You're going to Strongyle next."

He was? Yes, he was. It was an island in an archipelago, far to the east of Ogygia.

"Your mission is important to the survival of Atlantis. You must never again become so despondent that you consider giving up."

Darmon hung his head. He knew this. What was going on with him?

"No self-recrimination. It is a poor excuse to say we are only human. We are much more than that. This is the first lesson a student learns at the Mystery School."

"I remember."

"Even those of us given positions of great responsibility have very little influence over the actions of others. But inside, in our higher seat, we are our own masters. You can choose not to let worry and negative emotions steal your ecstasy. Every person you interact with can be uplifted by the fact that inside you are centered, clear, and filled with enérgeia."

Darmon nodded. He knew she was right.

"Achieving a position of consul in the physical world doesn't mean anything if you are incapable of forming a sacred geometric configuration and maintaining its shape in your inner world. You should have stayed in school."

"I see that now."

"I am not a prognosticator. I have no idea how long it will take you to accomplish what has been asked of you. But I know you cannot fail."

"I won't."

"Being a Master on the Court does not make me unsympathetic to human emotions. I am touched by your plight—the separation that destiny has forced on you and Hathorah."

He chewed his lip and wondered where this conversation was going.

"I accept the limitations your incomplete education has left you with and I'm inspired to give you a small boon."

"A gift?"

"A trifle. A hundredth the size of a grain of salt." She leaned toward him. "Close your eyes."

He felt her bony finger press on his forehead at the point between his eyes. With her other hand, she pressed on the hollow at the base of his skull. He saw a blue line appear inside his brain, connecting the two points. She let go, and the line remained. Next, he felt a pat on the crown of his head and saw a vertical line descend and intersect with the first line. Then both lines disappeared.

"There," she said.

He didn't feel any different.

"You can open your eyes."

Her eyes were fixed on his. Especially the one with the white star in the pupil.

"Inhale. Breathe your enérgeia up to the seat in the center of your brain."

He did.

"Can you feel a small lattice, shaped like a star tetrahedron but made out of enérgeia?"

"I don't know. Maybe."

She laughed. "Well, it's there. A star tetrahedron formed by two interlocking tetrahedrons."

"What does it do?"

"The one pointing up is male. The downward facing one is female. An adept who can cause the two to rotate in opposite directions can move through time and space. You, however steadfast in your meditation practices, are not adequately prepared to translate into higher realms. For you, it will only be a semaphore. I am leaving for Atlantis and may not be able to return should you fall into despair and need to reach Hathorah again."

"I'm better now. I won't let that happen again."

"Let's hope not. But should the need arise, the seed of the star tetrahedron I implanted can expand its geometry and activate for you. You only need call for it." She shook her finger in his face. "But don't waste it. Use it only if you have no alternative. Once it's expanded, you lack the training to ever bring it back. Therefore, you will lose it after one use."

Darmon nodded solemnly. "Understood. Thank you, Aigna, I'll be eternally grateful for all that you've done for me."

She held out her hand. "Help an old lady stand up, will you?"

Darmon stood and pulled her up. "Are we done here?"

"Yes. Would you mind walking me back down the mountain? That foot-path is treacherous in places."

Walk her? He owed her so much, he'd carry her on his back if she wanted.

"That won't be necessary," she said.

Ah, yes. He'd forgotten she could read his thoughts. "What about the torches? Should I put them out?"

"Leave them burning. It won't hurt anything."

She took his arm, and they stepped out into the moonlight.

CHAPTER 17

Months later, things were not going well for King Theop. Darmon still wasn't back, and no one had seen Hathorah. When the king didn't hear from Darmon after the message about continuing beyond Ogygia to Strongyle to look for additional resettlement space, he sent Milos to the school to inquire if Hathorah had received any letters. The school's response mystified him. She had apparently quit teaching and sequestered herself in the Temple of Poseidon. He hoped that wasn't his doing. He'd known women who became despondent over loss or prolonged absence of their husbands.

He shook his head. No. Surely not Hathorah. She would never succumb to melancholy. This was probably a spiritual retreat, the next step toward becoming a master. Not that he knew. Royalty were only required to take the barest minimum classes.

Meanwhile, he was being fenced in—literally—by an immense wall surrounding Atlantis that grew longer and higher every day. A stupid waste of stone and manpower.

If that wasn't enough, the barons reported that construction of aqueducts cutting across their lands was well underway, a scheme his techgnosists said would only hasten Atlantis's demise. He imagined the construction was making an unholy ruin of the outlying countryside, but he couldn't know for sure. He'd sent two survey teams into the countryside to find out what was going on, and both had returned bloodied and wounded. The barons, aghast, had sworn they would hunt down and punish the gangs of ruffians involved, but Theop wasn't sure they hadn't hired them. With the Plenum's constant political maneuvering, he dare not leave the capital to see for himself. While he could send Milos with an armed escort, he wasn't ready to let the barons know he had Milos in his service.

Theop called for a scribe and dictated a letter to Darmon, advising him of the chaos at home and urging him to complete his mission as quickly as possible. He signed it, sealed it, and sent for Milos.

When the prince appeared, Theop handed him the letter. "Give this to the captain of the next ship bound for Ogygia. If there isn't one leaving soon, you have my authority to order one to go."

He might not have his old friend on hand to confer with, but he felt better just getting everything off his chest. Now, if only the Court of Masters would render their opinion, he could get Nurlano off his mind.

A page entered. "The Overseer of the Treasuries is here, Your Majesty."

"Show him to the antechamber. Offer him some refreshment." Finances weren't his favorite topic, but at least it was something he understood. His overseer was precise and his figures true, but Theop's father had taught him to always keep abreast of the state of the Atlantean treasury.

By the time Theop entered the antechamber, the Overseer had everything ready. Accounting lists and summary reports were neatly arranged on the table in front of the king's chair.

The Overseer, waiting protectively next to his ledgers, bowed as the king entered. "Good morning, Your Majesty."

"Is it? I'm glad to hear it."

The Overseer frowned.

"So, not so good, then." The king sighed. "Sit. Let's see what you've got."

The man began by unrolling the tax ledger. "Due to the drought, tithes from the barons are down for the third year in a row." He turned it over. "Fortunately, merchant and foreign trade remains strong."

Theop noted the sums and nodded.

The Overseer unrolled another scroll. "But expenditures are out of hand. The wall is costing much more than the Plenum predicted, and they continue to build without any consideration of where the money will come from."

The king shook his head. "And yet they balk at any increase in taxes." He sighed. "What a waste—a wall we don't need whose only purpose is to keep Atlantean farmworkers from migrating into their own capital."

"Not my place to say, Sire. I'm just the keeper of the numbers." The Overseer stood by, not meeting the king's eyes.

"Well . . . Give me the rest."

The Overseer opened another ledger and put it before the king. "The aqueduct project is worse." He ran his finger down a column of numbers. "These expenditures seem outlandishly high, especially given how cheap manual labor has become. I hesitate to think any of our people dishonest, but . . . we could be looking at widespread fraud."

The king studied the numbers. "Thank you for bringing this to my attention. I need to have someone go out there and see how much work they're actually doing." He removed the corner weights and allowed the scroll to roll back up. "All this expense and not a trickle of water has reached the city."

"Again, Sire, not my place to say."

Theop stood and stretched his back. "Accounting is tedious work, but you're good at it. Atlantis is blessed to have you watching over its fortune. Do you feel fairly compensated? Is there anything you need? Ask, and if it's within my power, you shall have it."

The man looked dazed by the offer. "My wages are perfectly just. I would ask for no more."

"But are you happy?"

"I am, Your Majesty. It's a deep honor to serve Atlantis in my own small way. That is reward enough."

The king smiled ruefully. "Would that the Plenum had fifty men and women like you."

The Overseer blushed and then shook his head. "I'm afraid that wouldn't do. If they were all like me, there wouldn't be any debates."

The king's smile broadened. "I fail to understand why that would be a bad thing."

CHAPTER 18

"Darmon! You're back!" King Theop beamed at him. "I see you got my letter."

Darmon bowed. "Your Majesty."

The king raised him up and embraced him. "It's been too long. I missed you and wished a hundred times I'd sent someone else. But then I'd remember no one else would have succeeded like you have."

"Thank you. I can't express how glad I am to be back. But what letter?"

"Yes, the one I sent to Ogygia urging you to return."

"Sorry, sir. I must have gone on to Strongyle before it arrived."

"Strongyle?"

"An island far east of Ogygia that looks like a promising site for a third colony. I've put it all in my report."

"So, you came back without knowing I'd sent for you? That must mean your work is finished."

"I hope so. I haven't seen Hathorah since—"

"About that—"

"Don't tell me something happened to her while I was away!"

"No, no, nothing bad. I don't think. She simply disappeared into the Temple of Poseidon months ago and hasn't been heard from since. Not even a message from her king got a response."

He breathed a sigh of relief. That he knew about, and that it involved something esoteric that the Masters had her doing. But why was she still there?

The king patted his shoulder. "Don't worry. Do as I did and tell yourself it's merely some extended meditation retreat required for her spiritual evolution."

"I'm sure that's it," Darmon said.

"You're probably anxious to try to see her. Let's have your report, so you can go home. Or have you already been there?"

"No. I came straight here as soon as we docked."

"Oh. Do you want a bath and a meal first? You can use one of the palace rooms."

"Do I smell like a sailor?"

"No, no, I was only thinking of your comfort."

Darmon smiled. "Thank you, my friend, but I'm ready to present my report. Do you want me to go over it with you, or shall we send for the leaders of the Plenum and do it together?"

Theop made a face that told him everything.

"So, just you and me, then. We'll present it to the Plenum later."

"And the Supreme Nine."

"Really? Why?"

"While you were away, the Plenum and I reached an impasse, so I referred the matter of climate change to them."

Darmon had also learned that from Aigna when he was still on Ogygia. "Hasn't the Court responded yet?" It was like time had stopped here.

Theop shrugged. "You know as well as I do how slow they move. If your report has any bearing, sharing it with the Court may speed up their deliberations."

"I hope so."

The king motioned for a servant. "Before we start, at least let me give you something to eat. We can discuss your report over lunch. I'll read while you chew."

An hour later, the table was strewn with dirty dishes and pages of calculations of passenger loads, timetables, resettlement costs, and population growth projections.

The king pushed his plate aside and rested his head on the table.

A servant rushed over. "Are you all right, Your Majesty?"

Theop sat up. "I'm fine. All these figures have given me a headache. Send to the court physician for a potion."

"Do you want to stop for today?" Darmon said.

The king shook his head. "No. This place leaks information like a sieve. Rumors will be flying by nightfall. We'd better finish this afternoon."

Darmon stood. "A short break, then. Until your medicine arrives. Let's go to the window and breathe some fresh air."

The king nodded, and they walked to the window together.

"It doesn't seem possible," the king said. "It's been nearly a year since we stood in this very spot admiring the view."

"You're a lucky man. It's as lovely as I remember."

The king gestured toward the distance. "But I have no idea what they're doing out on the plains. I haven't been able to leave the capital since you left."

"You're the king. I thought that meant you could go anywhere you want."

"Not without risking that the Plenum would pull another stunt while I was away. Are you aware that they funded the aqueduct project?"

"I heard. That's terrible news. We scrapped those plans as soon as the techgnosists pointed out they'd do more harm than good."

"I agree, but the barons tell me work is progressing at full speed."

"Are you worried the barons might be . . . shading the truth a little?"

Theop laughed. "This is why I missed you. You're not shy about saying what's really going on. Listen, as soon as you get rested, I want you to ride out there and see what's what."

So soon? Time at home with Hathorah after she finished in the temple would have been nice.

The servant returned with the court physician.

"I don't need him," the king said. "I only asked you to bring me a potion."

The servant studied the floor. Darmon felt bad for him.

"The kingdom can brook no peril to your health," the physician said. "I'd be derelict if I simply handed out medicine without an examination."

The king waved him off. "It's only a headache, and it's nearly gone now. The fresh air has cured it as well as any of your potions could have."

"Yes, Your Majesty." The physician did not move.

"You're not leaving until you examine me, are you?"

"No, Your Majesty."

"Fine. Be quick about it. Darmon and I have work to do."

After a brief bout of squeezing, prodding, peering into the king's eyes, and asking a few questions, the physician set a small vial of colorless liquid on the window sill. "You seem sound. If the headache returns, take this. If it gets worse, send for me."

"Thank you. You can go now." He turned to Darmon, "Let's get back to your report."

They returned to the table where servants had cleared the dishes and left the pages of Darmon's report neatly stacked.

Theop flipped through the pages. "One of them has read this and run off to tell Nurlano. Let's discover our spy. Guards! Bring in all the servants and have them form a line."

"A waste of time," Darmon said. Besides, questioning the servants would only delay his reunion with Hathorah.

"They wouldn't have time to get to the Plenum and return," the king said. "If we see which of them is missing, we'll know our culprit."

"The Plenum is getting the report, anyway. Let's just finish before they do."

"All right. I know you probably want to get home. Guards, don't bother bringing the servants in. Just find out who's missing, and tell me later."

"So, Your Majesty," Darmon said, "in the likelihood we have to abandon the capital completely, the figures clearly show our whole populace won't fit in our two existing colonies."

The king looked like he could cry.

"However, I've just come from Strongyle, an unoccupied island. It's completely undeveloped, but if we relocated skilled builders and our best farmers, they could have a thriving agricultural colony established in less than the hundred years techgnosists predict we have left here."

Theop studied the pages. "The Plenum's really not going to like this part. I can hear them complaining about the expense already."

"They'll cry harder once Tartessos and Ogygia are full and they have nowhere to go. Plus, Strongyle is part of an archipelago if we require further expansion later."

The king sat back in his chair. "I'm so glad you're back. We'll celebrate your return with a banquet in your honor. Bring Hathorah."

Not too soon, he hoped. Any feast at the palace would undoubtedly turn political.

As if reading his mind, Theop said, "Rich food to make up for the plate of manure the Plenum's going to hand you."

"Thanks a lot, old friend." Oh, well, dealing with the Plenum leadership came with his job.

* * *

Darmon left the palace possessed with three certainties. Where Hathorah was; that he longed to see her; and that he dare not disturb her. What he didn't know was how much longer she would have to remain inside.

He did the only thing he could, climb the stone stairs up to the temple, sit outside against one of the columns, and wait. Presently, a priest came out, saw who he was, and went back inside without a word.

He determined to stay all day and night if necessary. Whatever his wife was doing in there was beyond his ken, but he deserved to know at least how long it would take.

It was a given between them that her capabilities in the esoteric realms had exceeded his years ago. This was undoubtedly the next stage in her spiritual evolution. Since he knew nothing of that, he could hazard no guess how much time she'd require. The only thing he had to offer was patience. He could wait. He could meditate. He could tender his meager contribution of enérgeia to her advancement.

He concentrated on the point between his eyebrows and tried to imagine a river of stars flowing from him into the temple and surrounding her with their faint light. No doubt his minor effort added little to her endeavor—whatever that was—but it gave his waiting a sense of purpose.

CHAPTER 19

The Milky Way had swept its way across the heavens and faded in the fuchsia-tinged hint of impending dawn by the time Hathorah came out. Her husband had lost track of the hours, but she had lost track of the days. Or weeks. She could have been swimming with the pod for a month or a year, she wasn't sure. Only that this morning she'd sensed Darmon out here, offering her support.

Her body felt small. The air, so thin, gave no resistance—nothing to push against. However long she'd been in the whale, she'd grown used to the sense of ocean pressing around her. She needed something to hold on to.

Darmon, standing before her, opened his arms and pulled her into his embrace.

Ah.

His tears and kisses wet her cheeks. She found his mouth and kissed him back.

Ah.

He parted and stepped back. "I've missed you so. Let me look at you."

She pulled him back into her arms. "Later. Hold me some more."

He kissed her again. "For as long as you'd like. Let us never again be apart for so long."

She couldn't promise that, but she certainly agreed with his sentiment.

"Let's go home," he said.

"You go ahead. I have to report to the Nine, first."

"Now? The Court's not open this early."

"They're expecting me."

"All right, I'll accompany you."

"Thank you, but I don't think they'll let you. They don't allow visitors in their sessions."

"The king wants me to present my findings to them. I'm sure he sent word, and they're expecting me, too."

Hathorah pushed a lock of hair off his forehead and smiled. "I didn't know that."

Arm in arm, they descended the stairway and walked through the empty streets to the white columned Court of Supreme Masters.

A woman in a flowing robe waited outside. "You're expected. Please go in."

The first birds of morning had just begun to chirp.

They crossed the threshold together, and Hathorah whispered, "You haven't been here before. It's this way." She led her husband along the hallway to the room where she had met with the masters previously. Unlike last time, the Nine were already there. This time, two empty chairs had been placed in the middle of the circle—so they were both expected. Holding his hand, Hathorah brought Darmon to the center, and took her seat. He did likewise.

She leaned toward him and whispered, "Don't be startled. This whole platform swivels when they speak."

The pinkish-lavender light cast by sconces along the stone walls comforted her. So opposite the deep blue-green light that had filled her whale's eyes.

"Darmon," Aigna said, "I see your journey's end has reunited you with your wife."

Darmon burst into a broad grin and nodded.

Hathorah grabbed her husband's hand when the platform rotated. The male member of the Court said, "The king has asked us to hear your report. He believes your information has a bearing on the matter before us."

Darmon squeezed her hand and cleared his throat. "If it pleases the Court, I'll summarize my findings and leave a copy of the full document for you to reference later. This information hasn't been presented to the Plenum yet, officially, but I shall have to do so, soon."

The old man nodded. "Please proceed. Be brief."

Darmon concisely and precisely reviewed what he had learned. He let go of her hand to gesture and write invisible numbers in the air. Hathorah beamed at her husband's brilliant presentation.

When he finished, one of the women said, "Very thorough and informative. We'll give your report careful study."

Another said, "Don't delay your presentation to the Plenum. They need this information. The factions keeping each other in the dark causes half our political problems."

Was her husband being chastised? Hathorah felt an urge to defend him.

But Aigna beat her to it. "Don't blame Darmon for what's been going on. He's been out of the country for most of the year."

Hathorah saw the woman give Aigna a sharp look. She'd always imagined the Nine to be above mortal foibles. Apparently not.

"My colleague's not wrong," Aigna said. "Darmon, share your report with the Plenum as soon as feasible. We thank you for attending us, and you are now free to go home."

What? Hathorah reached for his hand and sensed Darmon wasn't inclined to go anywhere yet.

"But you haven't heard Hathorah's report yet," he said.

Aigna pursed her lips and fixed Hathorah with a stare. "Consider if the ins and outs of how you came to the knowledge you are about to share wouldn't be better explained to Darmon in the intimacy of your own home."

She was right. Darmon held a high station, a position of trust. It'd be an unkindness to thrust the unexplainable upon him in front of the nine most important Atlanteans. Hathorah patted his hand. "Aigna is wise. I have so much to tell you, and we don't want to take up the Court's time. Go home. I'll be there shortly, and then we'll have as long as we need to share our adventures."

Hathorah felt his reluctance and nudged him.

He stood and bowed to the members of the Court. "Thank you, Masters. Hathorah, I'll wait for you outside."

"No," Aigna said. "Darmon, you are more fatigued that you realize. Go to your bed, and we'll send Hathorah straight home when we've finished with her. I promise."

She saw Darmon hesitate in front of Aigna and falter.

Then he yawned, one of those yawns that goes to the bones. "I guess you're right. I *am* more tired than I thought. Hathorah, I'll wait for you at home. Wake me when you get in."

Once Darmon had left, Aigna said, "Tell us what the whales said."

"Well, 'said' isn't quite the right word. Their minds are huge and the memories vast. It was rather like trying to find the right book in the library of a foreign country where you didn't know enough of the language to even read the titles."

"But you succeeded?" a woman said.

"With a bit of fortunate timing."

"Explain."

"At a certain stage of life, the whales begin transmitting the species' collective history to maturing juveniles. I happened to be present as a youngster reached the right age. They unraveled a whole chorus of information. I had to wait until they reached the parts I was sent to find."

"Fascinating, I'm sure," the old man said. "But tell us what you learned."

"Three things are particularly germane. But most important, before I left, I was able to get my host to ask the collective whales for their advice."

"Which was?"

"The whales tell us to have our people take to the sea."

"Of course that's their advice," one of the women said, "because that's what they did eons ago."

"They once lived on land?" Hathorah said.

The woman nodded. "Long, long before people existed. Didn't she communicate that information in the transfer of memories to the young?"

"Possibly," Hathorah said. "Not all of it was entirely clear, and I was only watching for certain bits."

"It makes me wonder what else you missed."

Hathorah watched her lower self become slightly irritated at the woman. She took a deep breath and cleared the emotion. "If you already knew this, then why did you send me out there?"

Aigna smacked her lips. "She's only saying they once lived on land because there are ancient whale skeletons east of Atlantis that have hind legs. But that doesn't tell us about the weather. Our archives only go back to the beginning of Atlantis. We need them to tell us what transpired before that."

The old man nodded, or maybe he was nodding off.

"What else?" he said. "You said three things were germane to the question at hand."

Nope, he wasn't sleeping after all.

"They said that people had to leave Atlantis once before, but they returned after a thousand years."

"We have a record of that, yes. What else?"

"That the monsoons won't bring heavy rains this far north for another twenty thousand years. Apparently, the pattern repeats—twenty thousand north, then twenty thousand farther south."

"How do they measure these years?" he said.

"Much the same as we do," Hathorah said. "Different mental symbol for it, of course, but they surface regularly and are aware of daylight, nighttime, sun, moon, and star movements. I suppose they count the changes in some way."

The old man straightened up. "Twenty thousand years before the rain returns? That should make our deliberations short."

"I agree," the woman next to him said. "But it's very early. We haven't had breakfast or much sleep for that matter. I move that we adjourn until noon."

The rest of the Court agreed.

Aigna said, "Hathorah, please wait for me outside. I want a moment of your time before you go."

* * *

Hathorah leaned against a column in front of the Court, waiting for Aigna. The stone had shed its warmth last evening, and morning air carried a chill.

Then Aigna was next to her, having approached her absolutely silently. She wore an odd expression, unexpected in an old master. A childlike curiosity danced behind her obsidian eyes. "Thank you for waiting. I wanted a word in private." She removed her shawl and wrapped it around Hathorah. "You're shivering. I expect you're used to a few more layers of insulation."

In a way. that was true, but her body had never really left Atlantis. Perhaps Aigna referred to blankets the priestess had laid over her form before locking her in the chamber.

Aigna took her hands, but she had the cold hands of an old person, and they did nothing to warm her. But Aigna's eyes beamed. "What was it like? Tell me everything. None of us have done what you have."

"Where to begin? In many ways, I was like an infant, able to comprehend only the smallest fraction of what was going on around me."

Aigna squeezed her fingers. "You already told us what they said. Tell me what they felt. What you felt."

"Oh, they are wonderfully sensitive, aware of even the most distant changes —every volcano that erupts anyplace in the ocean or on any land that touches a sea. They anticipate every earthquake before it happens. On the surface, they can sense changes in the air as a hurricane forms, and they all leave the area."

"And they remember it all?"

Hathorah nodded. "Every change to our planet that's occurred since they became whales."

"Imagine that. Though I suppose you don't have to."

Suddenly, she remembered something. "Oh, this will interest you. They naturally do a technique we teach our students."

Aigna raised her eyebrows.

"While hunting food, they dive to extraordinary depths and go without breathing for a long time."

"That's to be expected. They're underwater, after all."

"Yes, but what I found amazing is that they also stop their heartbeats."

"Really? Only our highest adepts can do that."

Hathorah smiled. "I thought that would interest you." She let go of Aigna's hands and looked out at the city.

"I sense you're anxious to get home."

"Yes."

"At this moment, Darmon is peacefully snoring, waiting for your arrival. But don't worry. When you wake him, he'll be completely rested and ready for whatever you want to tell him. Or do with him."

She sighed. "He isn't the only one in our marriage who's been missing their partner. I'm only human, too."

"No," Aigna said. "After the last year, you know better. You're a spirit having a human experience."

Hathorah removed the shawl and handed it to Aigna.

The old lady accepted it with a smile. "All right. Go to him. You've both done well."

CHAPTER 20

Darmon felt Hathorah's warm body pressed against him. Birds outside their window chirped in a delightful exchange that seemed to echo his mood. He yawned. He sensed it was time to get up, but he felt pulled to stay in bed with his wife. That's what they'd done yesterday after she returned from Court. Undoubtedly, the laziest day either of them had ever indulged in. They made love, told each other of their adventures—dear gods, she had been a whale! Then just lounged around the house, seldom outside of the other's embrace. He hated for it to end.

It had to end. In normal times, the king wouldn't begrudge him a few more days off. Both he and Hathorah had done their part for Atlantis and deserved it. But times weren't normal. No doubt by now the Court had rendered their decision, and the king would want his plan presented to the Plenum as soon as possible. That meant today.

He gently edged away from her, tucked the cover around her where he had been, and got out of bed.

"Darmon?"

He leaned over and kissed her. "I tried not to wake you."

"You didn't. I've been lying here listening to the birds, wishing it wouldn't end."

"Me, too. Beautiful way to wake up, isn't it?"

"You going to the palace?"

He nodded. "The Plenum, too. I have to."

She stood up and put on a robe. "I know. Let's have breakfast together before you go."

He hadn't expected there to be any food in the house with them both absent for so long, but when he arrived home, he found baskets of fruit, wine, bread, cheese, eggs, and other victuals on the doorstep. A consideration from the king, he was sure.

He wrapped his arms around her. "Absolutely. Look through the baskets and see what's left. I'll eat anything but squid."

She laughed. "It wasn't actually me eating giant squid. But I know what you mean. I don't think I'll ever enjoy squid again, either. I haven't told you about the beaks."

* * *

It took all of five minutes for the disharmony within the Plenum to ruin his mood. The day had gone as he expected. Soon after he arrived at the palace, the king asked him to accompany him to the Plenum. The Court's decision that Atlantis should be abandoned failed to quell the arguments. The Court had neglected to say when.

Darmon had spent the day going over his estimates of how many could be transported at a time and how long it would take to resettle the population. Sprydion, the chief techgnosist, warned they had less than a hundred years before the place would be a desert. In Darmon's opinion, they'd need all of it, especially if they were going to construct a third colony on Strongyle from scratch. That aspect of his report really fell on deaf ears.

"A new colony!" Nurlano shouted. "The barons will not stand for wrecking our economy and trade to build new colonies."

"Tartessos and Ogygia cannot fit everyone. That's not up for debate, it's simple arithmetic. We have to start construction now or Strongyle won't be ready."

Nurlano made a face. "Strongyle. I don't even like the name."

The king spoke up. "I'll rename it. Send me your suggestions."

"My suggestion is we don't build there at all. Several of the aqueducts are completed. Soon, water levels in the canals around the city will be back to normal."

"So far we're only seeing a trickle," the king said. "The techgnosists told the Plenum not to build them. It was a bad plan."

Nurlano pointed at Darmon. "It was your First Consul's plan."

It was never his plan. But he'd told them that many times and wasn't going to get sidetracked denying something he'd never advocated.

Nurlano smiled slyly. "I give him credit. It's bought us time, and when the rest of the aqueducts are ready, we'll have all the water we want."

"Until the lakes are empty," Darmon said.

"Nonsense. The lakes are vast."

The king rapped on the arm of his throne, and the room quieted. "I am not here to argue the merits of the aqueducts. The Supreme Nine has decided what we could not. We are bound by our laws to comply. The only issues I want to hear today are how and when."

"Your Majesty is right to correct us," Nurlano said. "I propose the Plenum form a committee to study Darmon's plan. His idea for the aqueducts worked out, and I'm sure his emigration plan has equal merit."

"I second the motion," said a member next to Nurlano.

Nurlano turned to the assembly. "All in favor, raise your hand."

Hands sprung up everywhere.

"The motion passes." Nurlano turned to the king. "As to the matter of when, the Court has clearly left that up to us."

A mistake. That's not a loophole you'd want to give the Plenum.

Nurlano looked at his cronies. "I, for one, can't believe we only have one hundred years."

"Nor we," they said on cue.

Suddenly, the chamber grew dark, although it was still afternoon. Attendants rushed to rotate the Tauoi receptor to power the room lights. Outside, the welcome sound of a downpour coursed through the city. The entire assembly ran to the windows and stared in wonder.

After a few minutes, the rain stopped abruptly, and the thirsty earth outside soaked up any sign it had ever happened.

"See that?" Nurlano said. "Proof that the drought is temporary."

Darmon shook his head. He doubted enough water had fallen to make a cup of tea.

"I move that we adjourn for the day," one of the members said.

Everyone agreed and began filing out into the richly humid air, ephemeral though it may be.

Darmon accompanied the king back to the palace. "It's like Nurlano has a curtain behind his eyes that closes whenever he starts to see something that doesn't suit his purpose."

"You'll note they adjourned without forming their committee." Theop said.

"Why didn't you stop them?"

"Everyone was so enamored with that pittance of rain, nothing would have been accomplished by holding them. When we get back, I'll send a formal request for the committee to report to me. That'll force them to do it."

"So you don't believe today's rain means the drought is ending?"

"I trust techgnosia. . . and the decision of the Supreme Nine."

While in school, Darmon had once asked a teacher why the Nine always had eight women and only one man.

"Even numbers are female and odd numbers are male," his teacher said. "Since Atlantis is ruled by a king and the Plenum is predominately male, the court was weighted with females to balance the decisions of men with the intuition of women." Never had that wisdom been more evident than times like these.

Theop cleared his throat. "Ah . . . um . . . I hesitate to ask."

Darmon looked at him. "Whatever Your Majesty needs."

"Someone has to go out and actually lay eyes on that aqueducts project. A lot of money is sailing out of the treasury and too little water is flowing into the capital. The Treasury Overseer fears corruption on a grand scale. I need an honest assessment, and I trust you above all others."

Darmon sighed. "How soon?"

"This week—tomorrow if possible."

He closed his eyes. Leaving Hathorah—again.

"I know you just got back. Take Hathorah with you. Make it a holiday in the countryside. You both deserve it. While you're out there, see what the situation is."

"Thank you, that's very kind."

"Enjoy yourselves. Don't bother sending reports. Just tell me when you return. This isn't an 'official' trip, and it'd be better if there weren't any letters a third party might intercept."

CHAPTER 21

Darmon wrapped his arms around his wife's waist and drew her close. "I know we both just got back, but the king wants me to visit the countryside and examine the aqueducts. There have been serious cost overruns, and he's worried there's corruption." He felt her body stiffen. "Theop suggested I take you along. It'd be a holiday we both well deserve."

She sighed. "Time in the country would be lovely, but I have my students."

"Hasn't one of the other teachers been covering your classes?"

"Yes, but—"

"Let them continue a bit longer."

"Oh, I don't know if that's fair to them or the students."

"I'm sure whoever the instructor is has a lesson plan they'd like to complete."

"You're right. It's just that . . . I miss teaching."

"I miss my wife."

"And I you."

"Then let's go. I'll requisition an elephant. We'll travel in style."

Two days later, Darmon and Hathorah, each carrying a light travel bag, entered the elephant compound at the palace. A man took their luggage up a flight of stairs to a mounting platform the height of the adult elephant that stood patiently waiting. He tied their bags to a strap that girded the gray beast and motioned for the couple to follow.

Darmon climbed on the elephant's back, centering his weight over its front shoulders, and held out his hand to Hathorah. When they'd dressed that morning, he'd advised her to wear long pants beneath her tunic.

"This isn't my first elephant ride, you know," she'd said.

She accepted his hand, threw her leg over the elephant's back, and he pulled her the rest of the way on. When he felt her arms tighten around his waist, he tapped the elephant's shoulder and it set off for the gate. It was early, and the streets had few people on them. They crossed the three canals that encircled Atlantis and reached a tall set of gates in a thick wall. The gates stood open. Four guards, clustered in conversation, glanced up and waved them through. The wall extended as far as Darmon could see in either direction. Nurlano's pet project. The whole idea of it disgusted him.

But soon the wall was behind them and the vast agricultural lands lay before them. The fields were surprisingly green, considering the drought.

Their elephant followed the well-worn road and required little guidance from him. Later in the morning, he spotted a pond fed by a ditch that crossed a fertile field. This was new. They stopped to water the elephant. At his command, it kneeled to let them off. Not his favorite way to dismount, but the surrounding area was flat and offered not even a high boulder they could use to step off.

Once the elephant had drunk its fill, it started toward the crops in the field, but Darmon guided it to the ditch, encouraging it to eat the plants growing on the banks. Hathorah drank from their flask of water and offered it to him. He took a deep pull while she opened a kerchief containing bread, dates, and cheese. They lay on a soft patch of grass, watching the elephant graze. Darmon ran his fingers through the lush turf and wondered that it was there at all.

He kept an eye on their elephant. When he judged it had roamed far enough, he got up and went to turn it to the other bank, encouraging it to eat its way back toward the place Hathorah lay waiting. He returned to her and stretched out on the ground. "Odd, isn't it, seeing everything green?"

"They must be using that ditch for irrigation," she said.

"I suppose. But it's too small to be one of Nurlano's aqueducts."

"I certainly hope not. If this is an aqueduct, it would explain why so little water is reaching the capital."

"No, this has to be just some baron's irrigation scheme."

"Didn't you say we're spending the night with a baron?" she said.

He nodded.

"Perhaps he'll explain."

"Perhaps." Darmon stood and stretched. "Shall we continue, my love?"

She smiled and held up her hand. "Yes."

He pulled her up.

"This is nice. I'm glad you brought me."

He hugged her. "I'm glad you agreed to come."

The baron's house was not particularly impressive, especially compared to the regents' mansions on Tartessos. Then he sensed Hathorah's reaction. This level of luxury was new to her. At home, he and Hathorah chose to live simply—one of the principles of the Mystery School. Four rooms, with a single servant who came in every third day to clean. Certainly, she'd accompanied him to palace events, but the opulence there was a state function. The palace belonged to all of Atlantis.

This mansion belonged to one man and his family.

"Doesn't this seem excessive?" she whispered, when their host was out of earshot.

Darmon shrugged. "We knew they were rich."

"I wonder if his tenant farmers fare as well?"

"I'm guessing not."

The baron returned, rubbing his hands together. "I've just checked on dinner. We have a few hours, yet. Would you care to have drinks and a light repast, or go to your rooms and freshen up?"

"Freshen up," Hathorah said.

"Of course." The baron crooked his finger, and a servant stepped through the doorway. "Show my guests to their rooms."

"Oh, Darmon and I will share the same room."

"I assumed you would."

Hathorah looked puzzled by the baron's reply.

The servant led the way. When he opened their door, her expression changed to amazement. Their "rooms" were a suite nearly the size of their house in Atlantis. They entered a parlor large enough to entertain a good number of guests. A set of double doors opened onto a terrace. The bedroom connected to two bathrooms, each with its own dressing room, where their bags awaited. Darmon stepped into the nearest bath and found a girl filling the tub. Flower petals of some kind were floating on top of the steaming water.

"I'm sorry, sir, but this is your wife's bath. Yours is the other one."

Hathorah appeared at his side. "Did you ask for this?"

Darmon shook his head.

"I understood you told his Grace you wanted to freshen up," the girl said.

"So, we did." Hathorah smiled at Darmon. "Was this what it was like for you on Tartessos?"

"Pretty much. Though here we get to feed ourselves." Darmon went to his own bathroom, where a man had the tub ready for him.

After they bathed and dressed for dinner, they joined the baron for drinks. Soon, other guests entered—several neighboring barons. Darmon hadn't expected it, but wasn't surprised either. The servants brought out trays of appetizers and did not offer to push food into his mouth. Once everyone had arrived and drunk enough to be merry, their host served up a fine feast.

In the morning, the baron suggested his wife keep Hathorah company while he showed Darmon the aqueduct and irrigation system. At last.

The aqueduct seemed sturdy. Its bed and sloping sidewalls were paved with smooth, squared stones, tightly fitted and covered with a layer of lime to eliminate water loss. He judged it to be as deep as the height of two men, if one stood on the other's shoulder. It appeared to be about half full.

At the end of each field, a spillway off the side of the aqueduct allowed water to flow into irrigation ditches that had been dug across the fields. Wooden gates across the spillways could be raised or lowered to control how much water flowed into the ditches. The baron praised Nurlano for saving agriculture in Atlantis.

That hadn't been the purpose of the aqueducts, but as Darmon looked over the green fields, he had to agree it seemed to be an unintended benefit. The control gate system seemed wise and should have left plenty of water flowing into the capital.

So where was the water going?

He wanted to follow the aqueduct further east, but the baron suggested they visit a neighboring baron's fields. They arrived in time for lunch and were served another bountiful meal. Afterwards, their host offered them a bed for a nap, but Darmon declined. He wanted to see the fields.

This baron's crops were also doing well. He'd followed the same design for the spillways and gates. But again, when Darmon tried to explore further, he was diverted in another direction.

The second day was more of the same. That night, he announced they would be leaving in the morning. The baron protested, but Darmon sensed he was secretly relieved.

Once he and Hathorah were in bed, he told her, "I'm being manipulated. There's something they don't want me to see. Let's take a different route home."

In the morning, they thanked their host and climbed onto their elephant. When they were beyond sight of the baron and his workers, Darmon turned onto a side road that ran north. An hour later, they came to another aqueduct and followed it. As they proceeded, the mansions they passed grew more exorbitant, the fields richer, and the water flow in the aqueduct less. Instead of gates controlling the spillways, gates spanned the aqueduct itself, acting as dams, forcing water into the fields.

The aqueduct construction was shoddy, too. Instead of tightly fitted seams, the sides and bottom were covered in loose rock that might prevent erosion but leaked horribly. Theop was right in suspecting fraud. The barons had built a few perfect sections they could show the Plenum, cut corners on the rest, and no doubt pocketed the difference.

Ahead, a tall mushroom-shaped rock jutted out of the landscape. It looked like a convenient place for them to rest. He nudged the elephant next to the rock and helped Hathorah disembark. He slid to the ground and lifted her down.

Darmon led the elephant to a ditch where it drank and began grazing on the plants along the banks. Smart. The elephant remembered.

Hathorah walked around the rock to the shaded side and patted the ground next to her. He shook his head. "No, you rest. I'm going walk the length of this ditch and see what they've done at the other end."

He walked longer and farther than he'd intended, but the evidence grew more compelling the further he went. Side ditches extended from the main ditch, and additional smaller rills off of those. No wonder so little water was reaching the city. He glanced back the way he had come and could no longer see the rock where he'd left Hathorah and the elephant. Time to start back.

It was hot, and he was thirsty. He crab-walked down the bank, scooped water with cupped hands, and drank. When he came back up, four tough-looking individuals were waiting for him.

These were thugs, not farmers. He'd dealt with their kind before and wasn't afraid for himself, but this time was different. Hathorah was with him.

In the distance, three more came to join them.

No. Not three—two, holding Hathorah between them. "Look what we found," one of the men shouted.

No fear, Darmon told himself. Don't give fear a foothold.

Without warning, he broke into a run, sprinting to his wife. The men surrounding him made a clumsy grab to stop him, but they were too late. They gave chase, but he'd nearly reached Hathorah before they even started.

"Let her go. Now!" he said with authority. A vague recognition of the burly man walking on her right bubbled up in his memory. "I remember you. Two years ago, you tried to start an uprising among the farmers."

"Oh, it's you," the man said.

Darmon pushed himself between the men holding Hathorah and swiftly pulled her from their grasp. He wrapped his arm around her and began walking with her toward the rock.

"Hey, you," shouted one of the others. "We're not done with you."

To Hathorah, he said quietly, "Keep walking. Bring the elephant to the rock, climb on it, ride away."

"But—"

"No buts. I can handle these men easier if I don't have to worry about you."

She nodded, and he let her continue on, while he spun to face the men.

The rest of the men caught up, and Darmon was surrounded by all six of them.

"You're done here." Darmon jerked his thumb toward the agitator he'd confronted once before. "Ask him."

"Let them go on their way," the man said.

Darmon fought a strong urge to turn around to see if Hathorah had made it to the elephant, but that would only draw attention to her, and they seemed to have momentarily forgotten about her.

One of the men shook his head. "That's not what we were sent to do."

"Believe me," the burly man said, "what the baron's paying us isn't worth it."

The men crowded Darmon. "I don't see why you're afraid. We outnumber him six to one."

"You should listen to your friend." Darmon needed to keep them distracted until Hathorah was safely away.

"He's not our friend."

Darmon stepped next to the burly man. "He's a better friend to you than you know."

"Don't ask for trouble," the burly man said to the others. "This man is the king's First Consul."

"He doesn't look like a royal," one of the men said.

"I'm not. I serve Atlantis by serving our king."

"Prove it."

Darmon's royal vestments and his First Consul emblem were in his baggage on the elephant, which by now was hopefully carrying Hathorah to safety. No, he didn't have anything on his person to indicate his position. What he did have was the rule of Atlantean citizenship, which every schoolboy learned.

"I don't have to prove anything." He drew himself up to stand as proudly as possible. "Regardless of my position at court, I am a citizen of Atlantis, and everywhere in the world it is known that should anyone harm even one hair on an Atlantean's head, the retribution of our military would fall upon them."

The men's eyes blazed with fear. They turned and ran off. *Well, that little speech was certainly effective.*

Then, behind him, he heard thunder and felt massive weight pounding the ground. He spun around and saw Hathorah atop the elephant, charging at full speed. He looked back and his tormentors were nowhere to be seen.

The elephant slowed, stopped, and bent down as calmly as any elephant ever had. Hathorah extended her hand to him and he climbed up behind her.

He kissed her neck. "I told you to leave."

She turned around and returned his kiss. "It's so sweet that you thought that would happen."

He chuckled. "Where did you get so skilled at handling an elephant?"

"Compared to a full grown whale, this wasn't that difficult."

Would it be wrong of him to feel pride in his wife? He thought not. Still, this hadn't been the romantic getaway to the countryside he'd promised. She deserved better.

"Let's go home," she said.

He gave her an affectionate squeeze. "Yes, home."

CHAPTER 22

Their elephant plodded toward the capital in no particular hurry, but neither were they. Maybe the excitement of the charge that Hathorah had set him on had worn out the pachyderm. Darmon, riding behind Hathorah, felt her shake with laughter.

She turned and looked back at him. "Are your field trips always so dramatic?"

"Almost never."

He could see the concern on her face. Because, of course, she had picked up the falseness in his voice.

"All right. I've only run into a similar situation once before."

"You never told me."

"There was no need. I was wearing my First Consul emblem that time." He laughed. "I admit that shiny bit of metal didn't frighten them as much as a valiant woman astride a charging elephant." He kissed her. "Don't worry. The biggest risk I face on most trips is getting fat from too many banquets."

The elephant continued on without their guidance as they enjoyed the day and each other's company, knowing the challenges of their daily lives waited at home. Darmon could be forgiven for wanting to stretch out these final few hours alone with his wife on the dusty plains—far from wily politicians and city noises.

He looked at the barren fields surrounding them. "People in the capital fail to notice the effect of drought because the markets are always full of imported goods. To folks in the countryside, crop failure means hunger."

Hathorah laid her hand on his cheek. The plains were hot, and her fingers felt cool by comparison. He clasped his hand over hers and held it there. Then he noticed they'd left the road. "Where are we?"

Hathorah gazed across the field. "I don't know."

"Well, who's driving?"

She laughed. "The elephant."

A wind started to blow, but instead of mitigating the heat, it did the opposite, lifting up the scorching temperature of the cracked earth. Hathorah's hair whipped his face. He reached into her travel bag, pulled out a scarf, and tied it over her hair.

"Thank you," she said.

The wind intensified, and Darmon turned in its direction. The sky had taken on a sickly umber hue he'd never seen before. He tapped his wife on the shoulder. "Ever known the sky to be this color?"

She looked behind them. "No. What do you think it means?"

"Nothing good."

Suddenly, the yellow sky surrounded them. Sand and grit and even small pebbles whirled around in a tempest. Darmon slid Hathorah's scarf down over her face and pulled it tight, then pressed his face against her back with his eyes closed. Grit still got in his nose and mouth. Worried how Hathorah was faring, he pulled her scarf tighter.

Their elephant continued walking. It didn't trumpet with alarm or even seem to mind being blasted by sand. He'd often seen elephants pick up dirt with their trunks and throw it over their backs. No doubt he thought this was a free dust bath.

After some time—it was hard to tell how long—the storm disappeared as quickly as it had come. The elephant had stopped moving. Darmon used his water skin to rinse his face, then handed it to Hathorah. She uncovered her face, gave it a quick rinse, and took a drink.

"Are you all right?" he said, his throat still a little gritty.

She nodded and handed him the skin. "You?"

"Yes. That was really something."

Her eyes crinkled with mirth. "Traveling with you is just an endless adventure."

The elephant tilted his head forward, filling his trunk from a waterhole.

"How did he find a pond in that sandstorm?" Hathorah said.

"Don't you know? Elephants can smell water."

"Good thing. I'm filthy."

"Pat his left shoulder and he'll let us down."

When Hathorah did so, the elephant bent his knee. Darmon jumped down and then reached up to help Hathorah. They bent over the pool where the elephant was drinking and washed their face, hair, and hands.

The elephant ignored them and continued to drink. When he was sated, he walked over and ate the top branches of some acacia trees growing nearby.

After they'd rested, Darmon said to their mount, "Come. Let's go home. There's better forage at the palace."

They climbed on, Darmon riding in front this time. "Find the road," he said. They started moving across the open field.

"Are you worried that he can't?" Hathorah said.

Darmon shook his head. "Elephants have excellent memories and an uncanny sense of direction."

Hathorah hugged him. "Then what's bothering you?"

"That sandstorm—that's what the future of Atlantis is going to look like. I feel an increased urgency to get everyone out."

She patted his back. "A foreshadowing, for sure. But the techgnosists estimated a century or more. You have time, and this is not your burden alone. Storms like today's may even help you prove the climate crisis is at hand."

"Not to the barons," Darmon said. "They'll drain the lakes and prevent the farmers from leaving until they squeeze every smidge of profit from the land."

"No one in Atlantis is *that* selfish."

"Can you say that after having spent this past week with them? They agree the drought is a serious problem. They merely find it inconvenient to admit. I have no doubt that many of them are already building mansions on Tartessos against the day when Atlantis no longer profits them."

"If that is true, then the Mystery School had failed them," Hathorah said. "Every baron and their progeny have been educated in our system. We gave them first-hand experience of the ancient mysteries. For them to act against our ideals means that we haven't lived up to our mission."

Darmon sighed. Well, this holiday certainly hadn't brought Hathorah the happiness he'd hoped it would.

PART II

CHAPTER 23

A decade later, the aqueducts were barely delivering a trickle of water into the canals surrounding the capital. The water level was hardly deep enough to allow ships to navigate. Darmon realized that soon, emigrants to the colonies would have to walk to the ocean and board outbound ships there and incoming cargo would eventually have to be offloaded and carried fifty stades inland. That was going to be problematic, as camels had replaced elephants. The strange, new creatures ate less, drank less, and fared better in the ever-growing desert, but they lacked the elephant's strength and placid demeanor.

For centuries, elephants had not only carried goods but pulled the ropes that hoisted nets of cargo onto the docks and pushed blocks of stone up ramps for construction projects. Camels could not do that. Some of that work could be done with enough manpower, with treadmill hoists and drag gangs of a hundred or more. But Nurlano's wall had proved effective at stopping immigration and forcing the workers to return to the farms, resulting in fewer manual laborers. When would that ruinous policy end?

Even worse, when the farms most distant from the lakes had started to fail, the Plenum had finally decided to obey the Supreme Nine and start shipping emigrants to the colonies—starting with the barons. And enough workers for them to support their lifestyle in a new place.

Darmon had told the king ten years ago that the aqueducts were shoddy and would lose precious water, and the king warned the Plenum. And the

Plenum swore up and down that the barons had made the necessary repairs, and their own inspection teams had confirmed it. But Darmon was certain they were lying, and after his last trip into the fields, the king felt he couldn't risk Darmon's life to find out the truth. Even so, recent reports indicated the water levels in the lakes were low. He expected it wouldn't be long before the king sent him out to look at the lakes.

He hoped that would prove unnecessary. There was enough to do planning Strongyle. After the king committed to establishing a third colony, he tasked Darmon with the planning. Was there no one else in Atlantis who could do this?

"No one I trust as much as you," Theop had said when he'd asked. "All around me I see graft. Every one of these big projects eats away at the treasury, and too many people are getting rich, though I can't prove how."

Meanwhile, ongoing emigration was filling Tartessos and Ogygia with wealthy Atlanteans who regularly complained to the king about anything that wasn't just as it had been in the capital. Then began protests outside the wall by ordinary citizens who felt they were being left behind. They were right, they were. But this time, it was Nurlano taking the blame instead of the king. Darmon probably took more pleasure from that than he should.

Colonies took decades to establish, and Strongyle still didn't have power. He'd hoped the techgnosists would locate another Tuaoi crystal. Until then, the colony would remain primitive and only poor Atlanteans would deign to settle there. Not that it was a terrible thing. The poor were less welcome in the other two.

Darmon and the king had once discussed the feasibility of settling portions of the populace in lands they traded with. "Those countries value our friendship. Might we not approach them about taking in Atlantean refugees?"

Theop shook his head. "Our people would never go for it. Even the least educated among us is more sophisticated than the backwater tribes we trade with. Making their lands livable for our people would be harder than simply starting a colony from scratch."

"Your Majesty is right. I was just putting another option on the table." Truth was, accustomed as they were to the conveniences afforded by the Tuaoi, Atlanteans would never settle in backward countries that still used torches for light, open-pit fires for heat, and didn't have running water.

The Tuaoi didn't do everything, but what it did, no one would give up. Its power lit their cities, villages, and buildings. Its ability to move water had been harnessed to pump fresh water for thousands of years. Even the deadly rays from the terrible crystal had been channeled by doctors to kill tumors. Atlantis was clean, comfortable, and well lit.

Darmon left the palace for an appointment at the complex that housed the Tuaoi stone. He really preferred to meet with techgnosists at the palace—a meeting at the Tuaoi installation involved too many elaborate rituals. But they said they had something to show him, so he agreed.

He climbed the first level of steps to a wide terrace, where he no longer could see the entire pyramid. Well, most people saw it as a pyramid, but techgnosists, priests, and Atlanteans who had attended the Mystery School knew it was actually the top half of an octahedron—two congruent square pyramids connected at their bases with the downward-pointing pyramid below ground.

A techgnosia initiate with a towel draped over his arm was waiting for him. "Good morning, First Consul."

"Call me Darmon, please."

They walked to the first altar, where he had to remove his shoes, jewelry, and anything containing metal. These he placed in a wicker basket with a lid, which was latched and stowed. Next, they would proceed to the laver, where he would be required to wash his hands and feet. After that, he would pad barefoot across the smooth stone terrace and stand before the outer doors with arms upraised. A techgnosist holding a pinecone-shaped object would walk around him, waving it up and down. It was all very ritualized, like they wanted to be priests instead of techgnosists.

This time, when he reached the laver, a techgnosist, covered head-to-toe in a white tunic, met him. "You're being granted admission to inner chambers today. I'll need you to immerse your whole body this time, and then put on these." He gestured toward a stone bench on which lay a tunic identical to the man's, a pair of cloth booties, gloves, and a headscarf.

Darmon sighed, stripped, and slipped into the laver. When he stood up, the man handed him a towel. He dried, slipped on the tunic—which was strangely stiff—booties, and gloves. They walked to the entrance where, as on previous occasions, there was the customary waving of the pinecone. When the door opened, he stepped inside and was greeted by Sprydion, the chief techgnosist, and four others, all dressed in white tunics and booties.

Unusual. He'd been here before, and though the gatekeepers acted like want-to-be priests, the techgnosists he met with usually dressed like . . . people. Now they had apparently all found religion and initiated him into the cult.

They entered the room where they had met on previous occasions, but the refreshments customarily laid out for their meetings were missing. Sprydion introduced the women techgnosists first, Maoyl and Corval, then the two men. "This is Forva and Katoric."

The group crossed to a door on the opposite side of the room. It opened to reveal a small closet.

Sprydion turned to him. "I'm sorry. This only accommodates two at a time. We'll send the two women first, then you and I will follow."

Maoyl and Corval entered, covered their heads and faces with their scarfs, and closed the door.

Darmon heard no sound, but in an instant the door opened and the closet was empty. Some sort of secret passage, he presumed.

Sprydion stepped inside and motioned for him to follow. Once Darmon was inside, Sprydion took the white scarf from him and draped it over Darmon's head, pulling it down until it completely covered his face. "Whatever you do, don't lift this up."

Then what was the point of coming? He couldn't see anything except the cloth.

Suddenly, he was weightless. His intuition told him that they were descending, but he no longer sensed a floor in the closet. Queasiness hit him, and he thought he might be sick. Then the closet door opened to a room filled with light. He peeked at his feet through the gap at the bottom of his scarf and saw he was standing on . . . nothing. Now he definitely felt like throwing up.

The covering over his eyes, which a moment before was too dense to see through, now seemed transparent. So much so that he touched it to make sure it was still in place. Maoyl and Corval, who had preceded them, reached inside and pulled him out of the floorless closet. They moved him out of the way, and instantly the two male techgnosists who'd remained behind stepped into the room.

Darmon's jaw dropped. Hovering before him was the Tuaoi, a faceted crystal capped with a six-sided pyramid on the upper end. He'd seen illustrations since his school days, but this was the first time he had been in its presence. Its height was about that of three tall men standing on one another's shoulders. Each faceted side was the length of a woman of average height lying prone. Its transparency was perfect, clearer than the purest quartz. Inside was an ever-changing array of colors.

"Your first time?" Corval said.

Darmon nodded. "Is it . . . a prism?"

"Not an ordinary one. There exist rays emanating from the sun and stars that are too fine for eyes to see." She pointed toward the top of Tuaoi. "When the rays enter the hexagonal cap, it directs them at a facet, which reflects them to the next, and it to the next. The beam circles around the axis six reflections per revolution, following a helical path for many thousand revolutions."

It was only because Darmon had found sacred geometry one of the more fascinating subjects in school that he could follow her explanation.

"When the beam reaches the last facet at the base of the crystal, its course is reversed and its helical path proceeds back to the starting facet. There it repeats the circuit anew, increasing in intensity."

He tore his eyes from the dazzling sight and looked at her. "How am I seeing through this opaque veil?"

"One characteristic of the rays given off by the Tuaoi is their ability to penetrate solids as easily as your hand moves through air. We use these in healing centers to kill certain detrimental tumors that afflict some people. But the rays can kill healthy individuals. The garments we're wearing contain fine threads of orichalcum, which channels the rays away to protect us, yet the weave of our face coverings refract enough rays to let us see."

Sprydion interrupted. "I'm sure Darmon knows all that."

"Well . . . " He knew the basics, but techgnostics had never been his favorite subject.

"When the first techgnosists began to study the crystal," Corval said, warming to her subject, "it was noticed that soldiers wearing armor containing orichalcum were less prone to burns. That eventually led—"

"Come with me," Sprydion said. "This team has been working on your problem and has had an exciting breakthrough. One that is more important than ancient history."

They descended a circular incline that ended in a room beneath the Tuaoi stone. The four techgnosists he'd just met walked over and stood around an opalescent crystal like proud parents. It was a miniature of the Tuaoi, about the height of his forearm.

"You found one!" Darmon said.

Katoric radiated pride. "Find it? No. We made it!"

"Bred it, actually," Maoyl said.

"Bred?" Darmon said. "What, like mating elephants?"

Sprydion laughed. "Well, not quite like that, but yes, this team has discovered a way to take a pure crystal and use the Tuaoi's energy to cut and polish its facets, form the hexagonal capstone, and then charge it with rays."

Corval took over. "We beam Tuaoi rays into it, similar to the way the Tuaoi receives rays from the sun and stars."

Darmon's heart began to beat faster. This was exactly what they needed to start another colony, one that would preserve Atlantean culture for more than the very rich. Once they could create their own power-generating crystals, there would be no limit to how many colonies they could establish. Until now, the only three Tuaoi known to exist had been found, not created. Thousands of years of searching had never turned up another.

A common myth was that the Tuaoi stone came from the stars, but one of the things he did learn in the Mystery School was that the Tuaoi was born deep in the bowels of the earth. Poseidon's father, Cronus, found it when an earthquake raised an island to the west. While investigating the newly raised land, he discovered the giant crystal and two broken pieces on the floor of a cave. He thought his wife, Rhea, would like one, so he carried it out into the sun. It immediately began its colorful display. He knew he had something special and went back for the other two. Good thing he did, because a subsequent quake sank the island, and he'd never have been able to retrieve them later.

For many years, the magnificent crystals were just decorative. Then someone, whose name is lost to history, began to polish the facets and more precisely shape the capstone. As he or she improved upon nature, the stone began to glow. Not long afterwards, the polisher died of strange burns. As did anyone who spent too much time near the crystal.

Poseidon was the first to understand its potential—and danger. Initially, he called it the Terrible Crystal for its harmful effects. But Poseidon understood sacred geometry and ordered construction of this very octahedron to house it. He then set Atlantis's original techgnosists to figuring out how to channel the power it gave off.

And now they had figured out how to make more.

"The king will be more than pleased," Darmon said. "How did this discovery come about?"

"I was updating the historical records we keep on the Tuaoi," Maoyl said, "and I noticed it undergoes a fractional growth every year."

"She brought her findings to the team," Katoric said, "and we postulated that the perpetual push of the rays along the helical paths actually forces the crystal outward."

Forva, who had yet to speak, cut in. "So we thought if we put a crystal in close proximity to the original, it might be possible to use this growth potential to breed another. As you can see, it worked."

"How much power does this small one generate?" Darmon said.

"Enough to light a building," Forva said.

"Oh."

"Don't sound disappointed," Sprydion said. "You're looking at the greatest accomplishment since Atlantis was founded."

Darmon thought of another problem. "I know power from the Tuaoi extends throughout Atlantis, but I've never actually understood how it gets from this building to places where it's applied. Does it flow through some sort of invisible channels in the ether? If so, a new colony will need to build those, too."

"No, no. Crystals vibrate at particular frequencies. Lights, pumps, and other devices draw from the Tuaoi by being attuned to its frequency."

"Hmm. . . could it be used to power our ships?" Tuaoi driven ships would really speed up migration to the colonies.

"In what way?" Sprydion said.

"We already use the Tuaoi to power water pumps. What if we fitted ships with pumps that drew in water at the bow and expelled it with great force out a tube at the stern?"

"Thus propelling the vessel forward," Forva said. "I like your thinking. You should have been a techgnosist."

Sprydion shook his head. "Perhaps your scheme could push scows around the city canals, but it wouldn't work for sea-going vessels."

"Why not?"

"A ship at sea would quickly lose its connection with the Tuaoi."

"I don't understand. I've visited villages and barons' estates thousands of stades away, all of them powered by this Tuaoi."

"True. The crystal's rays reach to those places, but the key to reception at vast distances is the size of the receiver. A ship that could maintain connection with the Tuaoi while at sea would have to be larger than our whole harbor."

Too bad. A Tuaoi-powered fleet would have been a wonderful solution. Oh, well. Darmon returned his attention to what was achievable. "So, how long before this small Tuaoi will be large enough to power a colony?"

Maoyl stepped forward. "We estimate the baby will grow to the size of the one on Ogygia in less than a thousand years."

"A thousand years!" Darmon turned to Sprydion. "You predicted we only had a century left here, and that was a decade ago."

"True, but—"

"What if we increase the power we're feeding it by tenfold?" Katoric suggested.

Forva nodded. "If it could handle the increased flow, that should reduce the required time to one tenth. There's your hundred years."

Corval shook her head. "That's a big if. We don't know if the growth rate is continual or exponential. Accelerating the power might blow it up."

Sprydion turned to Darmon. "It sounds like we need to calculate the forces at work and the probability mathematics before we can give you a definitive answer. One thing I do want to caution you about is that if we divert power to the baby Tuaoi by tenfold, Atlantis might suffer significant power shortages."

Darmon nodded. "Fair enough. Include that factor in your calculations so we know the risk to Atlantis and not just to—Baby Tuaoi? Is that what we're calling it now?"

The techgnosists glanced at each other and nodded.

"Baby it is."

CHAPTER 24

Darmon was made to immerse in the laver again before he could change into his regular clothes and go to the palace. As he passed the Plenum, he noticed an agitated crowd gathered there. What was that about? Water, most likely. That had been the most pressing issue for a decade now.

At the palace, there was a queue to gain admittance. As the line snaked forward and he neared the head, he saw the holdup. Guards were stopping to identify everyone before allowing them to pass or turning them away. He stepped out of line and walked to the gate. "Darmon, First Consul to the king."

"Good morning, sir." The guard stepped back to let him pass.

He stopped. "What's going on here?"

"Trouble in front of the Plenum. They sent word we should keep any outsiders away from the king."

"Isn't protecting the king your job every day? Why is today any different?"

"I don't know, sir. I do what I'm told."

Darmon nodded. "Just as long as it's your king doing the telling."

He started for his office but changed his mind and headed straight to the king. Theop would want to hear about the techgnosists' discovery.

When he reached the king's antechamber, guards he didn't know blocked his way, but the door was open and he could see Theop pacing at the opposite end of the room. "Your Majesty?"

The king looked at them. "There you are! Guards, let him in. I said not to admit Nurlano, that didn't mean everyone else."

Darmon entered and made a scant bow. "Are we at war?"

"Not that I know of. Why?"

"The guards. I could barely get in the palace."

"Oh, them. Do you think they'll discourage Nurlano?"

"Not much does. Why?"

"He requested an audience with me. I've been stalling."

Darmon gave the king a wry grin. "You scared of that puny old man?"

"I'm scared of what he wants."

"Which is?"

"He wants me to order soldiers to protect the wall and put down the protesters in front of the Plenum."

"Do that and you'll just inflame the situation. The protests are aimed strictly at the decisions of Nurlano and his cronies. No one blames the king."

"And I intend to keep it that way," Theop said. "That's why I'm not receiving him today."

"Ah. So, you *are* scared of Nurlano."

"Have a good laugh. I'm sending you to the Plenum in my place."

He shrugged. Nothing unusual about that. "Before I go, I have news that will cheer you up." Darmon relayed to the king all that the techgnosists had shown him, and Theop was indeed pleased.

Taking leave of the king, he put on his indigo vestments, pinned on his First Consul emblem, and went to the Plenum. Into the bonfire.

* * *

One thing that surprised Darmon was that Nurlano hadn't snapped up a spot on the colony as the emigration began. Even he couldn't deny at this point that the drought seemed permanent. Perhaps it was because he would have no power on Tartessos. The barons no longer needed him, and the king appointed the colony regents. Nurlano had burned that opportunity decades ago.

He wasn't going to win the king's favor with his current rant, either. "If Theop refuses to take necessary and obvious actions to defend us against migrants attempting to breach our wall, then I call upon our military to solve the problem quickly." Nurlano's face turned the color of a beet, and spittle flew from his lips. "When our ancient kings faced an enemy, they were vicious, they were ruthless, but they put the invaders down with indomitable force. That shows you the power of strength."

"Ah, but this situation is different." Darmon walked to the front of the chamber, keeping his voice pitched low, the reasonable person in the room. "The people you speak of aren't invaders. They are Atlantean citizens the same as you or me—the very people the Plenum is supposed to represent." He directed his attention to the collective body assembled. "The fact is, Nurlano has created an incendiary moment here. He wants protection from his own failure to recognize and deal with drought. Now there's unrest because of the unjust wall that is keeping poorer citizens out of the capital where they might gain equal access to boats and a better life in the distant colonies."

"Drought, drought, drought!" Nurlano yelled. "Darmon's favorite topic. He wants to change the subject from the king's unwillingness to take military action. Well, unless the First Consul is blind, he may have noticed that the hordes are not only surging at the city gates, but are inside Atlantis already, gathered in front of this very building."

"And you, sir, if you were to remove your blinders and actually look outside, would see not the farmers you fear but our own youth—good and noble citizens of the capital. They have convened to show support for the farm workers and demand they be treated equally."

Nurlano held up a report. "To what end? In your very own words, this document plainly states that the colonies cannot hold everyone."

"Two cannot, but if we build a third colony—"

"Yes, well and good. But in the interim, the king should force those outside the wall back to their farms to wait for the harvest."

"I don't think you understand. There will be no harvest for most of them. These are the poorest of the poor. The drought has permanently desiccated their farmland. They are not wealthy barons able to leach off government-constructed aqueducts. They will be vital to develop agriculture in the new colony, but they may not survive until then if we do not care for them now."

"If Atlantis does not show strength in the present unrest, how much less control will we have when they are on a distant colony?"

"They are not 'they.' *They* are us. We are all Atlanteans, here and in the colonies, under the rule of one king. You'll notice the young people aren't gathering in front of the palace. It is you and your miserable wall and failure to take action on the drought that has them upset. You cannot ask the king to hide you behind his army because you don't want to face the people you are supposed to represent." With that, Darmon took his leave.

Nurlano shouted to his back, "Why aren't they in school?" But even he must have realized that didn't deserve a response.

Darmon returned to the king. "Your Majesty, you're right. Someone needs to tour the realm and ascertain the conditions out beyond the baron's estates. It's been ten years since Hathorah and I went. I'll go, but I'm leaving her home this time."

"I wish I had two of you. One to advise me here, and one to send to the hinterlands. I'll provide you with an armed guard."

"No, I don't think that's necessary. It's Nurlano the people are upset with, not me."

"And Nurlano wouldn't dare interfere with you because he knows I'd come down on him like the wrath of the gods. Well, take an extra camel, just in case yours gets injured. I can't risk you getting stranded out there."

CHAPTER 25

Darmon had completed his tour of the agricultural plains—now far less agricultural than they had been—and was on his way back to the capital. He entered a village of small houses typical of what the barons allowed the tenants to have. It was abandoned like so many hamlets he'd seen on this trip. In a sense, that was good. It meant people were heeding the government's advice to leave. Well, not the Plenum's, but certainly that of the king and court.

The harsh reality of their predicament had really hit him when he saw the once great lake reduced to a fraction of its former size. It was one thing to sit in the capital discussing water depletion and studying maps of encroaching desert with techgnosists, and quite another to stand on what was once the shoreline and barely see the gleam of water halfway to the horizon.

He hadn't been to the lake since before Theop became king. Theop's father had sent them on a year-long tour of the realm to instill in his son respect for the people and resources he'd someday rule. Darmon wasn't First Consul then, wasn't anything official, merely Prince Theop's best friend. He remembered the lakes as being so vast they couldn't see across them, so huge it took weeks to ride around the perimeter of just one. And there were three equally large. That was only forty, no, fifty years ago.

Nurlano should come out here and witness the depletion the baron's canals had wrought.

The plaintive cry of a young child caught his ear. Apparently, this village wasn't entirely abandoned. He tapped his crop on his camel's right haunch and the beast turned in that direction.

Soon he came upon the source of the sound. A waif sat on a stone step, sobbing. He commanded his camel to kneel. His pack camel automatically did the same. Darmon dismounted and began to approach the girl. She looked alarmed, so he slowed his step. "Are you hurt, daughter?"

She shook her head.

"Why are you crying?"

She sniffled.

"Where are your mother and father?"

"Mother's dead. Father is trapped under our cart. The axle broke." She started sobbing again, and between sobs poured out a stream of words. "He tried to fix it, (sob) but the cart fell on him (sob) and he sent me back here to bring someone, (sob) but nobody's left. Everyone's gone."

He'd edged nearer until he was close enough to scoop her up. He held her and patted her on the back. "Don't worry, I'll help you. My name's Darmon. What's yours?"

"Seia."

He and Hathorah had never had children. Their life, their mutual commitment to their duties, just made it impossible. He didn't really know what to do with one. "Let's go find your father. Do you know the way?"

She wiped her nose on the shoulder of his tunic and nodded. He looked at the wet fabric. Children were certainly leaky.

When they started toward his camel, she squirmed out of his arms. He caught her by the hand as she scrabbled to the ground. "Whoa, where are you going? I thought you wanted to help your father."

She eyed the camel and pulled farther away.

"What? Him? That's just Strider. Are you afraid of him?"

Instead of answering, Seia grabbed his legs and hid behind them.

"Have you never seen a camel? They're new to Atlantis, I know. I used to ride elephants, which were a lot more fun, but there aren't enough grasslands for them, so they've gone away." Like we will.

He stooped down, wrapped his arms around her, and stood. "He looks funny, but he won't hurt you. Will you, Strider?"

The camel curled his lip and snarled.

Seia made a piercing squeal directly in his ear. Children were not only leaky, but loud.

Darmon patted the camel's neck. "Now, now, boy. You're frightening the little girl." He took Seia's hand in his and stroked the camel gently. "See? You can pet him. He won't bite." Well, actually, camels would bite, just not this one. And, if aggravated, a camel could kick a man across the yard. Not to mention the spitting. No sense mentioning that to the child just now.

He set her on the camel's back and picked up the rope to his pack animal. He climbed on in front of her. "Now, Seia, I'm going to need both hands free to manage two camels, so you wrap your arms around my waist and hold on to me." He felt tiny limbs tenuously embrace him. He gave a light tug on the reins. "Up, big fellow."

The camel stretched his neck forward and came up on his front knees. Darmon canted backwards, pressing against Seia. The beast raised its rear haunches, pitching the two riders forward. She was not accustomed to that, and screamed, gripping Darmon with the strength of a lion's claws. The camel straightened its front legs, jerking them both upright.

Darmon loosened her fingernails from his stomach. "Keep hold, but maybe not quite so tight. Let's go find your father."

The child's short legs had not walked that far, and it took no time for the camel's stride to cover the same ground. Darmon saw the lopsided cart with a pair of men's legs sticking out from beneath it. The torso was too far under to be visible. All he could hope was that the man was still alive. Nothing had prepared him to deal with a grieving daughter.

Darmon halted the camels and made them kneel, with the same pitching back and forth. He slid to the ground. "Seia, wait here."

"No. I want to come." Even lying down, the camel was much taller than Seia, but the child somehow managed to climb off and reach the cart before he did.

Next thing he learned, children don't do as they're told. He hoped for the best.

Darmon got down on his hands and knees to peer under the cart. "Sir? Can you speak?" He heard a muffled grunt, thank the gods. Seia nudged him aside and squirmed underneath the cart.

"Get out of there before you're both trapped!" He lay down in the dirt to better assess the situation. The weight of the cart had the man pinned, but he didn't see any blood. "Sir, turn your head this way, if you can move."

The man shifted his head far enough for Darmon to see his eyes. Good, they were clear and observant. He might not be paralyzed. "Seia, help me unload the cart, and I'll try to lift it."

"Do as he says, daughter."

Good. The voice was scratchy and weak, but the man could speak.

She wiggled out and began carelessly heaping their belongings beside the cart. Darmon stood and helped. Seia started to climb on the cart to reach items farther in. "No, I'll get those. Your weight might press it down on him." She shied away, looking chagrined.

Once he judged it sufficiently empty that he might be able to lift it, he bent his knees, grabbed the edge of the cart, and straightened his legs. "Can you crawl out?" His straining muscles began to tremble. "Seia? Is your father moving? If he isn't, can you grab his legs and pull him? I can't hold this up much longer."

The girl bent down and peered under the wagon. "He's moving! Oh, he's moving!"

"I'm clear," the man said.

Darmon let the cart drop. He put his hands on the small of his back and rubbed. There'd be a price to pay tonight. He extended his hand to the man, lying in the dust next to the cart. "Can you stand, or do you need help?"

"I think I'm able." He accepted Darmon's hand and rose unsteadily. Seia clutched him, nearly knocking him back down. "Easy, child, let me get my footing."

Darmon found a tarp among the family's belongings, opened it flat, and began piling everything into it.

"What are you doing?"

"Taking you back to the city with me. I don't know how to mend your cart, but I have an extra pack animal. We'll strap your things on him and you and your daughter can ride with me."

"It's no good. The baron said we had to go east."

East? "That . . . makes no sense. Even if you repaired your cart, you'd never make it across the desert. Get a rope and help me tie this closed."

The man shook his head. "The wall, sir. The poor aren't allowed in the capital."

"Don't worry about the wall. You'll be with me. Now, are you strong enough to help me lift this bundle onto that camel?"

"I am, but won't that be too heavy for him?"

"No, these beasts, despite all their moods, can carry a surprising amount of weight."

They picked it up between them and wedged it atop the pack camel. The camel started to stutter-step to one side. Darmon grabbed his reins. "Stay still!" He turned to Seia. "Bring us ropes."

The man held his side of the bundle in place while Seia fetched ropes. "They said we have to leave Atlantis."

Darmon nodded. "That's true. But you'll go by sea."

"I don't understand how that's possible for the likes of us."

The likes of them? Nurlano wasn't the only one who considered the farmers to be lesser Atlanteans. "Don't worry. I'll take care of everything."

"Who are you?"

"Oh, I'm sorry, where are my manners?" He extended his hand. "Darmon."

The man clasped it with brotherly affection. "But who *are* you that you can get us past the wall and onto a ship?"

"Just a humble servant of Atlantis," Darmon said. "Much like yourself."

CHAPTER 26

Darmon had been back from his journey for a few weeks. He'd left the farmer and his daughter with a group of migrants waiting to sail to Strongyle. Protests were still going on in the capital and out at the wall.

Hathorah had made breakfast, and they'd finished eating when there was a knock on the door. She was already dressed for school and waiting for him so they could leave together.

"Please see who is at the door," he said from the bedroom.

He heard the door open, then his wife called, "Darmon?" Her tone wasn't fearful, but it had urgency.

He hurried into the foyer. "Is everything all right?"

Four armed guards crowded in the hallway. "Darmon, come with us. You are under arrest."

"By whose order."

"The king. Come along peacefully. Don't make us bind you in front of your wife."

"This is a mistake." Theop would never condone this.

"That's what they always claim," a guard said.

"What am I charged with?"

"Embezzlement, abuse of office, and defrauding the treasury."

"Where are you taking him?" Hathorah said.

"To the keep."

He gave Hathorah a pleading look. "Talk to the king."

The men took him by the arms and led him away.

His cell was furnished with a single stone slab that served as table, chair, or bed. He was lying on it with his eyes closed, trying to imagine why Theop had turned against him. Or how this could have happened with the king's knowledge. The only persons who could order the seizure of a citizen were the king or those he authorized to act in his name. Nurlano certainly wouldn't be one of them, although no doubt the oily codger somehow had a hand in his predicament.

But . . .

He thought back to an address by Nurlano to the Plenum that he'd witnessed earlier that week.

"Let our youth not claim our wall is unjust, for we protect our capital city and our way of life. Our passage of the act authorizing its construction means that it *is* just, for we are the definers of justice," Nurlano had said.

His cronies applauded. Darmon remembered feeling nauseous.

"We govern wisely and to the best of our ability; but we also govern for the good of the established," Nurlano had said. "Why indeed should it be otherwise? If our people are to prosper, it should be their obligation to support those who beget their prosperity."

Members of the Plenum cheered. They evidently weren't aware of how many weren't touched by prosperity.

Nurlano smiled and nodded. "No Member of the Plenum can be guilty of breaking a law, for we are the makers of the law. And if we say it is legal, then it is legal by our saying so."

A member next to him stood and spoke out. "But not all in government are Members of the Plenum."

Nurlano nodded. "True. And if they are found to have pressed their own selfish agendas, profited by alarming innocent citizens, then their actions will be deemed unjust, and punished accordingly."

Darmon had had enough and left the room. Perhaps he should have stayed longer, or told Theop. But the Plenum was always speechifying, even more so recently. He didn't bother the king with everyday rants. Too bad he hadn't seen where it was leading.

Laws legalizing the baron's bribery and corruption could not be labeled "just" simply because the Plenum legislated it. What Darmon didn't understand was why Nurlano's followers thought themselves to be above the authority of the true arbiters of justice, the Ascended Masters. He knew for a fact that every one of them had attended the Mystery School. How could they turn their back on the ideals that had served to bulwark Atlantis for millennia?

Truth be told, being married to Hathorah, he might be too close to the situation to see what was happening. To him, the Mystery School and its secret teachings were the end-all, be-all of human development. Were he a baron or a farmer like Seia's father, struggling to live with no prospects for improvement for himself or his future generations, it might be harder to be excited about the prospect of long-term evolution.

The saying "Wealth is power" had a certain truth. Money could buy power, or the resources to get it. But that was political power. Actual power, as he understood it, came with ascension beyond physical, emotional, and mental barriers. That wasn't bestowed by providence or inheritance on an anointed few. It took work and mastery. Frankly, more effort than he'd ever put in.

In the hours of reflection afforded by imprisonment, it occurred to him that what Atlantis had lost was a broad awareness among ordinary citizens of what the Ascended Masters actually meant for Atlantis. They were, as he saw it, what Atlantis was for. Somehow, the goal of political power replaced the spiritual quest among their leaders. With the great sea trade, merchants become more concerned with imports and exports, and barons with enlarging their estates. Nurlano had once said, "The easiest to manipulate are those who care most about filling their own treasuries."

Yet Darmon was not without his own faltering steps along the path. The cold slab on which he lay, the drab walls of his prison, bespoke some wrongdoing. He hadn't committed the crimes he was charged with, but if justice was whatever the Plenum said, he was guilty of something for sure.

Darmon heard footsteps. The bolt banged sharply, and the door opened. Hathorah entered, and he leaped to his feet. The door closed behind her, and the sound of the bolt sliding back into place echoed in the cell.

He rushed into her arms. Never had it felt so good to hold her. "What's going on out there? What did Theop say?"

She shook her head. "He wouldn't grant me an audience."

"What?" This was a betrayal he never expected.

"He sent one of his courtiers out to talk to me—the tall, thin one with the wide nose."

Darmon nodded. "Go on."

"It's the aqueducts project. There's a fortune in overruns, and the Overseer of the Treasuries has traced them to bribes, kickbacks, and faulty construction that had to be redone."

"I know," Darmon said. "We saw how shoddy they were when we went to the country on holiday a decade ago. But what does that have to do with me?"

"Nothing, of course. But your name is all over the original plans."

Darmon huffed. "It's a trap. Those plans were never intended to be implemented in the first place. The king knows that. Why isn't he helping me, and why wouldn't he see you?"

"Whoever set you up has Theop in a pincer tight as a crab's claw. He can't even talk to us without appearing to show favor. Not only that, the Plenum is blocking him from acting as your judge, claiming the two of you have too close a personal relationship."

"I *thought* we did until now."

She combed her fingers through his hair. "There's hope. Whoever did this to you failed to foresee what would happen. Because you hold the highest civil position, none below you may serve as judge. Since they have prevented the king from doing so, the only entity that can try you is the Court of Supreme Masters." She smiled. "I think we can trust them to see the truth."

"But the king. . . I've given my life to Atlantis. I never expected him to have me arrested. And with no warning? He could have questioned me about the aqueducts before sending guards to our house."

"He was manipulated into it. I'm sure they gave him no alternative."

"He's the king. There must be alternatives."

"I know, but he's going to get you out of this place. The courtier told me that since your crime was only monetary and not a violent offense, Theop is changing the order to house arrest until the trial. You can't leave home even to go to the palace, but at least we'll be together."

It was something, and he would take what he could get. "How soon?"

"We're just waiting for the order to arrive from the palace. I'll wait with you until it comes. Then we'll go home and make dinner."

He smiled. "That sounds nice. I can't wait to get out of here. It's been a terrible day."

"I know. I'll tell you one thing, though."

"What's that?"

"No one's talking about Nurlano, his wall, or his migrant policy anymore."

Darmon furrowed his brow. "That may well be the reason I'm sitting in the keep."

CHAPTER 27

In the days following his release, Darmon endured house arrest until he was going stir crazy. Hathorah continued to teach at the Mystery School every day. She had her students and fellow faculty for company. He had only the walls to talk to until she got home. All of his papers and anything that would interest him were in his office, beyond his reach. He'd read everything in their small home library years ago. With nothing else to amuse him, he tried meditation—it couldn't hurt. But a few minutes after Hathorah left for work was all he could usually muster.

The only word of the outside world he received was when she returned in the evenings. Her school didn't involve itself in politics, barely even acknowledging such a beast existed. So the tidbits of news she brought him were no more than what any pedestrian would have garnered walking through the marketplace. She informed him that protests continued, but now the crowd called Darmon's name and demanded he pay for the aqueducts with his ill-gotten money.

"Hathorah, I think I understand my error," he said when she returned one night. "I didn't snatch those aqueduct plans from Nurlano the day he brought them to my office." Darmon put his head in his hands. "We don't have some stash of wealth secreted away. If the court rules as the crowd demands, they'll take everything. I'll be imprisoned, and you'll be destitute."

She lifted his chin and looked into his eyes. "Then we will go through this with our heads held high, knowing what we know to be true."

"This all occurred a decade ago. I can't remember if I even met these canal builders."

"Your enemies may have fooled the masses, perhaps even forced the king's hand, but do you really think the Supreme Nine could be deceived? By Nurlano?"

He fell back in his chair. "I started to cook dinner, but we've depleted the pantry."

She slipped her sandals back on and picked up a basket. "I'll go to the market. I won't be long."

Hathorah started at the miller's, buying barley flour and millet. Next, she perused the vegetable stalls, selecting a large cauliflower. Behind her were whispers, "That's his wife."

"Let's see if she pays or steals it."

"We can guess what her husband would do."

Hathorah whirled around, face flushed. Everyone busied themselves examining fennel and artichokes. She walked over to the artichokes and the others moved on to the onions and garlic. Deciding not to buy an artichoke, she added a handful of garlic to her basket and paid the proprietor.

"You see? She paid," said a woman behind her.

"Yes, but where did the money come from?"

"Whatever wrong he did, she's not part of it. She's one of the high-ups at the Mystery School."

"I know. I had her for a teacher during my year there."

The urge to turn around and identify the speaker tore at her, but she resisted and walked to the next store, where she purchased a measure of fava beans and another of lentils. There, too, people looked askance and mumbled snide comments they thought she couldn't hear.

These were her former students, their friends and neighbors. They knew Darmon as well as anyone in the city. How could they suddenly believe him dishonest? They didn't strut around the town in fine linens or gold ornaments. They didn't throw lavish banquets or live in a marble palace or have retinues of servants following them around. Instead, they'd chosen a simple house in an ordinary neighborhood and lived on the wages they earned. Although their marriage wasn't perfect, they were united in the conviction that silver and gold were merely metals that society had decided to prize, but as cold, inert, and lifeless as any other chunk of rock. To imagine that Darmon craved wealth was absurd. Those who quickly presumed his guilt obviously didn't understand him.

So why were people so ready to believe the lies?

She thought of the farmer Darmon had rescued, and so many like him. Atlantis was suffering. People were being ripped from their homes, from a life they had known for generations, and scattered around the world to start again. They needed someone to blame, someone to hate. They couldn't hate the change in weather, and Nurlano had been presenting himself as the champion of the common folk for decades. Even if it weren't true, it was the image he had built up, and people were unwilling to give it up.

Darmon, on the other hand, was quiet, behind the scenes. He didn't have a public image. He never trumpeted the purity of his intentions, his dedication to Atlantis. So, yes, people might be ready to believe anything.

She almost had to admire the way Nurlano had managed to manipulate things to get where they were now. There was a near-genius to it.

She stopped at the fishmonger's, but the best of the catch had sold, and she didn't care for the smell of what was left. At the fruit stand, she selected a ripe melon, grapes, and fresh figs and went home.

Darmon was waiting.

CHAPTER 28

Theop tormented himself for days following Darmon's arrest. On one hand, he refused to believe his boyhood friend would pick his pocket. On the other hand, his trusted Overseer of the Treasuries had brought the discrepancies to his attention year after year. And every time, whom did he send to investigate? Darmon.

He shook his head. No. It didn't make any sense. Darmon was the one who reported the shoddy aqueduct construction. If he were the culprit, why would he even bring up the matter? He could have easily reported all was well. It was all so long ago, but the king was certain he remembered correctly.

The king called to a page. "Bring me all of Darmon's reports for the last ten —no, make that eleven—years. Get someone to help if you need it."

If only he could talk about this with someone. But the only person he ever discussed truly troubling matters with was the man he'd had arrested. He couldn't talk to him if he wanted to. It was in the hands of the Court now.

"Your Majesty?" the guard at the door said.

"Yes. What is it?"

"The Overseer of the Treasuries is here, requesting an audience."

Where were his pages? Oh, right, he'd sent them to the hall of records. Theop sighed. "All right, let him in."

The Overseer entered and bowed.

The king fixed him with a hard stare. As Darmon's best friend, Theop wanted to be angry at the Overseer for the trouble he'd brought them. But as King of Atlantis, he couldn't. Theop had told his Overseer to investigate, and the man's figures never lied.

"What is it now?" the king said.

"I'm sorry to trouble Your Majesty, but the Court has asked to see the treasury accounts for the period in question. I didn't want to send them without your permission."

"Does this mean the trial has started?"

"I believe it has. What shall I do about the records?"

"If the highest court asks to see your ledgers, you show them the ledgers. Also, don't be surprised if they call you to testify as to their veracity."

"They already have."

"Then comply with whatever they require, no matter whom it implicates."

"As you wish." The Overseer bowed and started to leave.

"No. Wait. Bring the records here first. This is a very old matter to have been suddenly brought to public scrutiny. I intend to review it thoroughly before it goes to court."

The Overseer cocked his head.

"Now, please," the king said. "And clear your schedule. I want your help to make sure I understand everything."

The king and the Overseer spent the rest of the day and evening poring over every entry. In the end, two facts were plain. A lot of money had disappeared, and someone had taken it. It was less plain that it was Darmon, but it didn't mean he hadn't. And yet . . . a man smart enough to be First Consul would be clever enough not to have his name on any of the payment records. Darmon's name was all over the original plans. That, the king couldn't dispute. He sent the Overseer on his way, telling him to deliver the accounts to the Court.

Theop stretched. They'd worked beyond supper. Even so, he wasn't hungry and was too agitated to sleep. He glanced at his desk across the room. Two huge stacks of documents awaited him. Common people might think it glorious to be king, but really, it was an unending nightmare of documents awaiting his review or signature. Oh, well, since he couldn't sleep, he may as well tend to the day's business.

Several questions nagged at him. How had these decade-old crimes come to the Plenum's attention now, and how had anyone known on which dates they occurred?

He walked to his desk, settled into his chair, and picked up a report from the first stack. Darmon's handwriting? Oh, these were the files he sent the pages to retrieve this morning. A renewed sense of purpose surged through him, and he vowed to read every letter and report in the pile.

When he reached Darmon's letters from Tartessos, he leaped to his feet. "Page!" He riffled through subsequent reports and letters. "Page! Get in here!"

A sleepy young man appeared in the doorway, rubbing his eyes. "You called, Your Majesty?"

"Yes. Get me. . ."

Who? This would require a courtier of high dependability. Normally he'd have sent his First Consul, but that wasn't possible. "Tell Milos to come here. Wake him if you need to."

The king wrote a note to the Court that he wished to present evidence in the trial of Darmon. He knew, by rule of law, that even a king couldn't just walk in and demand to be heard. He had to be invited, and that is exactly what his note requested. He was willing to beg if he had to.

When Milos arrived, he handed him the sealed missive and instructed him to take it to the court and return with their reply.

"Your Majesty, there may be no one there yet. It's . . . early."

Theop glanced at a window. It was, in fact, still dark. "Your instructions are simple. Take this to the Court. Remain there until you receive a reply. Bring it back to me. Speak to no one from the Plenum."

The prince bowed, backed out of the room, and left. The king returned to his desk, selected relevant reports and letters from the pile, and put them in a leather portfolio. He yawned, leaned back in his chair, and nodded off.

CHAPTER 29

Midmorning sun through the windows painted long tapered fingers of light across the floor by the time a servant gently shook Theop awake. "Your Majesty, the prince has returned."

Theop rubbed his eyes, stood up, and nearly fell over because his right leg was asleep. "Admit him." He shook the leg awake, then stretched left, then right, trying to undo a kink in his back.

Milos came forward and bowed. "Is Your Majesty all right?"

"Yes, thank you, I'm fine." He reached for the letter the prince was holding. "May I have that, please?"

The king tore it open and scanned the contents. He was invited to present testimony and evidence at midday. The letter reminded him that the Court worked beyond privilege or rank, and therefore could not receive him as king, but would be pleased to admit citizen Theop.

He refolded the letter, dismissed Milos, and went to change. His clothes looked like they'd been slept in, mostly because they had. Mindful of the letter's unsubtle dismissal of rank, he chose his most ordinary-looking clothes, fancier that any commoner owned, but the plainest he had in his wardrobe. His stomach grumbled that it hadn't been fed. He dismissed it, snatched his portfolio, and left for the Court, surrounded by four guards.

On the streets, he saw the protesters for the first time. The chanting crowd outside the Court building alternated between demands for justice and slurs against Darmon.

His guards had to form a wedge to part a way to the steps. In their wake, people began to recognize him and directed their calls for justice at him. If only he could prove who the true culprit was, he'd be pleased to hand the rascal over, but the scoundrel had covered his tracks well. He only knew for sure they were maligning an innocent man, but it would do no good to proclaim it at this point. He'd let the Court do that.

The king left his guards at the door, and a woman led him into a domed chamber. In all his years on the throne, he'd never been in here before. The old masters sat in a circle of nine chairs upholstered in deep green—not royal indigo, for the high court were not royals. In the center of the room was a single straight-back chair on a round dais.

"Please be seated," the woman said.

Their letter hadn't been kidding. The hard wooden chair was no throne.

He looked around the room for Darmon but didn't see him. This Court normally judged only points of law or matters of government, not individuals. Apparently, it made no provisions for an accused to be present during the proceedings.

The platform his chair rested on suddenly spun. "Your request to be heard has been granted," said an old woman to his right. "Please proceed."

The king cleared his throat. "I have always suspected there was a spy or spies on the palace staff who rifled through my reports and divulged information to members of the Plenum to use for their own ends."

The seat spun again, toward the only man in the circle of nine. "I fail to see how that is germane to the case before us," he said.

"It is. Because when the Plenum acts on the stolen information, they have only a fraction of the true picture. Or in the case of the aqueducts, no truth at all. It was never my administration's intention to build any aqueduct. The plans which bear Darmon's name were merely theoretical studies, nothing more. They were stolen and presented to the Plenum as a solution to the drought, even though Sprydion, our leading techgnosist, told the Plenum that aqueducts would only hasten our demise."

The old man waved his hand. "But this case isn't about stolen plans. We are asked to judge if a top government official pocketed bribes and profited from substandard construction of said canals."

"I'm certain someone did, but I now know beyond a doubt it wasn't Darmon."

"Then why did you sign the order for his arrest?" said one of the women, causing his chair to turn.

"Because as king, I must, like you, respect the rule of law and not hinder the process of justice. And while we are discussing respect, I would like you to stop this device from whirling me around."

She nodded.

"You wrote that you had evidence we need to consider," said another member of the Nine.

This time, the king's chair stayed put. "Yes, I do." He opened his portfolio and removed the stack of documents. "Yesterday, I reviewed the accounting records the Overseer of the Treasuries provided to the Court."

"We're aware," the old man said. "The Overseer mentioned during his testimony this morning that you and he had done so."

The king stood, stepped off the platform, and approached one of the women. "These are letters and reports I received from Darmon over a decade ago. Please pass these among yourselves and inspect them. Note the dates on each." He returned to his chair. "I had these records retrieved from the archives. After the Overseer left, I spent the night combing through them. Compare their dates to the accounting records containing overcharges or suspected fraud and you will see, as I did, that Darmon was out of the country the entire time. He could not have had any involvement."

The stack of reports made its way around the circle, scrutinized by each member, then passed on. Theop wasn't privy to the procedure by which the Court reached a decision, but he had every expectation that when the stack of documents reached the last member, Darmon would instantly be declared innocent. Then he would apologize profusely to his friend and try to rebuild the trust they'd once had.

The old masters took their time studying the reports while the king drummed his fingers on his thigh, mentally devising and revising variations of what he might say to Darmon.

Last to receive the documents was the lone man on the Court. After he reviewed them, he set them on the floor. "Yes, these appear to show Darmon was not in Atlantis."

The king sighed with relief and awaited the pronouncement of innocence.

"But . . ."

What now? He hadn't anticipated a "but."

"These reports could have been fabricated and sent to you from anywhere. You don't know he was on Tartessos when he wrote them."

At first, the king was too stunned to answer. They could really suspect that level of deception? When he gathered his wits, he said, "I have ten regents and a prince who can testify that Darmon was actually on Tartessos the whole time."

"Then we will hear them."

"That would involve great delay and expense to bring them from the colony to Atlantis, but there is one present whom the Court will trust above any other. Of course she will have to recuse herself from the trial if she is to testify."

The Supreme Nine exchanged puzzled looks.

Theop turned to Aigna. She seemed surprised, as if she'd forgotten. But Masters never forget, do they?

The old woman stood and walked to the center of the circle. "I hereby recuse myself."

"Hold on," the man said. "That will leave the court with an even number. What if our decision is split? Who will break the tie?"

"It won't be tied." Aigna prodded the king out of the witness chair and took his place. "I, Aigna of the Court of Masters, can testify that I attended a reception for Darmon held on Tartessos by the regents of the ten districts. After which, he remained in that colony for over twenty weeks, visiting each of the districts. When he left there, he sailed to the colony of Ogygia, where I again encountered him. After a fortnight there, he told me he was going on to the island of Strongyle before returning to Atlantis. I myself did not visit Strongyle so I cannot testify to his presence there, but I will affirm he was in our two colonies during the period covered by the reports we have just examined."

"I think the time has come for us to deliberate," one of the women, who hadn't yet spoken, said.

"King Theop," Aigna said, "would you wait out on the portico?"

"I could return to the palace," he said. "I could leave a guard here to inform me as soon as—"

"I do not think the decision will take long."

She was right. In less time than it would have taken him to return to the palace, the lone man on the court came out. "You were right about the tie," he said. "The vote was unanimous. Darmon is declared entirely innocent."

Theop didn't even bother returning to the palace but went straight to the Plenum instead. There, he informed the assembly of the court's decision.

Seldom had he allowed the Plenum to see the depths of his fury, but they had pushed him too far. Not only was the attack on the character of his First Consul an attack on a friend, it was an assault on his reign. And it would not stand.

He turned to the Plenum scribe. "Write this down, so there can be no misunderstanding. One. When I am finished speaking, this entire assembly is to go before the crowd outside and proclaim that Darmon is blameless and that you are diligently searching for the true culprits."

He fixed his glare on Nurlano. "Two, you will follow up on that promise by ferreting out every man or woman who illegally benefited from the aqueduct construction ten years ago. Third, you will bring me the names of those who perpetrated this scheme to charge a member of my administration with malfeasance which, in my opinion, was concocted solely to divert public attention from the Plenum's own failures."

"I take exception to your accusation," Nurlano said, "but we understand Your Majesty's wish for justice. We will form a special committee to investigate."

"I will let you decide the method by which you will go about the tasks I have set for you, but before I send you out to address the crowd, let us be clear about the weight that hangs over you." He turned to the scribe. "Are you writing all this down?"

The scribe nodded.

"Good. Then add this. Form your committees or whatever. But you have *five* days to provide me the names of everyone involved. If you do not, I shall exercise the king's right to disband this Plenum and order new elections." He took a deep breath. Every eye in the place was fixed upon him, as well they should be. "If you feel threatened, that's because I am threatening you. Now, if someone will move for adjournment, the citizens of Atlantis are waiting for you outside."

Nurlano nodded. "I move we adjourn and reassemble on the front steps."

One of his cronies seconded it. The members voted "yes" and exited in an orderly fashion.

The king held the scribe back and had him write a royal order, rescinding Darmon's arrest. He signed it and sent one of his guards to Darmon's house with it. At a run.

It felt good to get that off his list. Theop left by a side door and returned to the palace. Maybe he should have gone to Darmon instead. He could have delivered the release order in person. But, no, he couldn't. He might have told himself he was too exhausted, but truth be told, he was ashamed.

CHAPTER 30

Hathorah readied herself for the meeting with the governors of the Mystery School. With Darmon restored to his position at the palace, she could turn her focus to her own concern. She understood why the king and her husband were urgently relocating Atlanteans to multiple colonies, yet she foresaw a loss they hadn't factored into their plans. It had come to her clear as morning light one day during her meditations.

Initially, she saw the problem, but not the solution. She kept at her meditations throughout Darmon's ordeal, waiting patiently for inspiration while supporting him. Once the king freed him—and essentially begged for forgiveness—their life returned to normal. Hathorah continued to teach advanced courses during the day. In the evenings, after her husband fell asleep, she'd sit up and seek an answer from the Ascended Masters.

It finally came to her, inserting itself into her morning meditation. She pushed it away, telling her mind to be still. The idea strengthened as she was trying to teach her class. She still rejected it out of hand. It violated the school's most sacred tenets.

And yet, despite her resistance, her plan took shape. The way around the school's rules was through the board of governors. Now she only needed to convince them.

Hathorah entered the meditation room on the top story of the school. Members of the board, all masters themselves, were seated on cushions on the floor. She left her sandals by the door and padded barefoot to an empty pillow. She bowed to the images of Ascended Masters that hung on the wall and sat down. It was said that, at important turns in history, they'd made their presence known and righted the course of the school. Now would be a good time for them to do so again.

Deep silence filled the room. Sounds from the school and surrounding city did not penetrate its walls. No one coughed or sneezed. Absent was the rustle of fabric she frequently heard in class as students stretched or repositioned their legs. Here she was least among the greats.

It was not her first time here, but there had not been many. She did not sit on the board, and teachers were seldom invited. She'd not exactly been invited this time, but rather pressed for an invitation until one came.

A gong sounded. Its reverberations continued to infinity, eventually becoming faint, then indiscernible. Xander, one of the governors, spoke. "Hathorah, we welcome you. Please begin."

Hathorah closed her eyes and took a deep breath. She felt her enérgeia rise and knew she'd do better if she spoke from her highest center. "I've come to ask if we are not at a point when two of our founding principles are at odds."

She sensed a ripple, yet no one had moved. Was it from them or in her?

"Explain," Xander said.

"One purpose of the Mystery School is to preserve and teach secret techniques discovered by the Ascended Masters to those spiritually advanced enough to practice them."

"That is its sole purpose," one of the governors said.

Hathorah mentally projected a warm smile toward the speaker. "It was you who taught me that we serve Atlantis at large. Our students' practices of the techniques sustain a beneficial field of enérgeia that uplifts the whole country, even those who do not meditate."

"This is true."

"The ratio I learned and now teach my students is ten percent. If at least ten percent of Atlanteans are practicing a meditation that raises their enérgeia, the other ninety percent ascend with them, albeit at a slower pace. Is this not a way of saying a main purpose of the school is to use the secret teachings to elevate everyone."

"If they are ready."

"No," said Xander, "*when* they are ready, not if. In the end, all will attain higher consciousness. Even if it takes ten thousand lifetimes."

"Would that still hold true if Atlanteans lost their memory that higher states exist?" Hathorah said.

"The Mystery School would never let that happen," Xander said.

"A decade ago, you tasked me to investigate whether poorer Atlanteans received their final year of school," Hathorah said. "Now that climate change is forcing the dispersion of Atlantis, it is too late to remedy inequities in branch schools. Soon, the ratio of Mystery School graduates among the populace will fall below ten percent. Branch schools must be set up in the colonies. Eventually, I am now certain, even the school itself must be relocated."

A governor gestured toward the images on the wall. "The Ascended Masters will tell us where and when."

Hathorah bowed to the pictures. "I know they will. But even that will not be enough. What I have come to suggest . . . to ask you to ask the Ascended Masters . . . is whether we might be permitted to teach one of the secret techniques to people who are not adepts in the Mystery School."

Another ripple, definitely not her this time. Their reactions hit her. *Outsiders? The uninitiated?*

Her words came out in a rush. "Please, hear me out in this. Just basic instruction on raising enérgeia. The same lesson we give second-year initiates. Enough to make people aware of their potential."

The governor next to Hathorah shook her head. "Even the second-years take a vow of secrecy before being shown that."

This wasn't going well.

Xander said, "How do you see this working?"

She turned toward him. "Perhaps we can disseminate the knowledge through the temples. During the service, enérgeia would be transmitted by an adept. Temple attendees will experience the blissful state. Afterwards, training is offered. To receive it, a person must swear not to reveal the technique, instead they should refer interested friends to someone we have authorized. That will protect the secrecy of the technique and yet make the experience available to a wider population."

No one responded. Her suggestion lay still as a dead fish on a table in the market.

The silence of the school governors stretched on. Was no one even going to ask the Ascended Masters? Was she the only one who saw that unless everybody who left Atlantis carried the knowledge that the higher realms were real and attainable, there would be no future candidates for the Mystery School?

Through closed eyes she perceived a shimmer like the dazzle of light reflected off ocean waves. Intuitively, she knew that the masters had granted permission. The governors had not asked on her behalf. In this place and at this time, she'd been heard and answered directly by the ancients who had founded this school.

She opened her eyes, perhaps expecting the images of them to have jumped off the wall to hover in their midst. They hadn't, at least not on this plane. But the room buzzed like a hummingbird's wings.

Xander spoke. "Hathorah, you have your answer. You are now in charge of this endeavor. How do you plan to proceed?"

"We should start with the priests," she said. "They all attended our school at one time or another."

The governors nodded.

A woman next to Hathorah said, "This undertaking could be time-consuming. Do you want us to assign another teacher to take over your regular classes?"

No! Her students were important to her, and the work gratifying. If there was anything she missed more than Darmon during the months she was with the whale, it was teaching.

"That's a kind offer," Hathorah said, "but I believe I can manage both. I'll let you know if that proves too difficult."

CHAPTER 31

The Plenum met the king's five-day deadline and, as he had expected, pinned the plan to accuse Darmon of malfeasance on someone else. Nurlano escaped unscathed. Although Darmon felt certain the man knew more than he admitted, Nurlano had apparently never personally profited from the aqueducts or the wall. No, he did not crave money, only power. But he excelled at spotting avarice and trading favors.

In private, the king had apologized for ever allowing Darmon to be arrested, and kept apologizing even after Darmon had accepted his apology. Darmon squirmed at the idea of the king humbling himself. He reassured Theop that his loyalty and their friendship remained strong, then deflected the conversation. "Let us redouble our efforts and get every Atlantean a new homeland."

Theop agreed, but saying he was mindful of how he'd been manipulated into arresting Darmon, he made two decisions concerning Strongyle. First, it was to be settled only by those who could build it themselves, so there would be no profit made by defrauding the treasury. Second, Darmon would not be involved.

"The Plenum is not happy about Strongyle," the king said, "and I will not risk losing you to another round of false accusations."

He knew the king was only protecting him, but it stung. Strongyle had been his discovery, and he had laid out the plan to make it work. Still, he had more than enough responsibilities without it. Droughts had become a way of life. No one could argue they were a temporary aberration.

The Overseer may have uncovered the corruption, and the Court may have absolved Darmon, but now the aqueducts that never should have been built were the king's to fix. The barons tapping the aqueducts to irrigate their fields may have been wrong a decade ago. But in the intervening years, the smaller farms had dried up. The families that ran them, cut off from the capital by the wall, had migrated east. Like it or not, the barons' irrigated fields were the city's only remaining agricultural resource. Without them, Atlantis would be forced to import food, and that would take ships away from the migration.

To make matters worse, the expansive lakes that fed the faulty aqueducts had been drained faster than anticipated. The largest was seven-tenths the size it had been a dozen years ago. The choice was clear. The aqueducts had to be repaired and more efficient irrigation systems put in place, regardless of the cost.

When the Overseer of the Treasuries asked to be replaced by a younger man, Darmon and the king met with him. "You have served me, and my father before me, well. I once told you if you needed anything within my power, you should have it."

"Living out my remaining years away from palace intrigues is all I wish."

The king's eyes darted to Darmon and back. "Would that I could ask one more crumb of service. . ."

The Overseer dipped his head. "Your Majesty has but to ask."

"We'd like you to oversee the aqueduct reconstruction expenditures," Darmon said.

The Overseer pivoted toward Darmon. "I'm trying to retire, not spend my days on the back of a camel inspecting canals."

"You can hire men you trust to do the inspections," the king said. "It is your sharp eye on the ledgers that I need. You know better than anyone what a dent this project is going to put in the treasury."

The Overseer still seemed reluctant.

"I'll appoint a new Overseer to take over all your treasury duties. Your only task will be to scrutinize what's being spent on this one project. Can you give it . . . say, one day a week?"

The Overseer nodded.

"This won't be forever," Darmon said. "As more of the population moves to the colonies, we'll need less food to support those remaining behind. But meanwhile, we have to ensure water for the barons' crops until everyone can leave."

Darmon sighed. When would that be? Relocation was taking longer than anticipated. The problem was, as usual, the Plenum, gumming up his plans.

The Atlantis naval fleet of warships had been pressed into service to transport passengers to the colonies. Now, the Plenum demanded the king reassign those same ships to escort merchant vessels, which they claimed were threatened by raiders. The king had no choice. Darmon understood that. No one could be allowed to challenge Atlantis's dominance over the sea. But it seemed the Plenum wanted a war, even though the enemy was largely fictional.

Darmon couldn't see what the baronial faction would gain from a war, but that there were machinations in play was evident. As soon as the Overseer left, he and the king were going before the Plenum to discuss the issue.

It had started out well, with what Darmon hoped was good news. Ships returning from Strongyle had discovered the mouth of a great river spilling into the sea. An adventurous captain had sailed inland, exploring a rich delta. The river seemed to have no end, so eventually he reversed course and returned to the sea. On his way back to Atlantis, he hugged the southern coastline until he reached the familiar entrance to the great Atlantic. His conclusion was that this fertile area, watered by an endless river, was none other than the eastern end of land to which Atlantis had a rightful claim.

Most significant to Darmon was the possibility that poorer farmers, who were already migrating eastward, might be able to reach this new place by a land route. Although overland passage might be arduous, it could relieve the pressure on the navy to save everyone.

Upon learning of the discovery, the king dispatched a ship to explore the river. He also sent a camel caravan east to mark out a route a farmer could follow. When the ship returned, the captain reported that only at its southern extreme did the river lands seem to be inhabited, and that the area roughly east of Atlantis was unoccupied. That was not true of the coastline along their return voyage to the Atlantic, where the ship had encountered a primitive raiding party—a dozen desperate tribesmen with spears in hollowed-out logs. The captain had easily fended them off, and they had certainly never been a threat. But Nurlano was framing it as the act of an enemy nation.

When the hour for the meeting came, the king and Darmon put on the royal indigo vestments and left the palace together. At the Plenum, the assemblage stood and bowed as the king entered and took his seat on the throne. Darmon sat in his usual place.

Nurlano, alone, remained standing and began his address to the king and the assembled members of the Plenum. "A fortnight ago, a ship of the royal navy was set upon by fast moving boats launched from the northernmost point of the continent by worshipers of Tanit, a female goddess of war."

"I read the report," the king said.

"The attack was completely unjustified," Nurlano said. "The ship was on a peaceful mission, mapping the coastline."

"The ship escaped unharmed and there were no injuries to the crew," Darmon said, for all the good he knew it would do.

"For that, we are thankful," Nurlano said. "Although, I would expect nothing less. Atlantis has the fastest ships and the finest sailors."

Members of the Plenum proffered cries of agreement.

Nurlano nodded and smiled. "They are the brave fist protecting Atlantis, and for that deserve our respect. But an attack upon any ship of ours must not go unchecked. The Atlantean fist must be redoubled and the enemy navy wrecked."

"The Tanits navy consists of crude wooden dugouts," the king said. "The impression I had from the captain's report was that their 'navy' could be wrecked by a couple of new recruits armed with threshing flails."

"An attack against Atlantis is an attack against Atlantis!" Nurlano shouted. His cronies stood and cheered. "We must throw the full force of the Atlantean navy at them." More cheers.

When the noise settled, the king looked at Darmon. "Maybe we ought to hear from the captain first-hand. Have him found and brought to the Plenum."

"He's not available," Nurlano said. "He has already sailed back there with a pair of warships for protection."

They had? By whose orders?

"Do these Tanits have a chief or leader?" the king said. "Perhaps we should send an envoy before declaring war against them."

"That's not what your father would have done," Nurlano said.

True. Darmon knew that wasn't the way previous kings met provocations. But could these people even be considered challengers? Atlantis had always known that stone-age nomads lived on the other side of the Atlas Mountains and let them be.

"We live in a different climate now," the king said. "Our mission is to move the people and culture of Atlantis to new colonies where our legacy will continue to thrive. I am very optimistic about this latest discovery. What are we calling it, Darmon?"

"Khem, Your Majesty, for the rich dark soil."

"Yes. A fertile land with an unlimited supply of water that I'm told will produce more abundant crops than all the barons' lands ever could."

Nurlano frowned. "How will you take it or keep it, if you don't maintain our reputation as a force to be feared? If a state fails to defend the life and property of its people, its enemies will perceive weakness and take whatever they want."

The king shook his head. "You propose dispatching a force of armed men in hundreds of ships to deal harshly with a dozen stone-age spear-throwers in a handful of dugouts."

"No, of course not," Nurlano said. "Send as few ships and men as you need to punish the Tanits. The resolution before us merely includes a provision granting the military the authority to expand the numbers if they deem it necessary."

One of Nurlano's cronies called for a vote, and the measure easily passed.

Darmon sighed. Were he and the king the only men in this assembly who understood that diverting ships currently carrying citizens to safe colonies would cause the people left behind to suffer?

He said as much when he and the king walked back to the palace. "War gains us nothing and squanders time and ships we might use to get our people out of this ever-growing desert."

"I agree," the king said. "Why fight over territory we plan to abandon, anyway? The Tanits have never given us trouble and couldn't give us trouble now if they wanted to."

"Especially now that they're selling us camels. Lots of camels."

The king looked back at the Plenum building. "I can't imagine why the barons would have their minions demand a war."

"Could it be the camels? They had Nurlano build a wall to keep their tenants from reaching ships. Perhaps they fear camel caravans will increase the migration east."

"No one would create a war for that."

Darmon shrugged.

"I'll tell you one thing, I not sending the fleet or starting a war."

"You're just going to ignore the Plenum's resolution?"

"I am. For years, if they opposed a project of mine, they'd just let it wither without funding. Nurlano said I should send as few ships and men to punish the Tanits as I deemed necessary. I deem that number is none."

PART III

CHAPTER 32

Darmon could see that Theop was in a foul mood the moment he stepped into the king's antechamber.

The king picked up a report and waved it. "Another ten years have passed, and the lakes are down to thirty percent of their original size. In a decade there may be no water at all."

"Khem has a great river and rich delta," Darmon said. "I understand there's already been some farming established."

"Yes, but not enough to sustain a culture. According to this report, very few crossing overland made it that far. It's too great a distance to expect farmers to walk. Many only go as far as the lakes and settle there."

"I know." Darmon grimaced. "Techgnosists say the lakes will dry up, and the lake dwellers will be stranded. Again. Our best hope is to press immigration beyond the lakes, following interconnected stream beds and oases eastward while they still have water in them."

"Do that," the king said. "Organize as many caravans as you can and send them overland to the Khem. Tell them to spread the word and pick up stragglers as they go."

"Do you also want me to recalculate how much room is left in each colony?"

"Yes. The rest of our people will have to go to Khem. How are the techgnosists coming with the new Tuaoi crystal?"

"Um. I haven't checked in a while. They originally told me it would take a hundred years. It's only been twenty."

"Well, find out its status, and how they plan to move the Tuaoi crystals when we're ready."

"I don't think that will be an issue. Some effect of the stones' power makes them weigh less than ordinary crystals." Considering the king's mood, this probably wasn't the best day to bring up the matter, but given the way things were going, there was unlikely to be a better day in the future. "Your Majesty?"

"So formal? What happened to calling me Theop when we're alone?"

"Yes. Have you given any thought as to which colony you want to go to?"

The king made a face. "I try not to think about it."

"Construction of a new palace could take years."

"I know."

"Tartessos may be your best choice. It has a sophisticated society, and its Tuaoi power station is well established."

The king rubbed his heart. "I belong to the land of my birth. All the kings of Atlantis are buried here. I don't wish to be the first who left."

"Not so. Hathorah learned that previously Atlanteans left for a thousand years and then returned."

Theop laughed. "I'd be the oldest man alive if I could pull off that trick."

"Joking aside, let's choose a site on Tartessos and begin work."

Theop sighed. "I trust your judgment. If that's your recommendation, then visit the ten districts and see who will give up some land for their king's new home."

"They all will, sir. They'll fight for the prestige of having you near."

"Well, make it clear that I won't be coming anytime soon. I'll stay in Atlantis as long as my people are here."

"The colonists are your people, too."

"Yes, and so are the farmers walking to Khem. It is them I worry about. Set plans in motion for Tartessos, but keep your attention on the people migrating east on foot."

CHAPTER 33

Hathorah dismissed her class early and went to the meditation room on the top floor, where the school governors met informally. During lunch, she'd received word that they were going to meet after school and had "invited" her to attend.

An invitation from the board was more of a command. It was likely she was being called to account for the failure of her decade-long project to awaken in ordinary citizens the recognition that each soul possessed the capability to reach higher realms.

The governors of the school were already there when Hathorah entered. She removed her sandals and made her way to the only empty seat—an isolated cushion at the head of the room in front of the masters. The arrangement reinforced her assumption that they intended to question her.

She bowed to the images on the wall and took her seat. Her mind automatically quieted as she raised her enérgeia to the realm of the masters. Worry fell away. The outcome would be whatever it should be.

The gong sounded, and Xander said, "Hathorah, we welcome you."

Hathorah opened her eyes. "You undoubtedly recall that the Ascended Masters and this board granted permission for the priests to teach a previously secret technique, so when people migrated from Atlantis, the sacred knowledge would not be lost. My original proposal presumed that the priests would cooperate." She waved dismissively. "True, the enérgeia people receive from the priests during the temple service raises them to a blissful state, but the effect doesn't stay with them after they go home. The priests were supposed to teach people how to do it on their own. They aren't."

"I've generally found it impossible to get the priests to do what I wanted," Xander said. "The Mystery School graduates who choose priesthood are seldom our most original thinkers."

"They've turned it into a religious rite," Hathorah said.

He shrugged. "Rituals are what temples do."

A woman governor on the end said, "Hathorah, do you think we called you here to scold you for the priesthood's actions?"

She looked down at her hands. If there was a different reason, she must not have been paying attention to her intuition.

"The drought is forcing everyone to leave," Xander said. "That includes the school. We do not have enough qualified masters to establish Mystery Schools on multiple colonies. We must choose one location and move everything there."

She hadn't considered that there might not be a school on whatever colony the king chose. But surely she and her husband would have to live where the king did.

"We are aware that as First Consul, your husband visited each of the colonies. Consult with him and recommend where we should relocate our school."

A governor across from her added, "It's our understanding that you and he are also going to visit the new land of Khem."

They were? Darmon hadn't said anything.

"We like the idea because it is on the same continent as our present capital."

"But the whales said—I mean, the Court said we should take to the sea."

A governor laughed. "Yes, I suppose the Supreme Nine are the whales of Atlantis government. But they never said which place to go, did they?"

Another added, "Their decision was undoubtedly based on the fact that we had enough years and ships to move everybody. Decades of the Plenum dragging its feet to prevent migration by sea has run us out of time. Were the matter put to the Court today, might they not say 'take the route east?'"

A woman behind him said, "All we ask is that you give Khem due consideration before making your decision."

Wait. Were they putting the fate of the Mystery School on her?

We are, came a collective response.

But how? I am not a—

"We should have led with that," Xander said. "As of today, you are a member of our board."

"But . . . only masters are governors."

From the images on the wall behind her, a thought penetrated her consciousness. *Hathorah, self-doubt is beneath you.*

She bowed to her fellow governors. "I am honored. Beyond words." She turned and bowed to the Ascended Masters. "I will rely on your guidance that I may act just and true."

The sense of honor didn't last long, as a new weight sat on her. No matter where Theop and Darmon resettled, she had to choose the best site for the school—her school—regardless of what it meant for her marriage.

* * *

That evening, Darmon entered their house and took off his sandals. He sniffed the air but didn't smell dinner cooking. Either Hathorah wasn't home yet or had decided to wait until he arrived. He wasn't late—though that happened more frequently that it should.

He stepped into the front room and saw her sitting stiffly in her favorite chair. Smiling, he crossed the room and kissed her. "Hello. How was your meeting?" Something about her felt off. Perhaps it hadn't gone well.

She raised her eyebrows. "Unexpected."

He sat facing her. "I'm listening."

With her fingernail, she drew an abstract doodle in the fabric on the arm of the chair.

Failing to meet his eyes or answer him directly wasn't like her. "What's wrong?"

She shook her head.

"It feels otherwise." Taking her hands, he pulled her up and embraced her. "Tell me everything."

"Let's sit together." She led him to the couch.

He settled beside her, wrapped his arm around her, and pulled her close. "Whatever's happened, we've seen worse. We'll get through it."

She wiggled free and made a quarter turn to face him. "I didn't say it was bad."

"You sure gave me that impression."

"No, just . . . unexpected." She pursed her lips and closed her eyes. "I've been elevated to the board of governors."

He grabbed her and kissed her. "That's wonderful." He cocked his head. "Isn't it?"

She glanced at her lap before meeting his eyes. "It means they think I'm a master."

"Anyone privy to your experience with the whales understands that."

"That was never anything more than my duty to Atlantis."

"Hathorah, even the Supreme Nine hadn't done what you did."

"But I don't feel any different."

"You're not. You achieved a higher state of consciousness long ago. That's why the Supreme Nine chose you for the whale mission. The Mystery School governors may have just figured it out, but Aigna and I recognized it long ago."

"That's kind of you."

"That's the truth." He let the notion of it hang in the silence.

She took his hand. "There's something else."

"What?"

"Why didn't you tell me the king was sending you to Khem?"

Darmon's jaw dropped. "Because he hasn't. He asked me to keep watch on the eastern migration, but he's said nothing about sending me there."

"Well, the board of governors says we're going there together."

"I wonder where they got that idea."

"From the Ascended Masters, I suspect."

"If they foresee it, it'll probably happen. But I've always heard time works considerably different for them. They could be seeing the distant future."

"I've heard that, too."

"Hey, you're a master. Can't you just ask them?"

"I wouldn't presume."

He kissed her. "You've always been humble."

"Well, whenever you get sent to Khem, I want to accompany you. The board is considering it as a possible site for our new school."

"I'd love to have you with me. In fact, I need to go to Tartessos at some point to negotiate a new palace for the king. Fancy a voyage?"

"I'd rather be with you than apart from you, but . . ." She bit her lip. "I'm not sure what duties being a governor of the school entails, or if I'll still have classes. I hope so. I so enjoy teaching. On the other hand, the board wanted me to consult with you about the colonies. Let me ask if that might not include visiting the colonies in person."

He hugged her tenderly. "I'd like that."

CHAPTER 34

The next morning, Darmon applied himself to the tasks the king had set forth. He began by considering all the up-and-coming courtiers to see who should help run the caravans to Khem. The ideal candidate would be young, with a thirst for adventure. Someone like Theop and he before his friend became king. He settled on a cousin of the king, too far removed to be in line for the throne, yet related close enough to wear royal vestments. The man's friends said that he was brave but had itchy feet. Darmon set up a meeting and brought him before the king.

"This is your choice?" Theop said.

Darmon nodded.

"Cousin, I understand you desire to do something on your own."

The youth smiled.

"The exploit we have in mind for you is arduous and contains an element of danger."

"I welcome it."

The king shook his head. "Reminds me of us, Darmon."

"That's one of the qualifications I sought," Darmon said.

The king led his cousin to a table with an open map. "How are you with camels?"

"They never give me a problem."

"Good. I want you to organize a number of caravans to Khem." He pointed out a route on the map. "At first, your duties will be administrative—acquiring camels and supplies, finding competent leaders for each caravan. Their mission is to encourage the outlying farmers to migrate east, and to help them with the move. Once you've dispatched the others, you may leave with the last one."

"May I lead it?"

"If you wish." The king pointed out distant lakes on the map. "It's been reported that many only traveled as far as these lakes, then stopped and planted small fields. Our techgnosists tell us that the lakes are also drying up, and these people will end up having to move again, anyway. When you reach them, unpack your royal vestments and tell them you come under my authority. Say that I wish them to continue on to Khem with all haste."

The man grinned. "You can count on me, Your Majesty."

"Excellent. Darmon will arrange for our techgnosists to educate you on the reasons the lakes will disappear, so you can explain it clearly to the farmers when you meet with them."

"Another incentive for them," Darmon said, "is that we've received reports that the soil in Khem is dark and fertile. Better than where they are now. And the king is granting each of them their own parcel. There'll be no barons telling them what to plant."

Theop raised an eyebrow. "I am?"

"That's what Atlas did, gave each family land. It was only later that the barons duped them out of it. If we're starting over . . . "

The king nodded. "Right. Tell them the farms in Khem will be their own. That ought to get them moving."

"One final caution," Darmon said, "sandstorms have buried some of the wells along your route. Anticipate having to dig them out to water your animals and men."

When the meeting was over, Darmon went to the techgnosia complex that housed the Tuaoi crystals. He should have checked on Baby sooner, but they'd told him it'd take a hundred years. From that perspective, two decades wasn't very long.

He remembered the routine from his first visit. He left his sandals, First Consul emblem, and everything containing metal at the first altar. At the laver, he stripped and immersed himself. When he got out, he changed into a white tunic, gloves, and booties. An intern handed him a white head covering. He walked to the entrance and waited while a pinecone-shaped object was waved over his body. Satisfied, the intern unlocked the door and admitted him.

The chief techgnosist, Sprydion, was waiting for him along with Corval and Maoyl, two women techgnosists he'd met last time. They exchanged greetings.

"You've come to see Baby?" Maoyl said.

"I have."

"This way." Sprydion pulled his headscarf over his face and motioned for Darmon to do the same.

They entered the small floorless chamber, two at a time, and descended to a lower level of the octahedron. He experienced a brief period of weightlessness before hands pulled him into a room far underground. His head cover was now transparent. Above him hovered the great Tuaoi with its ever-changing array of flashing colors.

The techgnosists led him down the circular ramp to the room beneath the Tuaoi. He would have run, had there not been people in front of him.

Last time he saw the baby Tuaoi, it was about the height of his forearm. Now, it was at least twice as high.

"We increased the amount of rays we were feeding it," Corval said. "You can see how the growth rate has accelerated."

Darmon was pleased. "If we need to put it into service sooner, what could it power?"

"A small settlement, perhaps. Not an entire colony."

Maoyl stepped in front of it protectively. "Don't take Baby yet. It's still too small."

Darmon turned to Sprydion. "The problem is, your climate techgnosists tell us the desert is taking over faster than predicted and that we have less time than we thought. Yet this group tells me they need more time."

Sprydion nodded. "Both are facts. The lakes are shrinking not only because the barons are draining them, there is also evaporation. The drier the desert air, the more it thirsts. Smaller underground tributaries that flow through oases and empty into the lakes are somewhat protected from the sun and wind, but the large lakes offer their surface water to the fierce sun and dry winds."

"I understand," Darmon said. "Just today, the king arranged caravans to Khem for those who settled near the lakes. But how long before we all must go elsewhere—even this facility?"

The techgnosists exchanged worried glances.

Finally, Sprydion said, "That's . . . kind of a problem. The ancients called the Tuaoi the 'Terrible Crystal' for a reason. In addition to its bountiful power, it has deadly effects." He pointed to the pyramid that formed the upper half of the octahedron. "The geometry and make up of this structure hold the harmful rays in abeyance. An octahedron—or at minimum, a special pyramid,—needs to be constructed on the colony to house the Tuaoi before we can consider relocating it."

Darmon was struck numb. "Why didn't you say this earlier? Pyramids don't just fall out of the sky. Major construction projects take time. Builders on Strongyle could have started it two decades ago."

Again, the techgnosists exchanged glances before the chief answered. "We don't know how."

"What do you mean?"

"To design the building. The buildings that house the three existing crystals date back to the days of Poseidon. Whatever plans and methods they used to construct them were lost in antiquity."

"You're techgnosists. You've got three examples to study. Surely you can figure it out."

"I have a team dedicated to doing just that. Part of their task has been to devise a container that would let us transport Baby once it's ready."

Darmon clenched his jaw and massaged the back of his neck with his hand. How could men and women who excelled in logic miss the obvious? "What's the use of developing a transportation vessel before you know how to build the destination?"

Corval drew a circle on the floor with her toe. "We were so enamored with the ability to breed crystals, we just didn't—"

"Necessary techgnosia—know how—were lost over millennia," Sprydion said. "Legend has it that they used the Tuaoi itself to somehow carve out the harbor. That our buildings and palaces are made from the cut stones. But if there's any truth to that, it still doesn't tell us how it was done."

"Even if it was true," Maoyl said, "they must have used one of the smaller Tuaoi that were later taken to the colonies. They certainly did not use our big one."

"No," Sprydion said, "no one would let that big Tuaoi loose in the city."

"Of course not," Darmon said. "But time is short, and the desert is coming. Your own people told me that. Figure something out."

He turned and stalked up the ramp toward the lift. Another worry added to his list. Before the drought drove the last people from Atlantis, the techgnosists had better come up with plans to house the big Tuaoi and leave enough time for construction. It couldn't just be left behind.

CHAPTER 35

Hathorah quickly discovered being on the school board wasn't what she'd imagined when she was a teacher. In their meditation room, the governors reviewed each student's progress daily and mentally planted hints for the direction their individualized lesson plans should take. This surprised her, for as a teacher she'd always believed she guided her students from her highly developed intuition and years of teaching experience. Now, she wondered to what extent she had received a subtle nudge from the masters on the top floor.

At the end of the day, she spoke up, "I have meditated long and hard on this before mentioning it, but I must recuse myself from the decision of where to relocate the school."

A ripple of surprise moved through the room. "May we ask why?" "Shouldn't you visit the colonies before quitting the task?" "We thought you were going to consult with your husband."

Hathorah took a deep breath. "I started to. In fact, he's planning a trip to the colonies and offered to take me along. I can investigate them in person if that is what you think best."

"That would be excellent," said the woman next to her. "I don't see that as a hindrance to your duties here. Like the masters on the Court, we don't have to be in the same room to converse. So, travel with your husband and join us mentally."

"That's not the problem," Hathorah said. "My judgment won't be impartial. I have already learned that the king will eventually relocate to Tartessos. The First Consul will live where the king does. That will bias my recommendation for the school's new location. I can't allow that."

"You were chosen specifically for this difficult decision, and the Ascended Masters approved," Xander said. "You can't quit before you've begun."

"I'd be forced to choose between being with the man I love or the school I love unless I recommend Tartessos."

"No," said a woman who had been her teacher when she was a First-year. "It's like when you were swimming with the whales. You experienced the whale's body because you were in the whale's thoughts about being a whale. None of us in this room are any one place. We are all everywhere."

"So true," said another.

Yes, but Darmon hadn't attained their esoteric state. To be with him was to keep one toe in his world. In any case, she needed a favor. He'd ask her if the Mystery School archives contained the original plans for the building currently housing the Tuaoi. She didn't know, but promised to ask the other masters. She'd best do that before they fired her for refusing to choose them over him.

The room shimmered as beings who had become light made themselves known. Though the school taught that the Ascended Masters stayed out of mortal matters, this was the third time she'd been in this room when they'd done otherwise. She was glad. Perhaps they'd come to assign someone else the task.

A thought appeared, then disappeared just as quickly. *Hathorah and Darmon will sail to Khem.*

The other governors looked at her. Clearly, they'd heard it, too.

She bowed and sat up. "If I may ask . . ."

"Yes?" Xander said.

The room still wavered with light. It felt a bit audacious, but when would she get another chance? "Do any of you know where the plans for the Tuaoi containment building are hidden?"

The governors shook their heads. One of them said, "I don't think they exist anymore."

"Oh Great Ones, is this so?"

Hathorah, go to Khem with your husband and take the baby. Then she felt their presence no more.

She looked around the room, and like the other governors, sensed their audience with the Ascended Masters had ended. But . . . the message made no sense. She and Darmon had no children and didn't intend to start any.

So what baby?

* * *

That night, when Hathorah told Darmon she'd like to accompany him on his voyage, his heart swelled. Then it bumped against an incomprehensible wall. Something about Hathorah, an emotional quandary, surprised him. She rarely indulged moods longer than a microsecond.

He brushed her cheek with the back of his fingers. "What's wrong?"

She gave him a weak smile. Again, not like her.

"Is it the trip? Theop won't mind if we visit the other colonies. It's time I took measure of the state of the migrations, anyway. As for adding Khem to our itinerary, it'd be good to see the place in person. So far, we've been pressing farmers to go there based purely on reports."

She stiffened.

So that was it? He patted her hand. "You're concerned that we've sent our people to an unknown territory, sight unseen. Well, so am I. But what choice did we have? Without enough ships to move everyone, land migration seemed the only solution."

She put her hand over his. "That's not . . . I'm afraid my new job is going to separate us."

He kissed her. "I won't let it."

She shook her head. "There are forces at play we may not be able to control."

He frowned. "Okay. Such as . . . ?"

"Thrice I've been told to look at Khem for the new Mystery School. You've already decided the king should live on Tartessos."

"That makes the most sense. Tartessos has an established society, a loyal constituency. All we know of Khem is that it has rich, black soil and a plentiful river—if the reports are even true."

Her brow furrowed. "I admit I don't understand why the masters even suggest Khem. The same logic applies for the school as for the king. Wouldn't it be better to relocate where teachers, priests, and royals have all attended school in Atlantis? No one in Khem has."

"It would." He took her hand in his. "It's not like you to let your mind run ahead. You're worrying about having to decide between colonies before you've even visited one of them."

She sighed. "You're right. It's just that now I've been given a seat behind the veil, I see how subtle cues from beings on higher planes have always influenced us. When a wall of images transforms into light and says, 'Go with your husband to Khem,' they probably have a reason."

"You saw that?"

"Not physically. It was more of an intuitive experience. But I got the message."

He wondered again that such a wonderful woman had married him. His hand caressed hers. "Then we're definitely going there. But, of course, that doesn't mean it's the place you'll choose. Tartessos has a fully operational power station. We don't even have a Tuaoi to put in Khem."

Her eyes snapped to his. "Oh. Speaking of that, I asked if the plans for the original building were in the secret archives and was told that they no longer exist."

"Could you ask the Ascended Masters? Maybe it's in their collective memory."

"I already did."

"What did they say?"

"Go to Khem with your husband."

"Does that mean they're hidden somewhere in Khem? I don't see how. Khem was never part of ancient Atlantis. We didn't even know it existed until a decade ago."

"I have no idea. The whole experience was inscrutable."

"That's the way I felt about my meeting with the techgnosists today. If the plans are lost, they'll just have to study the Tuaoi building here and draft new ones."

* * *

Hathorah accepted that she would have to tour the colonies to find a future site for the school. Darmon didn't know when they would sail, but assured her it wouldn't be for a while. At work, the board surprised her when they said they were adding to her duties.

"We recognize that you miss teaching," said one of the members. "We'd like you to conduct one of the seminars in the teacher training program."

Her? What an honor.

"We're going to need more teachers, so each of us is going to pitch in and instruct our beginning teachers how to impart a particular subject. Since this is your first teacher training program, we thought you should lead the Sacred Geometry workshop."

Good. Something she'd taught for years. At least no one suggested she teach a class in how to sit in a whale's mind.

"All the seminar participants are recent graduates," the woman next to her said. "Many of them will be your former students, so they've already mastered how to form and manifest pyramids, octahedrons, and all other geometric solids. Your task will be to show them how to transfer their knowledge and skill to their future pupils."

She'd always taught young people how to *do* a thing. Now she'd have to instruct them how to teach it. She couldn't use any of her old lesson plans, so she'd have to start from scratch. Still, the challenge of preparing a new course invigorated her. She bowed. "Thank you for this honor. I'll do my best."

"We know you will," said one of the governors.

CHAPTER 36

Darmon asked that the techgnosists meet him at the palace. He'd recently seen Baby. No need to go through all the rigmarole of undressing, bathing, and putting on special garments that a visit to the Tuaoi complex required.

The party of techgnosists sitting in his office fidgeted, perhaps uncomfortable out of their long white tunics. Darmon had a servant bring in cakes and beverages to put them at ease. "Please, help yourselves."

The others glanced at Sprydion, who said, "Will the king be joining us?"

"No."

Sprydion nodded to the others, who quickly emptied the platter of cakes.

"I have bad news," Darmon said. "The Mystery School archives do not have the plans for the Tuaoi complex. The Ascended Masters were contacted and offered no information, either. You'll have to study the present structure and come up with something yourselves."

"I've put a team on it already," Sprydion said.

"Good. At some point in the near future Hathorah and I are taking a ship to Tartessos. If you haven't figured it out by then, I'll be glad to take one of your team with us. Perhaps comparing the architecture of the colony's containment structure with our own would reveal something."

"That's an excellent idea, Darmon. But is there any reason to wait for your voyage? I suggest we send one of my team to Tartessos right away."

"There are ships leaving daily." Darmon wrote a note, signed it, stamped it with the official seal, and handed it to Sprydion. "This is a command for priority passage. Fill in the man or woman's name and have them present it to any captain heading for the colony."

Sprydion glanced at it and slipped it into his case. "Thank you."

"It also serves for their return trip, so they can conduct their study and get back here with the results as quickly as possible."

"Thank you." Sprydion nodded to Maoyl and Katoric. "Proceed." They stood and unfurled a large detailed drawing across Darmon's desk.

"The team working on the transportation container has drawn up a plan. They propose building a stone ark, lined with orichalcum and covered with a lead sheath as thick as the width of your hand."

Darmon studied the planned dimensions. "This will be far too heavy. It'll sink any ship in our current fleet. We're going to have to design and build a much larger vessel. That's going to take time."

Katoric shook his head. "No. One effect of the Tuaoi is it reduces gravity. That's why the main Tuaoi crystal floats in its chamber. We aren't worried about it sinking the ship. We're trying to figure out how much ballast to put in the holds to keep the hull deep enough in the water to be navigable."

He'd never considered that. Good thing Atlantis had brilliant minds like these.

Maoyl ran her finger across the drawing. "The actual ark will be larger than these dimensions."

Darmon cocked his head and waited for someone to explain.

"As you suggested," Forva said, "we've increased the power we're channeling to Baby to accelerate its growth. The final size of the ark can't be calculated until we decide when to disconnect the two crystals."

"Meaning you haven't started making the ark yet," Darmon said.

"Um . . . yes," Sprydion said.

"Then how do you know it will protect the ship's crew from harmful rays, or keep the crystal contained at all?"

"Theoretical mathematics."

"Theoretical? Transporting a thing powerful enough to kill every person onboard and all you've done are a few sums? Shouldn't you build a prototype and test it?"

"Test it with what?" Maoyl said. "We only have the big Tuaoi and the baby."

Darmon sputtered. Maybe the techgnosists weren't as sharp as he thought. "Fabricate an ark and shoot Tuaoi rays into it. See if any leak out."

"Yes. Yes," Sprydion said. "Of course we'll do that. Also, before the time comes, you'll select a specific boat, and we'll outfit the crew and passengers with protective garments like those we wear in the techgnosia complex— just to ensure all are safe."

Hmm, he was going to have to solicit volunteer sailors and inform them about the danger. "All right, you can put away that drawing. What else?"

Maoyl rolled up the drawing and beamed at him. "We've created more seed crystals and are ready to breed another Tuaoi as soon as we separate Baby."

"That's good," Darmon said. "Forva mentioned earlier that you've directed more rays into Baby, speeding up its growth—"

"Her growth," Maoyl said.

"Baby is a she?"

"Maoyl has come to think of her that way," Sprydion said.

"Very well. How much power can she generate at her present size?"

"Enough for a city," Sprydion said.

"But not enough for a colony?"

Corval jumped in. "No, but since we now possess the ability to breed more, some of us believe that instead of waiting to grow one huge Tuaoi, we could arrange and link a cluster of smaller generators throughout a colony and achieve the same result."

Interesting. Darmon turned to Sprydion. "Why didn't you mention this before?"

"The team is divided on the issue. We don't know if multiple Tuaoi in close proximity will cancel each other out, or magnify the effect—"

"Or blow each other up," Katoric said..

Darmon raised his eyebrows.

"We have no reason to think that would happen," Corval said.

"Yet something caused the quake that pushed the cave containing the original three Tuaoi to the surface," Katoric said.

"Don't worry," Sprydion said. "Our best mathematicians are trying to project theoretical reactions."

Oh good, more reliance on sums.

"If linking small crystals proves feasible," Corval said, "it would allow you to take Baby sooner and provide Strongyle with at least enough power for their capital city. As for the subsequent stones, once Baby is out of the way, I want to try feeding multiple smaller crystals at the same time."

The chief glanced her way and turned back to Darmon. "Well, there's a lot of work to be done before we can try that." He ticked off the items on his fingers. "Research and draw up plans for a building. Devise a prototype ark and test it. Build the new building on Strongyle. Outfit a ship. Fabricate safety clothing for the crew and passengers, and train them how to handle the ark. Construct the full-size ark. Separate Baby from the big crystal and pack it in the ark. Transport her across the sea and install her in the new complex." He paused and looked around. "Have I missed anything?"

Sobered, the men and women collectively shook their heads.

"Just one," Darmon said.

"What?" Sprydion said. "You want us to put a man on the moon, too?"

"Not hardly, but I want you to develop a plan for how you intend to get your own people out of Atlantis when the day comes."

"My hope is that what we learn while moving Baby to a new colony can be applied when the time comes to transfer our main Tuaoi."

Darmon recalled seeing the giant crystal suspended in the techgnosia complex. "Now, *that's* going to require a big ship."

"No argument there," Sprydion said.

Forva, sitting nearest the empty cake platter, ate the few remaining crumbs. "Darmon, I've been thinking about your idea of propelling ships with water pumps."

"You said the size of receiver required made that impractical for ocean voyages."

"Oh, it does. But now that we're breeding multiple crystals, perhaps each ship could contain its own tiny Tuaoi. The power for the pump would only need to travel a short distance."

Maoyl gave Forva a hard look—a lioness protecting her cubs.

Sprydion slapped the desk. "We can't get into that. We have all that we can handle."

"I agree," Darmon said. Considering all he'd just heard about arks and protective clothing for the sailors, a fleet driven by Terrible Crystals plying the waters would be too dangerous.

Chapter 37

Hathorah was conducting her first teacher training seminar on sacred geometry. These future teachers had long ago mastered the art of forming the shapes mentally and manifesting them in a higher dimensional overtone. She was trying to show them how to impart that knowledge and transfer the skill to their students. It was a new skill set for all of them.

At this point in her course, she wasn't ready to let them practice on actual pupils. The chance of an inexperienced teacher creating false pathways in a novice's mind was a risk she wasn't willing to take. So she had them practice on each other. Once they understood and perfected the methods of transference, she'd send them into a classroom paired with an experienced educator. Today, they were teaching each other how to manifest basic pyramids.

At the end of the day, she arrived home to find Darmon already there. "No crises at the palace today?"

"No more than the usual daily dozen."

"How are the techgnosists coming with plans for the Strongyle Tuaoi?"

"Fumbling around, taking measurements and writing equations. I fear that unless you can pry more information out of the archives, it's going to take them too long. On top of that, the climate techgnosists have told me we don't have as much time left as they originally estimated."

She kissed him and smoothed the wrinkles from his forehead. "This may cheer you up. Today, I had my students creating pyramids on the twelfth overtone. While I was walking home, it occurred to me that a simple pyramid would provide an adequate framework for channeling the rays in and out of a small Tuaoi—or even a large Tuaoi, if the pyramid were big enough."

"How would it work?"

"It's the geometry of the pyramid itself. You remember this from school— the angles of the structure's sides refract and focus rays within a pyramid at different distances below the apex. We'll just have to figure out which interior point is ideal for the Tuaoi stone and leave a cavity there in which to put it."

"But the current techgnosia complex is an octahedron. It's not obvious because the bottom is below ground."

"An octahedron is just two pyramids joined at their base, with their tips pointed in opposite directions. I'm not sure what pointing the buried half toward the center of the earth accomplishes, but my intuition tells me the half pointing skyward is all you need. So a pyramid should do for Strongyle."

"Even so, nobody's built pyramids for thousands of years."

"I do it all the time."

He gave her a warm smile. "You do. But rather than an etheric creation, we need to put the Tuaoi in a massive formation built from slabs of rock."

"I have a premonition that if you and I teamed up, and you directed workers based on my vision, a pyramid of stone would manifest on this plane."

"To do that, you'd have to go with me. You'd be away from school for however many years it takes to build a pyramid."

"Let's meditate on it. I can probably reach the other governors to ask their advice."

She and Darmon entered their meditation room. He sat on his cushion while she lit candles. "We come to seek clarity," she said.

They settled, and she sensed he'd already calmed. She slowed her own breath, focused her consciousness, and waited. Soon, the answers came to her. When the masters were finished, she inhaled deeply, exhaled, and inhaled again. She opened her eyes and looked at Darmon. His forehead glowed in the candlelight. "You heard?"

He opened his eyes and gave her a soft smile. "No, but I clearly sensed that you did."

She nodded. "They want us to go together and take the Tuaoi with us. Once we arrive, you and I will link our consciousness. The masters will show me the creation of an astral pyramid while you direct the techgnosists traveling with us on how to cut and assemble stone blocks using the Tuaoi."

"Or not using the Tuaoi! I've only recently realized how dangerous Tuaoi crystals can be. I don't want you anywhere near her. The thing needs to stay locked in her ark until the building is finished."

"That's not the plan. The techgnosists have to use it to quarry and levitate the stones. Tell them to make preparations to handle—wait, did you call it 'her?'"

"It's become almost a living thing for the techgnosists. They call her 'Baby.'"

After a moment, Hathorah began to laugh.

Darmon smiled as well. "What's funny?"

"Oh, the Ascended Masters told me to travel to the colonies with you and to take the baby. This was the baby they were talking about."

He smiled. "I'd guess so. But just because it's called Baby doesn't mean it's not dangerous. I want you to follow on a separate ship to limit your exposure to its rays."

She laid her hand on his knee. "I appreciate your concern for my safety, my love, but the instructions were quite clear about us traveling together."

CHAPTER 38

"Darmon, you seem troubled," the king said. "What's worrying you?"

"My mother should have had twins, so there'd be two of me."

"That'd be fine with me. I could do with another you. But I sense that's not what you meant."

"No. I feel pulled in too many directions at once."

"You're more than a king's consul. You're my oldest friend. Tell me about it, and we'll figure it out together."

"It's most urgent we start construction of your palace. The climate techgnosists say the shrinking lakes indicate we have less time than we thought."

Theop nodded. "I approved your plan. I didn't realize there was an issue."

"It's just that I should be on Tartessos already, negotiating with the regents, acquiring land, supervising site preparation. Buildings don't sprout out of the ground overnight."

"They don't?"

"It takes years, especially if—"

The king laughed. "I did actually know that. I was only trying to get you to crack a smile. Don't fret. I miss your counsel when you're away, but I realize it's necessary, so go."

"I can't. It turns out that transporting the new Tuaoi to Strongyle will require a specially prepared ship and crew. We all have to undergo training at the techgnosia complex before we can leave."

"We?"

"Hathorah and I, with several techgnosists who must accompany it and supervise its installation."

"Hathorah?"

Darmon frowned. "It's risky. I didn't want her anywhere near that thing, but it turns out she's the only one who can access the plans for a containment structure. We're going to try to use the power of the Tuaoi to quarry and levitate the stones for its new home."

"Why is this the first time I'm hearing about it?"

"I didn't want to worry you."

The king ran his hand through his hair. "I see why. Two of my closest friends at sea with a Terrible Crystal, then waving it around out in the open cutting blocks of stone—the idea terrifies me."

"The techgnosists are designing protective clothing and a special ark. They say we'll be perfectly safe."

"The same men and women who told me we had a century to get everyone out?"

"Well, that wasn't their fault. They also told the Plenum not to build aqueducts and when Nurlano did it anyway, they warned us that draining the lakes would speed up desertification."

"You're right, as usual. Are you confident their methods will protect you?"

"As certain as one can be with a plan that exists only on papyrus."

"That's supposed to comfort me?"

"This has to be done, and it has to be Hathorah and me doing it. That injunction comes straight from the masters."

The king frowned. "I want this theory tested beforehand. Not Hathorah's part in it, of course. But the techgnosists should take this new Tuaoi into the desert far from the capital, cut up some rocks, and make sure it doesn't kill anyone."

"I don't know if they'll go along with that."

"I'm not giving them a choice."

Darmon nodded. "I'll tell them."

Theop sighed. "What else?"

"Originally, I planned to sail first to Tartessos, get your new palace started, then continue to Ogygia to see how our recent emigrants were adapting, and end in Strongyle, to install the Tuaoi. That was before I learned we can't build something to house it until we arrive there."

"And now?"

"We'll sail straight to Strongyle, get the Tuaoi off our hands, then visit the colonies on our return trip home."

"Makes sense. The sooner you secure that crystal, the better I'll feel about it. Plus, Strongyle having an operational power station will increase its appeal as a destination for remaining Atlanteans."

"I agree. The thing is, the masters want us to build a pyramid to hold it. That could take a decade or two, even with all the masons on Strongyle helping us."

"No! That long?"

"The Tuaoi structures here and in the colonies were constructed thousands of years ago. No one's built anything like it since. Now you see my problem? We can't wait ten or twenty years to begin your palace on Tartessos. Someone you trust has to go there now, and it can't be me."

Darmon and the king paced the floor, walking in circles around each other as if by their perambulations they could grind out a solution.

"Many years ago, on your first trip to Tartessos, you had a young prince carry your report to me," Theop said.

"I remember. Milos. He proved himself a competent and loyal emissary. What made you think of him?"

"I gave him an apartment in the palace, and over the past two decades he's served me unobtrusively, and several times I've sent him as my envoy to the regents when you weren't available. He's matured considerably since you first met him. I believe he's ready for even greater responsibility. We could send him to Tartessos in your place. After all, he's from there."

"Do you mean for him to choose the site of your new palace and negotiate with district regents for it?"

"He grew up a prince among the regents."

"True."

"And he knows how to get them to do what we want."

"He does?"

Theop nodded. "Don't you see Darmon? You can give Milos the building plans, and he can hire honest contractors to do the work. By the time you arrive in Tartessos on your return voyage, he'll have a palace built, and I'll be living in it."

"That would save me from having to be in two colonies at once. The problem is, I haven't seen him recently. He may have gone back home."

"No, he's around, staying out of sight of the Plenum. I'll have him come in for a meeting." The king rubbed his forehead. "Two decades . . . how will I manage without you?"

"Theop, you know it's not by choice. It's the will of the masters. Maybe it won't take as long as we think."

"You said it yourself, Darmon. Buildings don't spring out of the ground overnight."

CHAPTER 39

The next morning, Darmon sent for the techgnosists working on the Tuaoi ark. This time, there were no refreshments. He was all business. "The king wants the Strongyle Tuaoi and its containment vessel tested out in the desert before we leave."

"I thought you were in a hurry," Katoric said.

"We are, but not so much so that the king wants to risk sinking a ship or destroying the new colony."

"Oh, Baby wouldn't do that," Maoyl said.

"Then there's nothing to worry about," Darmon said. "Tracts of former farmland to the east are vacant desert. His Majesty suggests that we take the ark out somewhere far from the capital and see what happens when we open it. If at that point, we're not all dead, then we'll pick it up and see if it can cut stone like the masters' claim."

"Oh, it can facet crystals," Maoyl said. "I'm sure cutting ordinary rock won't be a problem."

Sprydion shook his head. "A test in the desert is a waste of time. We have a lot of training and preparation to ready the ship and crew. We don't have time for field trips. I trust our mathematical models."

Darmon was about to speak when the door behind the techgnosists opened. He dipped his head. "Your Majesty."

The others swiveled toward the doorway and bowed.

The king strode in. "When my First Consul says, 'the king suggests,' that's just a polite way of saying it's an order. I want this whole concoction—Tuaoi, ark, protective equipment—tested. How soon can you do that?"

Sprydion gulped. "Would by the end of this week be satisfactory?"

"It would. Thank you." Theop left as suddenly as he had appeared.

Sprydion turned back to Darmon. "How do you suggest we get it out to the desert?"

"How did you plan to move it from the techgnosia center to the ship?"

"We've constructed a special wagon."

"Well, there you are, then. Anything else we need to discuss?"

The techgnosists shook their heads.

Darmon stood. "The end of the week, then. Let me know the exact day. I'll be joining you."

"That won't be necessary," Sprydion said.

"I disagree. You're going to test it before we leave, and I'm going to be there to observe."

* * *

The test was scheduled for dawn. In the wee hours before sunrise, Darmon arrived at the techgnosia center with a dozen of the king's guards bearing lanterns. The techgnosists, in their protective tunics, hovered around a wagon containing something like an oversize stone sarcophagus with handles on all four sides. It was large, but not as big as he'd imagined. Of course, the baby Tuaoi wasn't that long. Ropes crisscrossed in every direction, securing it to the wagon bed.

While Darmon changed into protective clothes, Sprydion came over wringing his hands. "We don't have tunics for the extra men you brought."

"They won't be at the test site. Their purpose is to clear the streets ahead of us as we make our way out of the city."

"That seems extreme."

"Is it? We don't know that the ark isn't emitting harmful rays as we stand here."

"Yes, we do. We made sure the ark didn't leak Tuaoi rays before we brought it out of the techgnosia center."

"I'm glad to hear that. Still, there's no reason to risk innocent citizens along our route. I've also arranged for a temple priest to lead the procession."

"A priest! That is—"

"Necessary, yes. Anyone seeing us will assume it's a funeral for some baron wishing to be buried in the country."

The chief rolled his eyes. "Politics is certainly a devious business. What about when we return?"

"A baron from the country being brought into the city for burial."

Once dressed, Darmon was anxious to get underway, but he had one more detail to attend to. He'd brought a large funerary blanket, which he had the techgnosists drape over the ark. Another smaller blanket painted with symbols of mourning he threw over the back of the camel pulling the wagon. He only hoped it wasn't their funeral they were riding toward.

The previous night, he'd barely slept, unsure if he and Hathorah would have another night together. He'd tried his best not to disturb her. While she dreamed peacefully, he snuggled against her and worried that the test could leave everyone dead.

He'd never confessed his weakness on Ogygia, where he'd become so despondent Aigna had to contact Hathorah. She knew, of course, that they'd talked telepathically, but he'd never admitted how desperate he'd been. He considered telling her before he left that morning. The last thing he wanted was to die carrying a secret. Yet, in the predawn light, when it was time for him to go, he merely kissed her sleeping form goodbye and whispered, "I love you."

Fifty stades beyond the gate, Darmon told the priest and guards to wait for their return. He and the techgnosists continued to a barren, rocky patch a safe distance away. Or what he hoped was a safe distance. Who knew?

They untied the ropes binding the ark to the wagon. A brief discussion followed about whether the ark could remain on the wagon or should be taken off before they opened it.

"Just get it out of there," Darmon said.

"That could be dangerous," Corval said.

"Sprydion told me it wasn't," Darmon said.

"Let's just try it and find out what happens," Katoric said.

"I'll do it." Maoyl climbed up on the wagon and unfastened the latches. "Clear the area."

The other techgnosists stepped away. Why? What happened to their certainty that it wasn't dangerous?

"Cover your faces," Maoyl said.

Everyone pulled their protective scarves over their heads. Once she opened the lid and picked up the Tuaoi, Darmon's scarf became transparent, and he could see her holding it waist high. The sun glinted off the crystal, and colors began to swirl within it.

"Beautiful," Maoyl said. "So beautiful." She pointed it at a large brown rock and then took a small hand-size crystal from a pocket in her tunic and slid it along a faceted side of the baby. Instantly, a bright beam of light shot out the end of the crystal, slicing the rock like warm butter.

"Satisfied?" Sprydion said. "Now, lock it in the ark and let's get out of here."

Maoyl set the Tuaoi back inside and secured the lid. "You can take off your head coverings now."

Darmon pulled off his scarf and rushed over to examine the rock. The others joined him. Maoyl ran her fingers along the fresh slit. "Amazing!"

"It certainly is," Darmon said.

CHAPTER 40

Darmon and Hathorah leaned on a balustrade overlooking the king's banquet hall, which had been decorated for their farewell celebration. An elaborate feast lay upon the tables. Courtiers would once have crowded the room, but now most had taken residence in Tartessos, kissing up to the regent kings, while others had chosen Ogygia, where they'd be the bigger fish. To make the room seem less empty, the king invited courtiers of any rank who remained in Atlantis.

At Darmon's request, the guest list included the four techgnosists who would be traveling with Baby to Strongyle, Maoyl, Corval, Katoric and Forva. Sprydion, as head of the techgnosia center, would be staying behind. But to avoid hurt feelings, he'd been invited to the banquet as well.

Darmon, and to some extent Hathorah, had trained with those techgnosists who were going, learning protocols for safely conveying and handling the Tuaoi. He'd grown close to them—they had a real love of both Atlantis and advancing knowledge, even if they did tend toward tunnel vision about their own field. The sailors underwent safety training at the techgnosia complex, too, but they stuck with their own, so Darmon didn't know them well. Milos would have been invited, but he'd already headed for Tartessos with the plans for the new palace and a decree from the king giving him authority to procure a site and the funds to build.

Servants passed among the guests with flagons of wine, liberally refilling cups with the king's best vintage. Tonight, Theop was sparing no expense.

"It is unlikely we'll dine together in this hall again," the king had said. "If all goes as planned, I may be in my new palace on Tartessos by the time you make your return voyage."

That was a depressing thought. Darmon shook off the memory of the king's words and tapped Hathorah's cup with a clink. "To a safe voyage and a grand adventure."

"To my great husband," she said, and they drank.

Modifying a vessel to carry the Strongyle Tuaoi had taken time. Hathorah had been able to finish her seminar but had refused to do future teacher trainings. She told him the school governors understood. They should. After all, they were the ones sending her to choose a new location for the Mystery School.

Theop came from behind them and draped his arms over their shoulders. "Ah, my dearest friends. What's to become of us? Barely a hundred and thirty and already torn apart by fate. When we were young, I'd always imagined we'd celebrate our two-hundredth birthdays together in this hall."

The king was growing maudlin again and was apparently doing his part to dispose of the wine. "Why say 'When we were young,' Your Majesty? We've barely reached the halfway point. What's a few years compared to hundreds? Now, don't dampen your party with any more sad thoughts."

The king tightened his hold, squishing them to him. "Oh, Darmon, your words always put me right when my mind goes wrong. Hathorah, take care of this man, he is a treasure Atlantis can't afford to lose."

"I will," she said.

Darmon lifted his cup. "Shall we join the feast, Your Majesty?"

Theop nodded, broke his embrace, and signaled the major-domo, who banged a gong and proclaimed, "His Royal Majesty, Theop, King of Atlantis, Tartessos, Ogygia, Strongyle, and all seas."

Chatter in the room hushed, and everyone bowed. Darmon and Hathorah hung back, letting the king make his entrance. When they followed, the king announced, "Our honored guests, First Consul, Darmon, and Mystery School Governor, Hathorah."

Hathorah demurred and stepped behind Darmon. He saw no reason for her to hide. He was proud of all his wife had accomplished. But then, pride wasn't in her nature.

There followed rounds of toasts, and the guests drank until their cheeks were ruddy. He and Hathorah took tiny sips, making their cups last through a dozen salutes before requiring a refill. They were sailing tomorrow and did not need pounding heads while they were finding their sea legs.

Finally, Darmon quietly suggested to the king that they eat. Theop walked to the head of the table and sat down. "Let the feast commence."

Hathorah and Darmon sat on either side of him. Servants began with the king and then circulated around the table carrying platters of food. When everyone had been served, the servants retreated to the wall, where they stood watching, ready to refill anyone's plate or goblet. The clang of utensils striking dishes, commingled with conversations, creating a merry clamor.

Thunder outside brought the room to a hush.

Everyone looked toward the windows. Nothing happened. In recent years, the sterile rumbles from heaven had teased them, then failed to yield rain. They'd become accustomed to it. Still, each boom spawned a flutter of hope that quickly faded.

The babble of conversations resumed, and the king turned to Darmon. "Is everything ready for your voyage?"

Darmon nodded. "Except the Tuaoi. We'll load that in the morning, just before we sail."

"You're leaving with the fleet?"

"Yes, we'll be with them almost to Tartessos, and then turn to the inland sea and on to Strongyle."

The king frowned. "I know your plan, but I'd feel better if you took two or three ships along as escorts."

"We've discussed that. Four ships carrying emigrants to Ogygia will accompany us as far as that island."

"Warships?"

"There's no risk of attack."

"Isn't there? There are spies everywhere. If anyone discovered what you had aboard. . ."

* * *

They left the next morning with the tide. More than a hundred ships assembled along the ocean coast waited for them. Their vessel passed under the Atlantean bridges and down the long canal that connected Atlantis to the sea. It was Hathorah's first voyage, but not her first time seeing the capital city from the deck of a ship. Its magnificent buildings of red, black, and white stone took on a different perspective when seen from the concentric canals that ringed the city. Through repeated dredging, the canal levels in the center were deep enough to float their ship out. Darmon had been concerned that they might have to transport the Tuaoi fifty stades over land and board the ship at the coast.

A memory of her hundredth birthday came, unbidden. Theop and Darmon had thrown a surprise party for her on the royal barge. The king had even arranged for her great-grandparents to be there, and they were well over two hundred at the time. The boat was garlanded with sweet-smelling flowers. Several bands played in rotation, providing continuous music. She remembered dancing with her great-grandfather as the barge circled the canals. Later that year, he left his body.

Their ship left the port, and the captain took his place in the convoy. Fair weather and good winds carried them north. Hathorah spent her days admiring the powerful force of nature that was the sea. It meant even more to her now that she had seen it from beneath. In the evenings, she and Darmon strolled the deck and admired the star-scattered heavens. During private moments, she tried to describe the world beneath the white caps and swells, teeming with creatures and plants beyond imagination.

The first few days, Darmon frequently went to the hold to check on the ark. Lately, he'd left that to the techgnosists. "Changing in and out of the protective clothing every time is too much bother," he said.

When the convoy reached a pair of towering rocky peaks separated by a wide entry into the inland sea, the captain turned their ship into the morning sun. Four other ships joined them, while the remaining convoy continued toward Tartessos.

Waters of the new sea were dark and looked deep. Their small group of five ships stayed far from the coastal region. Winds shifted irregularly, causing the sailors to scurry about raising, lowering, and adjusting the sails according to commands from the captain that Hathorah didn't understand.

On their third day in the new sea, just after the accompanying ships had turned off toward Ogygia, sailors ran to the starboard side of the ship and pointed. Hathorah and Darmon joined them to see what the fuss was about. Six or seven giant whales breached and spouted and then dove back under. They repeated this twelve more times.

Darmon leaned in and whispered, "Is it them? Your . . ."

"My pod? No," she whispered back. "But they're in a hurry to leave this sea."

"Can you find out why?"

"You mean talk to them? It doesn't work like that."

"What do you think it means?"

"Killer whales could be threatening their young, but I didn't see any babies in the group that surfaced," she said. "Besides, they'd probably form a defensive circle, not flee."

"What else could it be?"

"Could mean a bad storm is coming, even an earthquake or volcano somewhere."

"Dear gods. Shouldn't you warn the captain?"

She took his hand. She hadn't meant to frighten him. "Come with me. Some of these old salts may not listen to a woman."

They approached the captain. "A word, sir," Darmon said.

"I'm busy here. Boson, tell those men to quit gawking at whales and get back to their posts."

The boson gave a whistle and relayed the captain's command.

"Sir, it's about the whales," Darmon said.

"Yes, yes, passengers are always impressed when whales breach. But my men have sailed long enough that they should be used to it."

"It's not that. The thing is, my wife is something of an expert on whales."

"Is that so?"

Hathorah nodded. "These whales didn't just surface to take a breath. They're preparing to swim hard and fast in the opposite direction from where we're heading. That usually means a severe storm or worse."

"I believe we should make for the nearest safe port," Darmon said.

The captain scanned the sky in every direction. "Well, thank your wife for that bit of whale folklore, but after a hundred years at sea, a captain becomes something of an expert on storms. I've checked, and there aren't any signs in the heavens. Now, let me get back to my navigation."

"And how much of an expert are you on earthquakes, Captain?"

"Look, I really do not have time—"

Darmon looked like he wanted to throttle the captain. Hathorah tugged his sleeve. "Let's go below and tell the techgnosists to make sure the ark is secure."

"Do that if it makes you feel better," the captain said. "But look ahead, the sea's smooth as a baby's bottom."

She and Darmon went below deck and gathered the techgnosists.

"We could be in for a rough ride," he said. "Double-check that the ark is well fastened. We should all put on our protective tunics in case it ruptures. You, too, Hathorah."

She did as he asked and donned the white tunic and headscarf, though she did not cover her face. The air in the hold smelled like pitch and worse, and the hull creaked. She thought about the whales and wondered if they were sending her a sign. Perhaps colonial islands were not the safest place to relocate the Mystery School, subject as they were to disastrous hurricanes. Twice, she had been told to consider Khem. Even though it had no colony —just a ragtag bunch of farmer migrants as far as she knew—it had the benefit of being on the same continent as Atlantis. As she had told Darmon, when Ascended Masters drop a hint, it's for a reason. She'd visit all three colonies and give each fair consideration, but the whales' race for safety left her predisposed toward Khem.

The fly in the ointment, of course, was her marriage. She had a responsibility to put the school above her personal feelings, but couldn't imagine being separated from Darmon again. After her time with the pod and his tour of the colonies, they'd vowed "never more." If Khem was to be the place, she'd just have to deepen her skills. Aigna had revealed that the Supreme Nine could be physically anywhere and still attend court. According to the school governors, they could do that as well. If it could be learned, she'd master it.

Resolved that she could act in the best interest of the school and still live with her husband, she went to stand beside him as he took command of the ark and soothed the techgnosists' fears.

"Act rationally and calmly," he said. "It's possible that nothing will happen. But remember your training and we will fare well whatever comes."

"You would have made a good teacher," she whispered.

He shook his head. "I don't think I have the temperament to teach."

She stroked his cheek. Perhaps not, but he had the ability to bolster the fainthearted. For whatever it was the whales feared.

CHAPTER 41

The boom was louder than a whole day's thunderstorm compressed into a single sound.

The water beneath them fled, dropping the ship into a trough deeper than the ship was tall. Great green walls on both sides had them surrounded. The only way out was straight down the trough, but the sails slacked and the captain had only forward momentum to make his escape.

Then the starboard wave crested, becoming an angry maw spewing white spittle. It crashed over them, smashing men into the rails and sweeping loose objects overboard. The ship righted and water poured off her sides like waterfalls. Tossed, soaked, but still afloat.

A few less intense waves followed, and then the sea returned to normal. The captain ordered the men to trim the sails. Darmon and Hathorah went below to check on the ark and exchange their orichalcum tunics for dry ones.

By the time they returned to the deck, the sun had disappeared and a great thunderhead appeared in the distance, spanning the breadth of the sea as far as the eye could measure.

"That looks like a storm to me," Darmon said.

The captain turned to a knot of men. "Secure the hatches and batten them down." He turned back to Darmon. "Still nothing to worry about."

"And the wave that almost swamped us?"

"A rogue wave. They happen."

Darmon made his way below. Safer than being on deck.

Suddenly, it was upon them, pelting rain from every direction, bringing with it the fiercest waves. A man washed overboard. Fortunately, the next swell banged him against the side of the boat and the sailors hauled him up. The captain ordered a thick rope strung along the center of the ship from bow to stern, and the men clung to it when they moved fore and aft.

Waves came from every direction, continually rising and intensifying. The captain pressed hard to go forward, but the waters were uncooperative and the vessel only spun in circles. He ordered the first mate to lash him to the transom, lest he lose hold of the steerboard.

When a particularly high swell lifted them above the rest, he turned the ship a quarter turn and let the storm take them in the direction it was headed. They raced forward, close hauled, the port side nearly skimming the surface. But the wrathful sea was not to be thwarted, and again it trapped them in a trough between two waves that seemed taller than the Atlas Mountains. When the wall of one collapsed against the other, it capsized the ship, and then rolled them completely over.

Below deck, Darmon, Hathorah, and the techgnosists gripped the bindings that held the ark in place. Briefly, they found themselves dangling upside down. Fortunately, the ark remained secure.

Righted, the ship groaned like an old man in the morning and creaked and snapped like an arthritic's bones. The captain brought her about and aimed for a breaker in front of them, catching a rising swell coming from behind. The surge thrust them skyward like a breaching whale. At the crest, they were propelled downward with the furious waters and up again with the next. After each set, the keel hit the water with a sickening crack.

Sailors, holding fast to the rigging, endured for hours. The captain navigated by hunch, unable to see naught but rain and stinging saltwater.

The angry weather wasn't through with them yet. It tore loose the anchor windlass, heaving the anchor skyward. The anchor slammed down onto the deck, piercing the boards. Water poured into the hold. Darmon and Forva and Katoric climbed on top of the ark and pushed the impaling anchor back out. Hathorah and Corval wadded up a spare sail that had been stored below and handed it to them. The men stoppered the hole.

On deck, the freed anchor slid about dangerously until two sailors lashed it to the rail.

A brief glimmer of sunlight above the clouds emerged over the bow, but was soon swallowed by the massive gray storm. The winds slowed to something resembling a gale. The swells became combers. To old sea hands, that meant the water was shallower here. The mouth of a wide river opened its jaw to them, and the sea spit them into it like an irate goddess.

Winds pushed them farther inland on the river for several hours, continuing to thrash men and ship alike. Eventually, the clouds lessened, and the tempest diminished to a gusty breeze. The pitching ceased, and the ship settled into a forward motion.

* * *

Darmon stared up at the plugged hole in the deck. "The worst of it may be over. Stay with the Tuaoi while I go up top and see what's happening."

He gingerly unfastened the hatch and poked his head out. Sailors were hurriedly checking the sails and making them taut. Darmon climbed out of the hold and saw they were in a wide river, proceeding upstream against the current.

"Never saw a storm like that," the captain said. "Should've listened to your whales."

"Where are we?" Darmon said.

The captain shook his head and glanced back the way they had come. "Don't know. I've not seen this place. I tried to make Ogygia, but we never even got near it. I think we're directly opposite, maybe."

A sailor stomped on the makeshift sailcloth stopper, pushing it back into the hold, then spread pitch around the opening and nailed a board over it. "That should keep 'til we make port," he said.

Two men on the bow held knotted ropes over the sides and called out numbers.

"Plenty deep," the captain said. "We shouldn't run aground,"

Darmon hadn't thought of that.

At a point where Darmon judged the river to be about twelve stades wide, the captain ordered the ship to come about.

"Where are we going?"

"Why, back out to sea," the captain said.

"Do you think it's safe?"

"Can't imagine two storms like that in one day."

Darmon watched as they tacked their way through a wide delta he had missed while sequestered below. After several hours, they reached the river's mouth, where the sea rebuffed them with strong tides and large waves. He tore open the hatch and dove below deck, bringing loads of water with him. Darmon secured the hatch, and after checking on Hathorah, turned his ministrations to the other members of their party. As the ship made repeated forays, those below deck were rolled and whipped around the cabin.

Finally, calmness settled. Darmon again took it upon himself to be the one to go up on deck. He found they were back on the wide river, proceeding inland.

The captain handed the ship over to his first mate and came over to Darmon. "My men are exhausted. I'm taking us farther upriver, beyond reach of that storm. We'll find someplace to tie up or anchor for the night and try again tomorrow."

The captain's plan was agreeable to Darmon. He went below and told the others they could come up. Hathorah did. The techgnosists stayed behind, checking the ark and Baby. That was fine with him.

He and Hathorah stayed out of the sailors' way as the ship proceeded. Ashore, the soil was rich and dark. Several hours later, the captain, minding the depths, nudged the boat close to the bank and dropped anchors fore and aft. By then, the sun was low in the sky. Darmon had to shield his eyes with his hand to look in its direction, but in the distance, he saw tall grasses. "Hathorah, look toward the sun. Does that look like wild marsh or some kind of crop?"

She blocked the sun with her hand and looked. "I can't tell."

The day had worn everyone out. They ate a cold meal and went to sleep early.

CHAPTER 42

Darmon was the first passenger up, just after sunrise. The crew, of course, had taken turns standing watch all night. The sun was behind him now, and as it began to ascend, it illuminated the lands before him. On the horizon, tiny figures began to move toward them. "Look!" he shouted to the man on watch.

The man cast his eyes in the direction Darmon indicated. "Captain! We've got company!"

The boson was the first on deck and looked where Darmon and the crewmen pointed. He blew a loud signal on his whistle that Darmon had not heard before. The sailors began to pour on deck, many carrying weapons.

The approaching figures were clearly human—some sort of tribe.

The captain appeared with the rest of the crew. "Hoist anchor, and put us out of range."

Hathorah and the techgnosists rushed up from the hold to see what the shouting was about.

"Best return below until we see if they're armed," the captain said.

With the anchors aweigh, the ship began to drift with the current back toward the sea, but not far enough from the river bank to suit the captain. He and the first mate yelled for the crew to get the sails unfurled. Darmon hesitated to go below and studied the approaching people.

Of course.

"Hold off, Captain. These men and women are farmers, not warriors."

"How can you be sure?"

By now, they were running toward the ship, waving and calling out in Atlantean.

"Because I sent them here. Don't you recognize your fellow countrymen?" He opened the hatch cover and leaned down. "Hathorah, come quickly. We've found the migrants. Captain, put us closer, where we can go ashore."

The captain anchored the ship as near as the water depth permitted and stretched a long plank out to the riverbank.

Everyone onboard went ashore, and the farmers greeted them as if they were heroes. Soon, more came bearing baskets of food and amphorae of a frothy drink they said was made from barley. It became a day of revelry and celebration, though it was unclear to Darmon exactly what they were celebrating. Perhaps for them, that their boat had survived the terrible beating the sea had given her. For the people of Khem, a reminder that they were once part of a great seafaring nation.

Farmers shared stories of the dire desert crossing they'd endured. The sailors rendered their recent trial at sea as a great battle with a god whose wrath they'd barely escaped.

The farmers praised the fertile soil of the delta and the yields of wheat, barley, and flax it wrought. The wives grew chickpeas, lentils, sesame, onions, garlic, and lettuce. Papyrus was so abundant in the swampy delta it didn't require cultivation. More than one farmer mentioned how good it was to tend their own land without barons controlling them.

Children, born after the migration, had never seen an Atlantean ship. They swarmed up the gangplank and chased each other around the deck.

Darmon located Corval chatting with a group of women and pulled her aside. "Who's watching the ark?"

She glanced around at the festivities. "I think we're all out here."

He pointed to the children dashing about the ship and swinging on the ropes. "Sooner or later, they're going to get curious and start exploring the hold. I appreciate that you've all been cooped up too long, but what will happen when one of those children opens the ark?"

"Nothing good." She grabbed Katoric and dragged him toward the ship.

Next, Darmon found the captain, who had been drinking and failed to notice his ship being overrun. He was appalled, and told the first mate, "Clear the vermin off the ship and post a watch."

The joviality continued throughout the day. Darmon and Hathorah were seldom together. Each of them circulated among different clusters of conversation, not unlike an event at the palace.

When the sun began to fall below the horizon, the farmers bid them goodnight and returned to their homes. Sailors who were tempted to follow those with single daughters were ordered back aboard ship by the captain. "We're leaving at dawn. I don't want to be searching the village for you," he said.

Darmon and Hathorah lingered on shore, holding hands and admiring the sunset. "Quite a stroke of luck finding our people," he said.

She smiled. "Wasn't it?"

"I'm amazed they made it all the way to Khem—most of them on foot. They have quite the tale to tell their great-grandchildren."

"I heard," she said. "I wonder what this place will look like in a hundred years."

"Well, it will never be another Atlantis."

"They realize that, and it pains them."

"What do you mean?"

"Didn't you sense it while talking with them during the party?"

"They seemed happy to have their own lands and be out from under the barons' thumbs."

"Oh, they are. But under the surface there's a deep melancholy among those who remember the grandeur of Atlantis. Even the ones who spent most of their lives at more distant farms were proud of being part of great Atlantis. Only the youngest, who were too little to remember, and those born after the migration, are truly happy. The rest are weighed by memories of their ancestral homeland. I wonder if that's what we'll find when we visit the colonies."

He shook his head. "Tartessos and Ogygia have well established Atlantean societies and have Tuaoi power stations. I'm sure recent arrivals from Atlantis felt immediately at home. And soon Theop will live there. Tartessos is about to become Atlantis reborn. Even Strongyle will advance rapidly once we get their Tuaoi installed. I regret we don't have another Tuaoi to give Khem."

She sighed. "I confess, after seeing the whales flee and riding out yesterday's furies, I'd realized islands were risky places to put the Mystery School. I'd made up my mind in favor of Khem. Then fortune brought us here and I saw it. Now, I realize it isn't developed enough to ever be the site for the school. I've decided to keep my mind open until we've visited all the colonies."

"That's better. It's so unlike you to not keep an open mind."

She slapped his shoulder. "It wasn't just that. The Ascended Masters had said we would visit Khem."

He looked around him. "And so we have."

"I just don't think it is a good candidate for a school, that's all."

"The masters trust you, and so do I. In the end, you'll make the right decision."

She squeezed his hand. "Thanks for your confidence. I only wish there was something we could do for the people here before we leave. I'm concerned our visit has brought up too many painful memories—reminded them of everything they're missing. You go to bed. I'm going to sit for a while and pray they forget."

"No," he said. "I'll stay up and meditate with you."

CHAPTER 43

In the morning, Darmon stood on deck with Hathorah, watching the crew ready the ship to sail. The techgnosists were below, double checking that the ark was secured. A small group of farmers came to the shoreline and asked if they were traders. Darmon thought he recognized them from yesterday's party, but he might be mistaken.

Hathorah leaned close to him. "I prayed the Ascended Masters would veil the people's remembrance of Atlantis. Apparently, they did."

He looked at her. "Just like that, and Atlantis is gone? Not even a memory?"

"Veiled, not erased. Nostalgia did them more harm than good. They can never go back. Their farms in Atlantis are already sand dunes."

"But—"

"Look, I didn't do anything to them. I only asked if the masters could relieve their suffering."

He'd certainly resent the masters if they'd tampered with his memories.

The captain ordered the anchors hoisted. Darmon and Hathorah waved goodbye to the people on shore as the ship got underway. They sailed downriver and through the delta, where the captain made two aborted attempts to enter the sea. Each time, huge waves rebuffed them, battering the ship until it moaned loudly.

Superstitious sailors cried that Poseidon was driving them from the sea. Darmon knew that wasn't true. Poseidon was merely an ancient king. Had the masters veiled the sailor's memories, too?

The captain finally withdrew, taking them back upriver to where they'd anchored previously. Instead of allowing anyone ashore, he divided the crew into teams and had them go over every inch of the ship. Some were lowered over the sides on ropes to inspect the planking and transom. Others crawled up the masts, searching for breaks or cracks. Those sent below checked the ship's stores and then donned protective tunics like the techgnosists wore to inspect the hold containing the ark.

The techgnosists, frightened by that morning's battle with nature, came on deck and begged Darmon to have the captain wait a week or more for the sea to settle before they ventured out again.

When the inspection was finished, the captain gathered sailors and passengers alike. His facial expression was that of a man learning his only son had died in war. "Well, you're getting your way, and more. We're not going anywhere soon. At least half her ribs are splintering—that's the frames that support the hull and give the ship its shape and strength."

Darmon looked at his techgnosia team. They shrugged and seemed as puzzled as he. "Captain, what does that mean?"

"It means if we try to reach Strongyle now, she'll fold right in half under our feet. She needs to be repaired. And that means we need a shipyard. Ogygia is the nearest."

It wasn't ideal. It would put them further behind, but he couldn't take the chance of losing the ark. Strongyle would have to wait.

"There's another thing," the captain said. "You're not going to like it. If we're to have any chance of making Ogygia, we're going to have to unload the cargo here. We'll come back for it, of course, as soon as the ship is refitted. But to even make it to Ogygia, I'll need her as empty as we can get."

The techgnosists looked aghast.

"Captain," Darmon said, "I see the wisdom of what you're saying, but to unload the ark we first have to build a structure to contain it."

"Well, we can't go anyplace until you do."

Hathorah tugged on his elbow. He took her aside. "Yes?"

"I didn't mention this earlier, but last night when I was praying for the masters to help the people of Khem, I had the strongest intuition that they wanted me to tell you to use the Tuaoi to build its pyramid on Khem."

He shook his head. "We estimated it will take ten or twenty years to build a pyramid on Strongyle."

"Not if we use the Tuaoi. It could be accomplished in a few weeks—or so I'm told."

"Well, now I'm sorry the people here can't remember where they came from. We're going to need a lot of help."

"You've got me."

He gave her a weak smile. "I know I do. Let's discuss it with the techgnosists and see what plan they can come up with. It doesn't have to be a great pyramid, just . . . the Tuaoi equivalent of a shed. We're going to return for the ark as soon as the ship's fixed."

Darmon brought the techgnosists into their conversation. "Hathorah has some thoughts. Let's go ashore and scout for an appropriate site."

"Perhaps the locals can help," Forva said. "They know the area."

"They definitely will." But first, he'd have to explain to his team why the farmers they'd partied with yesterday had never heard of Atlantis.

* * *

Although the farmers no longer remembered their connection to Atlantis, they were as friendly and helpful as they'd been previously. Darmon asked if they could show his team a good place to quarry stones.

"The arable land ends upriver, an hour's walk or so." said one of them. "I'll show you."

It took them more like two hours to get there, but the site was ideal—a vast wasteland of limestone. They returned and had the captain move the ship there.

The techgnosists, who had remained aboard with the ark, came ashore with Hathorah and studied the area. Darmon returned to the boat and sought out the captain. "I assume with your century of experience, you have not only learned to read the seas but also the high tide marks on a harbor wall."

"Of course."

"That's what I expected. The farmers say this river floods annually. Will you come ashore and identify the high-water marks for us?"

Once they'd worked out the minimum safe distance from the riverbank, the captain returned to the ship. Darmon and the techgnosists met with Hathorah on the rocky plain. They chose a limestone knoll with a flat top, well above the high-water mark as the site for the pyramid. He explained that his wife could mentally construct a pyramid of sufficient size on another plane.

Katoric looked skeptical, though he didn't say anything.

"Look," Darmon said, "All of you attended the Mystery School. You know this is possible. She's been teaching students to do it for years."

"Yes, small geometric shapes floating in front of you. We need a behemoth of solid rock."

"Size is not an issue in the higher overtones," she said. "It can be any dimension we need. But to manifest it on to this plane, I suggest we create stone blocks of manageable size and assemble them."

"Using the Tuaoi," Darmon said. "Like when we tested it in the desert."

The techgnosists nodded.

"I've not told Hathorah this," he said, "but the Tuaoi has a funny effect on gravity. It nullifies, or at least weakens it. Can't that be used to lift the stones in position once they are shaped?"

"This Tuaoi's not big enough," Corval said. "It can probably quarry rock without difficulty, but I doubt its power can lift much more than its own weight. We'll have to get the locals to drag the blocks there and build ramps to raise them in place."

"That will take decades to build even a small pyramid," Katoric said.

Darmon looked at his wife.

She shrugged. "I was told if we used the Tuaoi, it would be accomplished in weeks."

"Not if it can't lift the blocks," Katoric said.

"Well, it is too risky to carry the Tuaoi on a broken ship," Darmon said. "Besides, the captain wants everything out of the holds before he sails for Ogygia."

"So, we need a pyramid," Maoyl said. "Does it have to be stone? I mean, it's the sacred geometric shape that does the trick, right? What if we took the protective tunics we gave the sailors and sewed the orichalcum material into a pyramid-shaped tent? They're not going to need their tunics until they come back for us."

"What happens to the tent the first time there's a harsh storm?" Darmon said.

"It's . . . You're right, I hadn't thought of that."

"I'll meditate on this further tonight," Hathorah said, "and see if additional answers come."

Darmon nodded. "Let's return to the ship and start figuring out how we'll bring the ark ashore."

They worked until dark, building a wide ramp of planks connecting the ship to the riverbank. The sailors pitched in, but scoffed at the notion that the boards would hold the weight of the lead-encased ark.

The sun had already set when Hathorah told Darmon she was going out to the chosen site and put herself in a trance.

"I'll go with you."

"No, there's no need."

"We don't know that. Any kind of beasts might prowl this place at night."

He took her hand, and they walked together all over the knoll, until she said, "I sense the center of the pyramid should be here. Mark this spot so we can find it tomorrow."

Darmon gathered a few loose rocks and built a small pile.

Hathorah sat on the already cooling stone and began to meditate. He took a seat across from her. The heat of the day had vanished and the night air turned cold, but as soon as he connected to her enérgeia, he forgot his physical discomfort. And when she entered a deep trance, she took him with her.

Together they were shown a mystery he was sure even the techgnosists didn't know. The Tuaoi could liquefy the limestone, send it across the ether, and restore its solidity elsewhere on the plain. The rest of the session concerned ordinal alignment of the pyramid. The evening ended with a message to Darmon.

He hadn't been aware the masters even knew he was present.

"During construction, while Hathorah remains in a trance, you'll be connected to her, acting as her voice, guiding whomever is handling the Tuaoi at the time."

The masters might be over estimating his meditation experience. He couldn't imagine holding the connection and talking to others at the same time.

"The masters will be giving you some help," Hathorah said.

"Let me be the one using the Tuaoi," he said. "A direct connection from your thoughts to my hands would be simpler."

"If you must," she said.

CHAPTER 44

The next morning, Darmon told everyone, including the sailors, to put on protective clothing. They unloaded the ark off the ship and moved it to a limestone outcropping well away from the place he'd marked with the rock pile last night. Hathorah went to the center point of the future pyramid, sat down, and closed her eyes. Darmon double-checked his gloves and told the sailors to move away. He and the techgnosists pulled the orichalcum scarfs over their faces and opened the ark. "I'll operate the Tuaoi." He reached into the ark and lifted it out. The techgnosists gasped.

Why? Did they think him incapable? He picked up the hand size crystal that Maoyl had used to trigger it.

"Watch," he said from behind the headscarf covering his face. He closed his eyes and felt for the correct distance to hold the Tuaoi above the limestone and slid the triggering crystal along a faceted side of the Baby. A small tornado formed downward from its tip and a hole appeared in the rock. He moved in an ever-widening rectangle, the tornado tracking him on the opposite side, until he had carved a hole about four cubits square and two cubits deep. He lifted the crystal away from the Tuaoi, and the tornado ceased.

All eyes had been fixed on the operation. Now the techgnosists moved nearer and peered into the cavity. Darmon laid the Tuaoi back in the ark and closed the lid. He removed his face covering and directed their attention to Hathorah.

Before her was a perfectly formed block of limestone, two cubits high and four cubits square.

Darmon nodded toward it. "I think we've just solved the mystery of how Poseidon's original techgnosists built the octahedron and the techgnosia complex."

The techgnosists rushed over and began examining the block.

Hathorah stood and embraced Darmon. "You did it."

"Not me. All I did was allow your enérgeia to guide me."

"Not mine," she said, "the Ascended Masters'."

He turned to the techgnosists. "Now that we see how it can be done, work your equations and tell Hathorah the height the pyramid needs to be and the size of its base."

"We calculated those figures before we left Atlantis."

"Good." He handed each of them a rock from the pile. "Assume this first block marks the center line of the wall pointing toward sunrise. Determine the positions of the corners and place your stones there."

When they finished, he said, "Now we need to make absolutely straight lines between the corners, to define the base of the pyramid. I wonder if the captain has a long rope."

"A rope line won't be precise enough," Maoyl said. "Why don't we use the Tuaoi?"

"We will once we have our boundaries marked."

"No, no, shooting a straight beam of light is one of the simplest things a Tuaoi can do. I'll show you. Everybody cover your face." She opened the ark and took out Baby and the triggering crystal.

246

By the time the sun reached its zenith, the perimeter of the base had been outlined by razor-thin cuts in the stone. These they colored using a soft red rock.

They stopped for lunch and, while they ate, Darmon explained that on a higher plane, his wife had already formed the entire pyramid to their specifications. Over the next few weeks, she would divide it into manageable size blocks and pass the information to him as he manipulated the Tuaoi. With help from ancient masters, an ethereal receptacle would manifest to trap and re-form the limestone in position. "Your jobs will be to monitor the block placement to ensure we maintain perfect alignment. While this is going on, don't distract Hathorah by speaking to her. But you can give her messages through me."

After lunch, Darmon carried the Tuaoi to a nearby hill of limestone and went to work. By the end of the day, they had five large slabs in a line. He stowed the Tuaoi and walked over to inspect them. They were perfectly carved and fit so tightly that a piece of straw couldn't be slipped between them.

"I'm exhausted." Hathorah pushed herself upright and headed toward the ship.

"Me, too. I'll come with you." He turned to the techgnosists. "Someone should stay with the ark."

"Oh, we intend to," Maoyl said. "We'll take turns."

Aboard ship, Darmon shed his protective clothes and started to climb into bed. Hathorah pressed his bare chest with her fingertips. "You're sunburned."

He looked at his arms, which were bright red. "Wow. The orichalcum bends the Tuaoi rays, but obviously doesn't protect against the sun. I'll wear a shirt under my orichalcum tunic tomorrow."

The next day, they made good progress and completed the foundation row along one side. Unfortunately, the following morning, Darmon felt so lethargic he couldn't stir from bed.

After Hathorah shook him awake, twice, she pulled back the sheet. "You're whole body is red as fire!"

She rushed ashore to find the techgnosists, while he drifted off again.

When he woke, Forva and the two women crowded around his bed. Katoric must still be with the Tuaoi.

Hathorah pulled back Darmon's sheet. "Look."

Darmon saw the techgnosists exchange worried looks. That couldn't be good.

"It's the Terrible Crystal effect," Forva said.

The others nodded.

"Quick," Corval said. "Get him into the water."

They carried him off the ship and immersed him in the river. The cool current felt good on his skin.

Hathorah waded into the water and stood next to him as he floated on his back. "Is this caused by the Tuaoi?"

"I'm afraid so," Forva said.

"I thought our orichalcum clothing protected us."

"It does—for short periods, and from a distance. Your husband's been hugging Baby next to his body for hours at a time. No one's ever done that before."

Darmon was feeling more awake. "We need a pyramid, and this is our best hope. What if I wear two layers of orichalcum?"

"That may help," Corval said, "but I think how long you're exposed is the important factor."

"And water immersion," Maoyl said. "I don't know how we overlooked that. We need to build a laver—and *use it* every time."

Forva nodded. "I agree. We can carve out one in front of the pyramid, as we cut the next row of blocks."

"From the color of Darmon's skin, that won't be for a few days," Hathorah said.

Maoyl shook her head. "A few more hours in the river, and his skin will return to normal. But when we resume, we're going to have to take turns using the Tuaoi. No one should hold it longer than it takes to cut a single block, and we'll all wear double tunics and immerse in the laver after each turn."

"But how will you know what size and shape Hathorah wants you to cut?" Darmon said.

"You'll just have to tell us."

Hathorah pushed his wet hair off his face. "He can do that. Darmon, remember they said you'd act as my voice to whoever was using the crystal. They never said you had to do it all yourself."

No, they hadn't. He'd made that foolish decision on his own. When was he going to learn he didn't know more than the masters?

CHAPTER 45

When the farmers discovered the strange structure rising from the rocky plain, they came to watch. The techgnosists didn't have any protective clothing to spare and were concerned about them coming too close to the Tuaoi. Finally, Darmon asked the captain to have the sailors come ashore and form a picket line to keep them back. This was pleasant duty for the seamen, who merely had to stand around talking to the farmers and flirting with their daughters.

Not knowing what was going on, the sailors entertained themselves by making up fanciful explanations. One of the sailors told a girl that the whole thing was some kind of temple and the idea spread.

The pyramid was capped three weeks after it was begun. The techgnosists asked Hathorah to help them construct living quarters near the laver. Even though they intended to seal the pyramid, they'd decided to stay on in Khem to guard the Tuaoi while the ship underwent repairs. Darmon thought that was an excellent idea.

With the building finished, the ark containing the crystal was secured inside the pyramid. A fitted slab was pushed over the entrance and set in place. Without the gravity effect of the Tuaoi to assist them, moving the slab required Darmon and every techgnosist, and a complicated set of ropes and rollers.

The captain wanted the ship emptied as much as possible, so he gave the techgnosists all the ship's stores, keeping only what was needed to feed his crew and the two passengers, Darmon and Hathorah, who were going with him.

On the eve of their departure, Darmon and Hathorah met with the techgnosists. "We're going to Ogygia with the captain because we're already behind schedule. If repairs take too long, I'll exercise my authority as First Consul and commandeer a different ship. These provisions should hold you until then. But if you run low, set up a school to educate the farm children. Their parents will be happy to feed you."

"Probably be a good idea to do that, anyway," Hathorah said.

At daybreak, final goodbyes were said, the anchors weighed, sails unfurled, and the crippled vessel, riding high in the water, headed downriver. A calm sea welcomed them back. Within a few days, the captain found his heading, and they arrived in Ogygia later that week. The captain gave the crew shore leave and told Darmon he was going to inquire about shipwrights.

Darmon pointed toward an inn up the road where he'd stayed on a previous visit. "Hathorah and I will lodge there. Come find me when you have news about the repairs."

The captain nodded and turned on his heel to go.

After securing them a room, Darmon wrote a letter to the king explaining why they hadn't reached Strongyle, and another to the techgnosists still in Atlantis.

"Hathorah, I'm sending a report to the techgnosia center describing how we used the Tuaoi to construct a pyramid. But they won't be able to do what we did without help. Would you write the governors at the Mystery School and ask them to assist the techgnosists?"

She nodded and set to work. When they were both finished, they walked to the docks together and dispatched their letters on a ship bound for Atlantis.

In the morning, the captain reported that he had found a shipwright he thought competent. He promised to examine his ship and provide a cost estimate as soon as they finished the one they were working on.

"How soon will that be?" Darmon said.

"Not long, I think."

"Later today?"

"Not *that* soon."

"All right, Hathorah and I are going to hike up Mount Atlantis."

"That will be nice," she said

Hathorah would be glad to get away from the port, which stank of fish guts and rotting seaweed.

Mount Atlantis towered over the island and looked like it'd be a long hike. "Should we take a lunch?"

"That would be good," he said. "The market is on our way."

Hathorah bought a basket and selected olives, figs, goat cheese, and two barley loaves.

Darmon held up a tiny pear. "Buy some of these. You'll like them. They're sweet."

She bought a water skin, and he filled it with water at a spring in the town center.

They proceeded through the countryside until he found a narrow path he apparently recognized and they started up the mountain. The trail was overgrown, disappearing under tall weeds in places. Where it was bare, loose gravel forced them to climb carefully. They rested at an overlook on the edge of a steep cliff where Hathorah could see the ocean stretching off in the distance. Ships coming into port looked like tiny toy boats. They drank some water and continued to climb. Knotted roots, exposed by erosion, forced them to pay attention to where they were walking.

An hour later, they took another break. Hiking had made her hungry. Hathorah set the basket on a large flat rock, pried an opening in a barley loaf, and stuffed it with cheese and olives. She handed it to Darmon and made another. When they'd finished the bread and cheese, she fed Darmon a pear, then ate one herself. "These *are* sweet," she said.

Rested and refreshed, they resumed climbing. At the summit, she spotted an ancient temple. Darmon went to it, stopped beneath its portico, and held out his hand. She took it, and he led her into the inner sanctuary, apparently long unused. No roof, just an empty room surrounded by columns built from mud bricks. Black marks above torch holders on the columns showed where flames once blazed. Vines growing overhead formed a ceiling of green. Sun streaming through the leaves dappled the floor. "It's magical," she said.

It was magical in another way. Something about this old place struck her as very familiar, yet this was her first time on Ogygia.

"Shall we sit?" her husband said.

"Yes, let's honor whatever deity this place was built for."

They sat together. She closed her eyes and inhaled deeply, beginning her meditation.

"Do you recognize this temple?" Darmon said softly.

She opened her eyes and gazed into his. "It feels like I should, but I don't know why."

"This is where Aigna helped me contact you while you were swimming with the whales."

Ah, that explained it. "I sensed something special here. But then, I didn't see, I only heard you. Do you mind if we meditate a while?"

"Of course not, that's why I brought you up here. I knew you'd appreciate it."

"I do. I also think it may be a good place for me to make contact with the governors of the Mystery School."

"I'll be quiet now," he said.

Hathorah was as comfortable on the higher overtones of this plane and the next as she was in her old school. She could usually reach the governors in a single breath, two breaths if her enérgeia was low. That should not have been the case today, after the draining weeks spent manifesting the pyramid. But just the opposite was true. The frequent contact with the Ascended Masters guiding the construction had left her vibrating.

She inhaled, raising her enérgeia to the thirteenth overtone and held it there while she watched her body exhale. Another inhalation, and she moved into the next higher plane. Hathorah visualized the room on the top story of the Mystery School where the board of governors met, but it was empty. She looked for the wall that held images of ancient masters and couldn't see it. She'd obviously overestimated her abilities.

Humbled, she quieted herself further, and resumed the breathing practices that raise enérgeia, as she prayed to the Ascended Masters.

When they responded, the school governors were with them. "We have given up our earthly bodies," they said. "There's been an accident."

Oh!

Suddenly, Hathorah let out an exclamation. Darmon opened his eyes and saw her lying on her side. Darmon rushed to her, but stopped himself from touching her. What if she'd attained some high ecstatic state he couldn't even guess at?

It was unlike her to make any sound while meditating. In fact, in all the decades they'd been married, he couldn't remember it ever happening before. Still, if she lay in some deep communion with the universe, it wouldn't do to disturb her.

Yet, what if the food they'd bought in the market was bad, or the spring contaminated, or something? High on Mount Atlantis, they were far from any aid. He leaned close to her face and sniffed. There was no odor of indigestion. He felt no sign of illness himself. So perhaps it wasn't the food or water.

Darmon straightened up. Without actually making contact, he began slowly passing his hands above her body like a dowser searching for a well. He didn't know what to expect, but he'd seen healers do it.

Hathorah stirred and caught his hand. She pulled herself into a sitting position.

He stared. She was white as the snowy peaks of the Atlas Mountains. "Are you all right?"

She shook her head.

"What's wrong?"

She bit her lip.

"If you don't tell me, I can't help."

"You can't help." She embraced him and began to weep into his shoulder. "The Mystery School is gone."

What? He must have misheard. She was, after all, mumbling into his tunic. He pushed them apart and looked into her eyes. "Say that again."

"Destroyed. The Mystery School, the techgnosia complex, the Plenum building, most of the capital—"

"No!"

"It's true."

"What about the palace? Is Theop dead?"

"I don't know about the king, but all the governors at the school have transitioned. I'm the only governor still in a body—all that remains of the Mystery School on the earthly plane. We should have moved sooner."

"But . . . how?"

"As I understand it, the techgnosists back on Atlantis were trying to force the large Tuaoi crystal to generate more crystals. They lost control, and it caused a rupture in the earth, raising the land like a bubble, which then popped and collapsed. A series of earthquakes have followed in the weeks since. Atlantis is gone."

Now Darmon wept.

When his tempest of emotions had settled, he dried his eyes with the palms of his hands. "Weeks ago? That may have been the source of those terrible waves we fought." He stood and pulled Hathorah up with him. "Let's go. I need to get a ship back to Atlantis immediately."

"Me, too."

"No, it's too dangerous. You wait here and return to Khem with the captain. I've got to make sure Theop is safe."

"No, you don't understand. I've been given a mission to salvage certain secret teachings from the Mystery School before more destruction occurs."

"I won't risk losing you. Tell me where to find them, and I'll get them for you."

"You can't. Only a school governor can access them and, as far as I know, I'm the only one left."

"Oh, what a horrific thought!"

"I wouldn't have been given the task if there were anyone else alive who could do it."

He took her in his arms and embraced her, as much to comfort himself as her.

They walked out of the temple and began their descent as fast as the rugged path would allow.

CHAPTER 46

Darmon was 130 years old, still possessing the health of his youth, but heart-sick when he saw his city. He'd commandeered the fastest ship in Ogygia. They'd made good time, only to arrive and find the port canal obstructed by great stones and too shallow to navigate. He and Hathorah left the ship and walked the fifty stades to the capital.

Before leaving Ogygia, he'd found the captain of their broken ship. "Hatho-rah and I have to go to Atlantis. When your ship is repaired, return to Khem, pick up the techgnosists, and proceed to Strongyle. Tell them we'll meet them there, but just now I can't say how soon that will be."

The captain hadn't asked why, and Darmon didn't tell him, choosing to wait until he saw proof with his own eyes.

Now he had.

Try as he might, he could not accept that Atlantis lay in ruin. The bridges across the great canals were nothing more than stubs, forcing them to wend a crooked path from one concentric ring to the next. Wide chasms in fa-miliar streets caused them to double back and find alternate roads. Their route took them around the city, just inside Nurlano's spiteful wall. Now it was nothing but crumbling sections like the grimace of a gap-toothed old hag.

A wobbly guard tower stood next to the fallen gate. Darmon carefully climbed to the top and gazed over the Atlantean plains. On the horizon, a once vast lake was reduced to a mere mud puddle. Channels the barons had built to rob water from the aqueducts were full of sand, and their fields buried under dunes.

Atlantis was gone.

He descended the stairs, sat on the bottom step, and held his head between his hands. "Nurlano is surely dead now—beyond reprisal. But the legacy he's left extends as far as the eye can see."

Hathorah rubbed his temples with her fingertips. "Nurlano didn't cause the droughts, or the barons' greed."

"No, but he made them worse than they had to be."

"Shall we go? I need to check on the Mystery School."

Right! What was he doing sitting here stewing over Nurlano? He needed to find Theop.

Entering the city from the direction of the gate was easier going until they reached a gaping hole that had been the techgnosia complex. There, they split up. She headed for the Mystery School, and he stood seething.

Darmon knew better than to let anger get to him. He'd spent a career dealing with rogues and buffoons without losing his temper. Even when threatened by thugs or arrested unjustly, he'd resisted ire. But as he gazed at the surrounding destruction, his blood became fiery. He burned with rage against techgnosia.

The problem with techgnosists, was that when any of them came up with some bat-crazy idea, the others would say, "Sure, let's just try it and find out what happens." Even if an experiment seemed likely to destroy the entire world, no one in the room would say, "Let's think about this first. This sounds really disastrous."

He lifted a chunk of broken pavement and hurled it with all his might at the shattered laver dangling on the edge of the rent. "Look what you've done to our beautiful city!" The laver trembled, then tottered over the edge, and fell so far down that he heard no report.

He took a deep breath. Anger wouldn't help his mission. It was time to find Theop, if he could. He took more slow deep breaths to cool his wrath and worked his way through ruptured streets to the palace.

When he found it, the colorful red, white, and black stones which had once so proudly decorated it were strewn everywhere. Solid granite archways lay in crumbled pieces among splintered planks from once stout doors. Yet somehow the palace itself was still standing. He hoped Hathorah's school had fared as well.

It was dark inside. He should have expected that. Without power from the Tuaoi no building would be lit—even the king's. Fortunately, he knew every corridor of this place. Picking his way through the rubble, he made his way to the king's antechamber. The doors had fallen in, and a man's withered legs stuck out from under them. He had a moment of panic until he recognized the boots as the type worn by the king's guards. Not that he took comfort in the death of any man, but at least it wasn't Theop. He lifted the end of one door and slid a block from the fallen archway under the edge.

Darmon grabbed the man's boots and pulled him free. The man was lighter than a stout guard should have been. Gray molted skin clung to the face. He didn't recognize him.

Putrid air trapped under the door escaped into the room, causing Darmon to retch.

He'd bury the man later. He pressed on, hoping not to find Theop. Hoping the king had escaped.

Wishing did not make it so.

It was in the king's private chamber that he found his corpse sprawled beneath the heavy crush of the fallen ceiling. Darmon slumped to the floor and bawled like he had not since weaned from his mother's breast. Eventually, he got up and began casting aside debris that covered the king.

Theop would want to be interred with the ancestral kings. Darmon was sure of that. The question was, how would he carry him out of here? He needed help. He hated to expose Hathorah to the dread he had faced, but they'd yet to meet another soul.

Once he'd cleared the rubble, he pulled a blanket from the king's bed and rolled him up in it. At least she wouldn't remember Theop the way he'd found him. In an afterthought, he took a sheet from the bed and draped it over the guard's body, and then went to find Hathorah.

While walking from the palace to the Mystery School, a dog crossed his path. He whistled, and the pooch bounded over, wagging its tail. He held out his hand. The dog sniffed him and made a friendly bark. Darmon patted his head. "You look well fed." Then he realized what the dog might have been eating and shuddered.

A voice called from the next street over. The dog perked up his ears and dashed off. Darmon followed him.

When he saw the man who had called the dog, he waved. "Hello. I'm Darmon, First Consul to the king. Are there others still alive?"

The man waved back. "A few, but they'll thank the gods when they see you've come to rescue us."

"There's a ship. You'll have to walk out to meet it. The canal from the sea is impassible. How many of you are there?"

"Twenty or thirty."

"Oh, our ship can carry that number. I'm sorry more didn't make it."

"There weren't many people left. Ships have been taking everyone to the colonies for a while now."

That, at least, was a relief.

"Please gather the survivors and meet me outside the palace. We must lay the king to rest before we can leave." He choked back a lump in his throat. "Oh, I'm sorry. I didn't tell you, the earthquake killed the king."

"The King of Atlantis cannot be dead," the man said.

"No. I regret to say, I've seen the body myself."

"King Theop may have passed, but he had four generations of children, grandchildren, great- and great-great-grandchildren. One of his progeny is bound to be alive, and is now our king."

Legally, yes, but whoever the successor was, he would never be Darmon's boyhood friend, Theop.

"You're right, of course. But we must honor Theop, as well. He was barely a hundred and thirty. He should have ruled for another century or more. Assemble all Atlanteans who remain in this ruined place while I go to the Mystery School."

"There's no one at the school."

"My wife is there."

A few minutes later, he met Hathorah as she exited the destroyed Mystery School. "Did you recover what you came for?"

She shook her head. "It wasn't there. Someone hid it in the Temple of Poseidon."

"It should be safe there a bit longer," he said. "I need you." He took her hands in his and faced her. Tears ran down his cheeks again. "Theop is dead."

"Oh, Darmon, I'm so sorry."

He cleared his throat. "The good news is that there are survivors. They're convening at the palace now. I want Theop entombed with the other Atlantean kings."

"It's only right." She wrapped her arm around him and they walked to the palace.

A crowd waited. He whispered to Hathorah, "Stay with these people while we get him. See if any among them is a temple priest." He stepped forward and spoke to the group. "We have a ship that will take you to safety tomorrow. Today we must do homage to King Theop. Six of you come inside with me. The rest of you make your way to the tombs of the ancient kings."

Darmon led the six into the king's chamber, cautioning them not to step on the shrouded guard. He doubted if any of them had ever been in here before. It didn't matter. All the opulence that had once decorated this room was nothing more than tatters and desolation. He directed two of the men to remove a board from the side of the king's bed to use for a bier. They slid it under the king's body.

Carrying the king's bier on their shoulders, the men exited the palace and solemnly made their way to the mausoleum, where the small crowd was milling about. Upon arriving, Darmon saw that the entrance was blocked by fallen rocks. He would not allow Theop to be denied his familial rest. He began picking up stones and moving them away from the door. Others joined him without a word, and in no time, the entrance was cleared.

Hathorah had managed to locate a priestess who said the appropriate ritual words, consigning Theop to the eternal comfort of his ancestors.

When the service ended, Darmon held up his hands. "If I can have everyone's attention before you go back to your homes . . . Are your houses still standing?"

"Some are."

"Good, at least you had shelter. I mentioned earlier there is a ship that can carry all of you to the colonies, but you'll have to walk to the coast. It sails with the tide tomorrow night, so please start early in the day. It's a fifty stade walk. Also, don't bring much. You'll be able to obtain everything you need in the colonies."

With Hathorah at his side, Darmon moved through the crowd, shaking hands and offering words of encouragement. Suddenly, a little old man's bony fingers gripped his hand.

No. "Nurlano?"

"Thank you, Darmon. I'm glad that you gave the king a funeral."

"You're alive. But how?"

Nurlano shrugged. "I don't know. I'd have stood on the steps of the Plenum and held up the pillars myself if I were strong enough. Does anyone know what caused it?"

If Nurlano didn't know, he wasn't going to tell him. He could see no reason to cause the old man further pain. He guessed his anger was truly gone.

He looked into the old man's tired eyes. "It's a long walk to the ship. Let me find some men to help you."

"Thank you for that, Darmon. You have a good heart. But I'm not going with you."

"You can't stay here. Everyone will be gone."

"Darmon, Atlantis has been my home and my life for over two hundred years. I was born here. I intend to die here."

"There won't be anyone to bury you."

"That won't be necessary. When my time comes, I'll go to the graveyard and lie down beside my ancestors."

"I can't leave you behind."

"You've been a worthy adversary, Darmon. Go with my blessings."

"No!"

The old man smiled. "Surely you must have learned by now, I cannot be moved."

Darmon nodded. Nurlano had never spoken truer words.

Hathorah took Darmon's hand, and they walked away from the mourners. "Where shall we sleep tonight? Do you think our house is still standing?"

He surveyed the surrounding wreckage. "It would be a miracle if it is. And I'm not sure if there is a bridge sturdy enough to cross. Let's see if there is an undamaged apartment in the palace. From there, it'll be quicker for you to go to Poseidon's Temple in the morning."

CHAPTER 47

Hathorah! He had to find Hathorah.

Solid ground beneath his sandals had suffered small tremors all morning. He'd organized the refugees and got them started for the ship while his wife went to Poseidon's Temple. But when the shaking started, he made his way as quickly as he could, winding a crooked path through the city.

The shaking worsened. He leaped across ravines and scrambled over fallen blocks of stone. Fine houses, once the pride of their owners, now looked like derelict old men, with half fallen archways and missing cornerstones.

The stairway to the temple was impassible. He climbed the hill on a path of loose gravel. It was strangely silent. Not the chirp of a bird or squeak of a mouse, only the grinding sound of his sandals on the sliding pebbles and their subsequent tumble downhill as he took his next step. Had Hathorah come this way? Had she made it at all?

His voice gave an urgent cry to the stone pillars atop the hill. "Hathorah! Are you there? Can you hear me?"

No answer. Just an odd, distant thunder behind him. Rain Atlantis so desperately needed? He spat. A hundred years too late.

The path grew worse. He paused and called out again, "Hathorah!"

If she'd made it at all, she had to be up there. That was her sole mission. She'd have no reason to go elsewhere.

His sandals were doing him no favors. He unfastened them and started to cast them aside, then tied their thongs to his belt and let them bang against his hip as he continued.

The path became too steep to walk upright. He crawled on all fours, then on his belly like a skink, digging his bare toes into the gravel, and clawing rocks with his hands to pull himself forward.

He paused for a breath and looked up. The temple seemed as far away as ever. But he couldn't quit now. He had to reach Hathorah. The hill shuddered, and he slid backward in a shower of loose stones.

"Come on, Poseidon. Give a husband a chance."

He wiped the dust from his eyes and tried to find the path. It was gone. No, there it was, over to his left. But now there was a crevice the width of an elephant's back between him and the path. He'd have to forgo the path and climb the rocks. Perhaps the temple had a secret passage and she could just meet him below. He could slide down easier than he could climb up. He called for Hathorah, again.

Still no answer.

Nothing to do but press on. He reached for a handhold and cut his hand on a sharp rock. He sucked the wound, but it wouldn't stop bleeding. No way to continue climbing with one hand. With his teeth, he ripped a strip of material from the hem of his tunic and tied it around his hand.

The thunder behind him became a continuous roar, the loudest he'd ever heard. He drove his feet into the dirt to get enough of a foothold that he could turn and look out to sea. At first, he could not comprehend what he saw.

In the far distance, a blackish-green wall extended from the horizon line to the topmost edge of the sky, where the moon would have been if it were night. But it wasn't nighttime, and what force had built that wall? Darmon remembered the waves that had swamped their ship at sea and had a sick feeling in his stomach.

He had to reach Hathorah. Now! He redoubled his efforts.

The wounded hand throbbed, and between blood and dirt, his crude bandage turned rust-colored. His clothing snagged on the rocks and tore. He didn't care.

In a glorious moment, Hathorah appeared on the balcony of the temple and pointed to him. Had he ever seen a happier sight? He waved, and she pointed emphatically. From her vantage point, could she see a better path? Or was she telling him she would meet him below? He glanced left and right and failed to spot an alternate route. He looked out toward the canals.

The wall of water was nearly upon them.

He turned back to see Hathorah swept toward him as they were both brutally slammed by a force of water too intense for description. He lost sight of her as the retreating water dragged him into the harbor and out to sea amidst a tumult of stones, blocks, pillars, and mud. He fought to hold his breath while his body was slammed and churned by a harsh undertow. His fingers grappled the water futilely, desperately hoping to catch the hem of Hathorah's tunic. It was senseless, he knew. They were nowhere near each other when the wall of water took her.

Fear tugged at him, but he refused to give in. Hathorah was here somewhere, swirling in the same maelstrom as he was. Fear would do neither of them any good. Fear would make his heart race, which would rob him of breath faster.

He put his complete concentration on the point between his eyebrows and tried to apply the techniques he'd learned as a student over a century before. They came back to him as if he'd done them every day. He gave thanks for that.

The first thing he needed to do was to stop the fear. The antithesis of fear was always love. He centered all feelings in his heart on Hathorah and let them expand until there was no room for fear. Next, he had to end the craving to breathe. He consciously slowed his heart until its beat was imperceptible. No heartbeat, no need for air. He relaxed every muscle in his body and surrendered to the ebb and flow of the water. The tide's strength far surpassed his, so it was pointless to waste enérgeia trying to fight it.

Now he was ready to find Hathorah.

With all of his emotional, mental, and spiritual bodies, he stretched out into the ocean as far as he could, mentally calling for her.

Nothing.

In these matters, she was so superior to him, it should have been her reaching out to him. He stopped pushing and started listening.

Still, nothing.

Darmon refused to consider that the fall might have killed her. But she could be unconscious or even farther out to sea than his unpracticed skills could extend. He stopped wasting time thinking and tried again. No response, no sense of her nearby. He mustered all of his concentration and gave it his all.

Failure.

Wild currents roiled detritus about him. A nautilus shell struck his temple, unleashing a pain so sharp it temporarily pulled his attention from the point between his eyebrows. As he struggled to refocus, a memory surfaced of the gift implanted in him by Aigna years before on Ogygia. The old master had warned him he could use it only one time, so he'd saved it for so long he'd forgotten that he had it.

Would it still work, or did it require Aigna's enérgeia to function? She'd undoubtedly died in the cataclysm.

An immeasurable weight of water slammed him into the seabed and dragged his face across the sediment, scraping it like a dull blade.

Well, if he could only use her gift once, and if still worked at all, now seemed like a good time.

Terrible waves continued to thrash him about, but he refused to be distracted. They were outside, he was inside. Darmon brought to the forefront of his consciousness the mental image of the outline of a star tetrahedron Aigna had hidden near the midpoint of his brain. The few sentences of instructions she had imparted decades ago came back clearly. He concentrated and found it. Inside the tetrahedron was a tube torus, a spiral that moved in on itself. At its center was an infinitely small pinhole. That was his goal.

When the old master had given it to him, she promised the tube torus would bring Hathorah to meet him at its center. This would be the ideal moment, even if it were their last.

He let go of every thought, memory, and worry, and dove straight for the small white point of light at the center of his consciousness. He caught the curve of the spiral and went round and round, falling ever deeper, a seemingly infinite number of times.

When he hit the bottom, no Hathorah, no nothing. The gift must have aged poorly, perhaps the framework had distorted over the years. Or perhaps she was gone. He'd never know.

His lungs finally spent the last fraction of air. His world turned black, and he slipped away without ever finding Hathorah.

PART IV

CHAPTER 48

He woke up in the cold, dark room with an urgent need to pee.

And he was naked. Where were his clothes? He scuffed his feet over the stone floor, feeling for them. Failing to come across them, he decided his bladder couldn't wait. He bumped into the stone wall and followed it with his hand until his palm touched an opening. He leaned into the corridor and listened for sounds that anyone else was around, but the place was silent as a tomb. Barefoot, he padded up a long hall, fingers lightly trailing the wall in search of a doorway. A power switch to turn on the lights would do.

The corridor seemed to run uphill, causing him to wonder if he was going the right direction. It only added to his feeling of failure. He doubted there was a trace of Atlantis left at all.

Wait! Ahead was a light. He quickened his pace. Then he saw sky and realized the light was streaming in through a door or window. Naked or not, some urges could not be denied. He covered his genitals with his hands and hoped that no one was around. He reached the end of the corridor and stepped out into sunlight. Instantly, its brilliance blinded him.

"Darmon?" Katoric said. "What are you doing here?"

He shielded his eyes with one hand, keeping himself covered with the other. "Where is here?"

"Why, you're in Khem, standing in the entrance to the pyramid."

"Excuse me, I really need to . . ." He dashed into the latrine.

When he came out, Katoric handed him a tunic.

"Thank you." Darmon slipped it on. "I have no idea what happened to my clothes. Have you an extra pair of sandals?"

"Yes, let me get them." He went into the house near the pyramid that the techgnosists shared and returned with a pair. "Your clothes are the least of the mysteries. In fact, your appearance is a miracle. Hathorah thought you were dead."

"Hathorah! She's alive?"

"Yes, she wandered up from the river a few days ago. We thought the captain had returned with the ship, but she said no. But she hasn't told us—"

"Where is she? Take me to her."

"Last time I saw her she was on the plain, talking with the farmers."

"Please, show me where."

Katoric led Darmon around the side of the pyramid and pointed toward a group of people in the distance. Forva and Maoyl, who were marking out the perimeter of a new building, dropped their implements and ran toward them. "Darmon! How did you get here?"

"I don't know. How did the pyramid get opened?"

"Oh, we had the farmers help us move the slab covering the opening. Hathorah wants to build another—"

Darmon broke into a sprint, waving and calling, "Hathorah!"

She whirled around. "Darmon!" and hurried to meet him. They collided, mid-stride, in a tight embrace.

"I thought we were both dead," he said after they caught their breath.

Hathorah said, "I went under the ocean and came up in the river. I never knew how."

He glanced at the crowd gathering around them. "I'll tell you how when we're alone. But I didn't think it worked. I failed to reach you, and I ended up in a stone tomb."

She hugged him tightly. "I had a constant sense you were somewhere in the ether, but I couldn't find the plane you were on. It never occurred to me to look on this one."

He whispered in her ear, "I didn't know I was in the pyramid. I can't imagine how I got in there."

Hathorah proposed a day of celebration. She sent Forva to the group of farmers to ask permission to hold a feast in their village as thanks for helping them open the pyramid.

"Is the ark still inside the pyramid?" Darmon said.

"Yes," Katoric said, "We only got the entrance opened this morning. Then you came out."

"Good. Leave it in there. It's more dangerous than we could have imagined. Did Hathorah tell you what happened to Atlantis?"

"No."

Darmon and Hathorah had them sit down on the ground and slowly filled them in on what they had seen and what they had guessed about the strange storms that had battered them.

The techgnosists' heads slowly nodded. Tears began to fall. By the end of the story, they were all holding one another, weeping.

Eventually, Maoyl stood and faced the pyramid. "That won't happen here. It can't. This Tuaoi isn't that powerful."

"You think not?" Darmon pointed to the pyramid. "It did that. I held it in my own hands and watched it devour, then reconstitute, solid blocks of rock taller than a man and as wide as an elephant."

"We can . . . manage it," she said. "Hathorah wants to construct a school building and a temple next."

Darmon didn't want to deny his wife's wishes, but he was wary. The deluge they experienced had certainly swept whatever remained of Atlantis into the sea. If the same force extended further up the coast, it may have destroyed Tartessos. The captain had never made it back from Ogygia. Perhaps that colony was lost as well. They may be all that was left of Atlantis.

He turned to his wife. "Look, let's have that day of celebration. The farm families are waiting. We can put this discussion aside and just rejoice that we are both alive."

They selected goods from the provisions left by the ship's captain and carried them to the settlement. The locals added more food and drink, and there was music and dancing. When sunset neared, they thanked the villagers and headed back to the pyramid while it was still light enough to see where they were walking.

Darmon and Hathorah, holding hands, drifted away from the techgnosists, the way young lovers do. The air was beginning to chill, but he was perfectly content strolling with her. When they reached the building where the techgnosists lived, he said, "Hathorah and I are going to meditate on the plain. We'll be in later."

"We are?" she said. "I can't recall a time you ever suggested it first."

He simply gave her hand a squeeze. They walked together around the pyramid and then toward the area the techgnosists had been marking when he'd arrived.

Hathorah broke the silence. "You promised to tell me how we got here."

They stopped walking and faced one another. "I don't know, not for certain. But I'm pretty sure I did it. Twenty years ago, when you were with the pod of whales, Aigna put a star tetrahedron inside of me. She said I could use it to connect us if I ever again became desperate."

It all suddenly came back to him. He swallowed, and his saliva tasted like saltwater.

She hugged him.

He cleared his throat. "Well, with the entire ocean slamming us to the seabed, and you nowhere to be found, it seemed the time had come. So, I opened it, and . . . somehow it brought us to safety."

Hathorah kissed him. He'd been waiting to do that since he'd first seen her this morning. Finally, alone, they could kiss until the sun came up for all he cared.

From a distance, Corval called his name.

"Out here," he said. "What is it?"

"We're discussing if we need to put something over the opening to keep out wild animals."

"Have you seen any wild animals about?"

"No."

"Then do whatever you want. Hathorah and I are busy." He took her in his arms and kissed her again.

After a time, she said, "I thought you wanted to meditate."

"I do. Choose where you want to sit."

They walked across the lines marking out the perimeter of the intended new building and sat in its center.

"The night before we first built the pyramid, you communed with the Ascended Masters," he said.

She nodded.

"I'd like you to try to reach them again tonight. The techgnosists are enamored with their newfound toy. But they never saw the remains of Atlantis. We have. Before we release that Terrible Crystal in Khem again, I'd like the masters' assurance that we won't harm what may be the last remaining citizens of Atlantis."

"As the only governor still corporeal, I received a mandate to build a new Mystery School."

"But that doesn't mean they intended for us to use the Tuaoi to do it. We should ask."

"That's reasonable."

She closed her eyes, and he did the same. He calmed his breath and felt his enérgeia conjoin with hers and ascend. Darmon became lightheaded, as if floating above his body. He witnessed his wife conversing with beings of light. Among them, he recognized school governors he'd known, and ancient sages he'd only seen in paintings. Aigna and the rest of the Supreme Nine were there, too. They must have died in the earthquakes. He looked for Theop, but didn't see him or any of the previous Atlantean kings. Perhaps deceased rulers don't enjoy the company of masters.

"Darmon, haven't you learned to control your wandering mind yet?" said a familiar voice.

"Aigna?"

"Yes. But let's withdraw from the others so you'll stop interrupting their communication."

"Sorry."

"I know you are. Try not to think so much."

"I'm glad to have a chance to thank you for the gift you gave me on Ogygia. Do you remember it?"

"Like it was yesterday."

"I finally opened it when I was desperate to reach Hathorah. I didn't know what I was doing, but somehow I managed to bring us both to Khem."

The surrounding ethers rippled with mirth.

"My dear boy, you're not even a hundred and fifty yet. I was well past two hundred and I couldn't have managed such a feat on my own. No, that tetrahedron's only function was to connect you to Hathorah—and to me, of course."

He felt like a child given a pat on the head and told to go wash his hands for dinner.

"Don't misunderstand. You played your part perfectly and alerted me. But it took a host of Ascended Masters to slingshot you both all the way to Khem."

With reverence, he mentally bowed to her and to the assembled masters.

"You'd better return your attention to the *now*. Your wife is getting the answers you wanted."

CHAPTER 49

Satisfied with the masters' assurance that the Tuaoi, if handled carefully, would not cause earthquakes in Khem, Darmon allowed the techgnosists to use it to construct a new Mystery School for Hathorah. Warned about the dangers of the Tuaoi, the locals kept away whenever the ark was outside the pyramid.

In the evenings, after the Tuaoi was secured, he, Hathorah, and the techgnosists mingled with the villagers. Years of serving the king had honed his skills with people, and he set about establishing a unified community.

Darmon had accepted that this tiny settlement might be all that was left of the once mighty Atlantis. The captain had never returned, and that seemed a pretty sure indicator that Ogygia was also lost in the deluge. Strongyle might have survived, but development there had stalled, waiting on the arrival of the Tuaoi, which was now in Khem. Without the Tuaoi, any Atlanteans there would slowly sink back to the level of the tribesmen they traded with. The people would survive. Atlantis would be gone. The loss of Theop still bothered him, but he realized even if he'd gotten his friend to Tartessos, he most likely would have died there. At least, he'd entombed Theop with his ancestors, even if that tomb had washed out to the sea the following day.

He and Hathorah made a good team. He had the expertise on how to govern. She had the secret teachings and knew how to share them. Once the school was built, development around the pyramid could continue, adding a temple, another laver, and a techgnosia complex. It was the seed from which a new Atlantis might grow.

Two tall obelisks were cut from black granite. Unlike the limestone blocks, which had been dematerialized and reconstituted in place, these were cut as whole pieces and moved using the Tuaoi's anti-gravity property. They were erected, one on each side of the temple entrance. The techgnosists beamed with pride at their latest accomplishment.

Darmon's main concern was that without the merchant trade they'd enjoyed in Atlantis, there was no way to obtain more orichalcum. He limited future use of the Tuaoi and instituted rituals like those he'd undergone each time he'd visited the techgnosia complex in Atlantis. "We need to treat the protective tunics as sacred garments to preserve them as long as possible. Once they wear out, we won't be able to make more, unless we find a source of orichalcum."

They had to face facts. Khem had farmers who grew plenty of crops. What they didn't have were shipbuilders. Even though the Tuaoi could create marvelous stone works, a ship made of rock couldn't float. They'd remain cut off until someone figured out how to build a boat or one of their old trading partners stumbled upon them. Considering how far inland they were, that didn't seem likely.

Hathorah had her challenges, too. During their evenings among the villagers, she tried to suss out likely candidates to become teachers. One evening over dinner, she said, "Darmon, I see that Atlantis did a great disservice to the farmers and people living outside the capital. Except for the barons and upper class, citizens never got the type of education necessary to prepare them to teach at the Mystery School—a fact I was blind to when I taught there."

"Hathorah, you have plenty of time. You've only turned a hundred and thirty. Over the next century, you can train four generations, at least. It may go slowly at first, but you'll find your prodigies. Among them will be teachers, priests, even future governors. And don't forget. We're not alone in this. Powerful beings of light are helping us."

She smiled and kissed him. "Thank you for reminding me."

Chapter 50

The journey from Atlantis to Khem took many Atlanteans years. People continued to straggle in over the course of the next decade, as the last of the lakes dried up. Unlike the first settlers, whose memories of Atlantis the masters had veiled, latecomers brought with them bits of their history and shared stories of days long ago. Most of the established community took these to be myths.

If a new arrival suggested that the pyramid or Mystery School resembled those in Atlantis, well, the people of Khem had their own stories, too. They had witnessed the pyramid and other structures magically rise from the limestone plain, surely the work of gods.

"Hathorah," Darmon said after hearing them talk of the gods in the marketplace. "Shouldn't we disabuse them of this fantasy?"

She shook her head. "Remember that terrible storm that forced our ship from the sea and landed us in Khem?"

"I never intend to forget it."

"The superstitious sailors thought Poseidon was a god keeping them from reentering the sea."

"Yes, I heard them, but I assumed it was just a seafarer idiom."

"It may have been more than that. Some of the previous school governors have suggested that, in periods when literacy drops, the way to preserve and transfer important information is through myth. A good myth can preserve core knowledge for thousands of years."

"Yes, but at the cost of turning the kings of Atlantis into gods. And they weren't."

"Not as you and I remember them. Twenty thousand years from now, when the monsoons return and the desert greens again, would you rather the people carried on their lips the names of dead kings? Or that they just look upon this pyramid in wonder at its meaning?"

"Hathorah, perhaps if I'd stayed in school and done advanced studies like you, I could see twenty thousand years into the future. But I didn't. My world is where you and I happen to be, building whatever we are directed. I don't socialize with those who have ascended to higher planes. I'm only privy to their counsel because you and Aigna have let me eavesdrop."

"Don't be so modest, Darmon. You're able to reach high meditative states with only a few breaths."

He scuffed the dirt with his foot. "We are a good marriage. I hold the community together, while you teach them the secret mysteries."

"Yes, but for their children's children to want to seek the knowledge of ancient Atlantis, the mythology has to contain symbols that they will have to tease out. Students learn best by trials that engage them the most."

Darmon smiled at her. "Here is how I have come to understand it. If I cover first one eye, then the other, my left sees the same thing in a different position that the right. One eye watched drought destroy our beautiful homeland, the other saw us challenged to cross new thresholds. But the third eye watches divinity increase beyond the bounds of the universe, beyond all sacred geometry and symbols."

"Well put," she said.

"Not bad for a Mystery School dropout?"

"If you were my student, I'd say you'd passed."

"Hathorah, I am forever, and always, your student."

"And through myth, our memory of Atlantis will ever be remembered."

The End

And so, to grasp the full value of the mythological figures that have come down to us, we must understand that they are not only symptoms of the unconscious (as indeed are all human thoughts and acts) but also controlled and intended statements of certain spiritual principles, which have remained as constant throughout course of human history as the form and nervous structure of the human physique itself.[1]

—Joseph Campbell, *The Hero with a Thousand Faces*

[1] From Joseph Campbell's *The Hero with a Thousand Faces* Copyright © Joseph Campbell Foundation (jcf. org) 2008. Used with permission.

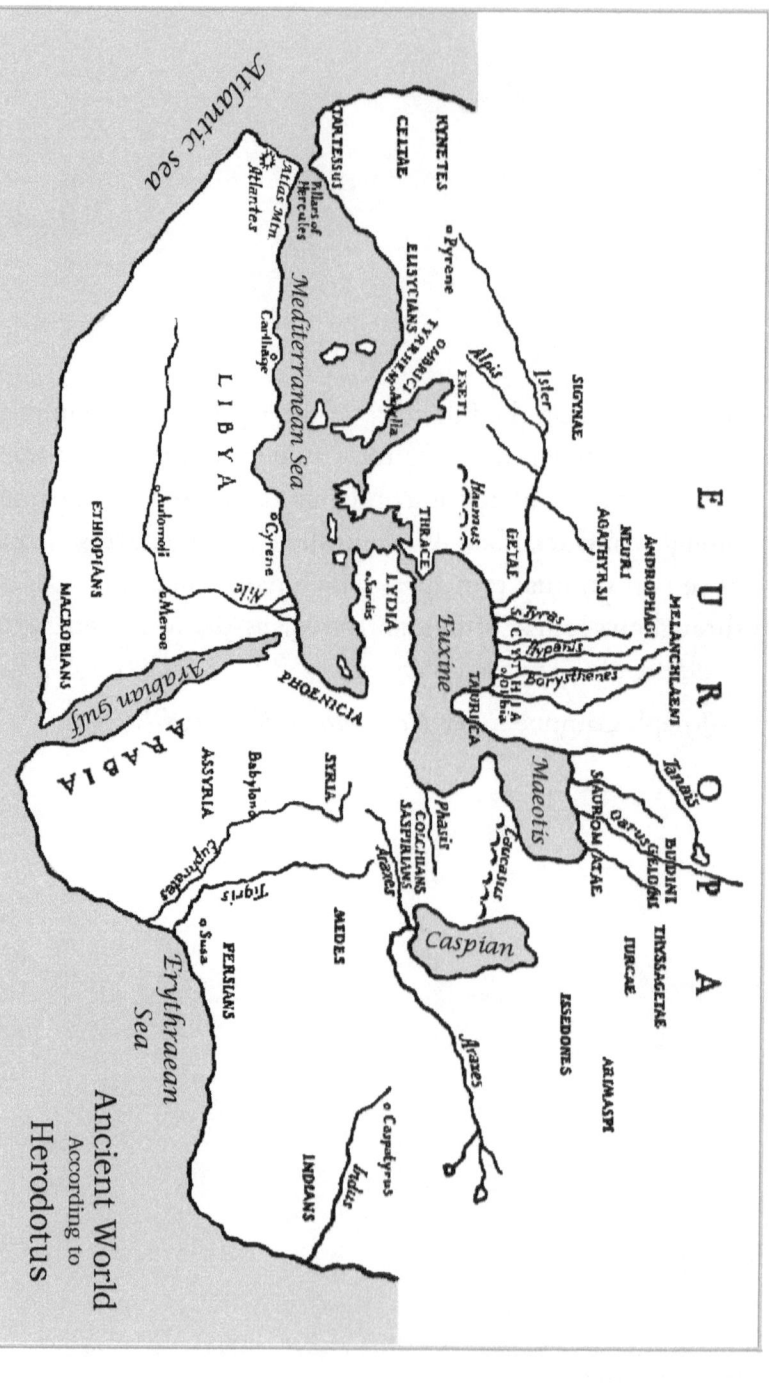

Map by Greek historian and geographer Herodotus places Atlantis on the west coast of North Africa.

Ancient World
According to
Herodotus

Author's Note

My inspiration for a novel often comes when unrelated pieces of information appear in my life and coalesce. This was the case with *Atlantis Dying*. Amid politicians' denials that we are currently in a climate crisis, I learned that science had proven that the vast Sahara had once been lush, tropical wetlands, which completely turned to desert over the span of one or two hundred years. I had also read Michael Hübner's theory (discussed below) that Atlantis had been located near the coast of North Africa, where a land formation uniquely fits Plato's description of Atlantis.

Since the days of Plato, people have searched for and argued over possible locations for Atlantis. What little we know of Atlantis comes to us through Plato, who claimed the source of his information was the great Greek statesman, Solon, who first learned of Atlantis while visiting a temple in ancient Egypt.

Plato passed on many exacting details about the size of Atlantis and its whereabouts. One clue searchers ignored was his statement that Atlantis was larger than Libya. In the same passage, he also said that Atlantis ruled over several other islands, over parts of the continent, and had subjected parts of Libya.

An even earlier Greek reference to Atlantis is found on a map created by the first historian and geographer, Herodotus, who lived about sixty years before Plato. His map, showing the known world of his time, accurately positioned the Atlas Mountains in northwest Africa. Adjacent lands south and east of them, he labeled "Atlantis."

Before the twenty-first century, North Africa was never seriously considered as a possible site. Why should it? Nearly its entirety—an area equal to the size of the continental United States—is the Sahara desert. Each year the central desert receives less than two-and-a-half centimeters of rainfall. That's hardly conducive to a seafaring nation.

Then, in 1956, French oil exploration discovered vast quantities of fresh water two hundred feet below. Twenty-five years later, NASA used a new type of ground-penetrating radar to scan a forty-eight-kilometer-wide swath of the Sahara from outer space. The scan revealed a buried network of ancient waterways crisscrossing the desert.

Dr. Nick Drake, from the Geology department of King's College London, linked NASA and other satellite images to GPS coordinates and visited those locations. There, Drake found shells of millions of freshwater mollusks along the former shoreline of an ancient lake. Once he identified the land formations that delineated the lakeshore, he realized these mega-lakes, as he called them, had been massive.

Investigations at other GPS positions on the satellite images provided evidence that mega-lakes had once existed all across the Sahara, including Chad, southern Libya, and Tunisia. Professor Drake estimated that when filled with water, they would have covered ten percent of the Sahara. In contrast to its appearance today, that Sahara would have been lush, green, fertile, and teeming with life. Yet, North Africa is too close to the equator to attribute mega-lakes to snowmelt. Vast accumulation of fresh water would require monsoon-like cycles, and dips in the desert floor provide that geological evidence of monsoons.

For millennia upon millennia, winds across the Sahara's arid surface deposited layers of its soil into the Atlantic Ocean. In 1995, oceanographer and paleoclimatologist, Peter deMenocal, published a scientific analysis of core samples extracted by drilling deep into the ocean floor off the coast of North Africa. The samples, representing hundreds of thousands of years, contained alternating sediment layers. Reddish sections were accumulated dust from the Sahara blown into the sea during its desert periods. Dark green and brown layers came from minerals that make up the normal seabed. These accumulated during periods when the Sahara had sufficient water to support groundcover—marsh or grassland—which prevented the soil from blowing in to the sea. The core samples showed that the Sahara had switched from wet to dry regularly every 20,000 years. Astronomers found the reason why.

Our planet's rotational axis isn't straight up and down. It is tilted, and the angle of tilt varies over time. In 1984, NASA scientists computer-generated more precise formulas to measure this tilt. Building on NASA's work, Parisian astronomer Jacques Laskar was able to compute that the shifts in our axial tilt repeat in 20,000 year cycles. Although these fluctuations are less than two degrees, they are enough to alter the pattern of monsoons in Africa. For twenty millennia, monsoons water grasslands and fill mega-lakes. Then the earth's tilt changes, the rain belt moves farther south, and the Sahara becomes an arid wasteland until the axis returns to its previous angle.

Across the Sahara, scientists have excavated signs of man's presence on the shores of former mega-lakes. Fekri Hassan, PhD., who holds degrees in both geology and anthropology, investigated the site of a settlement in Libya radiocarbon dated to about seven thousand years ago. Stones quarried from local bedrock form the foundations of a group of houses in a settled farming community. Animals lived along the lake, too. Throughout the site, Hassan's team found beads and pieces of the ostrich shells the beads were made from. At similar sites, Hassan's colleagues excavated the remains of gazelles, elephants, hippos, and crocodiles. Human bones found in gravesites elsewhere along the lakes range from 6,000 to 10,000 years old.

In hills above the settlement, Hassan found a cave containing animal droppings preserved by the sand. These provided excellent material for radiocarbon dating and also allowed scientists to learn about the climate of the period from the diet of the animal. Exploring deeper into the cave, he found human handprints on the walls. He also discovered a cave drawing of a cloud with long wavy lines coming down, which he interpreted to mean rain.

The importance of Dr. Hassan's cave discovery was that it dated the Sahara's most recent return to desert, documented in cave paintings by a generation that saw it happen. Hassan believes this latest great drying of the desert led to widespread migration. From different places in the desert, people migrated toward the Nile. Along its fertile valley, they reestablished their villages, and within a short time, gave rise to the Egyptian civilization.

Peter deMenocal's core samples more precisely dated the latest change. Every quarter inch of a core represents two hundred years. In a segment spanning the last eight thousand years, he found a point about 5,500 years ago where the proximity of the two different layers showed him that a wet, completely vegetated Sahara suddenly switched to one that was bone dry within just a century or two.

Satellites and NASA technology provide new tools for discovering previously unknown geological and archeological sites. Yet with billions of satellite images to sort through, it helps if you know where to look. That's where German researcher, Michael Hübner's algorithms came into play.

Michael Hübner created computer algorithms to refine a range of geographical details and other data. His result identified a site in the Republic of Mauritania, a country in northwest Africa near the Atlas Mountains and in the area Herodotus had labeled Atlantis. When Hübner checked photos on Google Earth, he spotted the Richat, or Eye of the Sahara, exactly where his calculations pointed. It was a caldera-like structure with unique characteristics: a central hill, surrounded by concentric rings that appeared to be dry riverbeds, and a deep crevice that extended out to the Atlantic Ocean, terminating in the possible remains of a harbor. Hübner traveled there and found the specific geomorphological formations and ruins of ancient buildings built from white, red, and black stones that matched Plato's details.

Richat, or Eye of the Sahara (photo courtesy of NASA)

Unrelated to Hübner's work, but also located in Mauritania, southwest of the Richat, is a desert, discovered in 2007, that is covered with whale bones thousands of years old. No one knows how the whales ended up so many miles inland from the ocean, but one possible explanation is a massive tsunami.

Now that there was proof that North Africa once had plentiful water, Hübner's theory became more probable. If true, what would it be like for the Atlanteans to watch their entire country become a desert? And that became the basis for this novel.

While Atlantis's climate crisis was caused by a wobble in the Earth's orbit, and ours is manmade, the common element might be how their leaders and ours meet the challenge. Do elected representatives refuse to deal with the climate crisis because doing so conflicts with interests of wealthy supporters?

Almost daily I find myself astounded at, and befuddled by, political maneuverings to obstruct any efforts to remedy our situation before it is too late. To put a twist on an old cliché, when you're up to your ass in alligators . . . is no time to deny that water in the swamp is rising. Or, in the case of Atlantis, drying.

I was putting the final touches on the manuscript for this book, when the CBS news show *Sixty Minutes* broadcast a segment about the twenty-seven-year-long drought afflicting seven Colorado River Basin states. After reporter Bill Whitaker showed that the water level of Lake Mead had dropped 150 feet, he traveled to St. George, Utah, where in the midst of this drought, Utah is proposing to build a pipeline to bring twenty-seven billion gallons a year from dwindling Lake Powell. Whitaker asked the manager of the water district about the plans. "You're talking about siphoning off water from a lake that is already at a critically low level to help a city grow in the desert." The official replied, "Utah wants the right to do what every other basin state has done."

I couldn't believe it. Real life was making it increasingly difficult to write plausible fiction.

This is a work of fiction, intended to entertain, and perhaps inspire, not to offer a master plan to end global warming. But it might lead readers to ask questions. Who benefits from delaying the inevitable? Do we have modern barons trying to squeeze every last cent of profit before giving up wasteful irrigation methods? Are oil magnates trying to drain every last oil well before retiring the internal combustion engine?

Equally important, the sage advice, "Follow the money." Learn who is backing a politician or writing environmental loopholes which are then enacted.

Pay attention to what we're being sold and its impact. A cell phone carrier recently announced that all customers will get a new phone every two years. On one hand, people are committed to end global warming. On the other, they crave the latest smartphone without considering the impact of throwing away billions of perfectly functional phones to scratch the itch of a well-targeted advertising strategy. I could list other examples, but I won't.

Atlantis tried to save its people by sending them elsewhere. That's not a choice for us. We have to fix the place we live.

Acknowledgements

Thank you to fellow members of Writers Alliance of Gainesville who critiqued the book as I was writing it: Ken Campbell, Pat Caren, Allison Durham, Bonnie Ogle, and Fran Sweeney; beta readers, Richard Beal and Daniel Blumberg; my editor: Dave King; and proofreaders: Pat Caren and Cindy Elder.

Bibliography

All the scientific studies referenced above in the Author's Notes are actual findings reported in reputable journals by the scientists named. The novel, of course, is a fictional story, not intended to prove or disprove the existence of Atlantis. However, several resources about Atlantis are included in the bibliography.

Adams, Mark, *Meet Me in Atlantis: Across Three Continents in Search of the Legendary Sunken City*, New York: Dutton, 2015

Davidovits, Joseph, *The Pyramids: An Enigma Solved*, New York: Hippocrene Books, 1988

deMenocal, Peter B., "Plio-Pleistocene African Climate," *Science*, New Series, Volume 270, Issue 5233, pp. 53-59, Oct. 6. 1995

Drake, Nick, et al, "Three North African dust source areas and their geochemical fingerprint," *Earth and Planetary Science Letters*, Volume 554, London: King's College, Jan. 15, 2021,

Hassan, Fekri, *Droughts, Food and Culture: Ecological Change and Food Security in Africa's Later Prehistory*, New York: Springer, 2007 updated 2002

Hübner, Michael, *Circumstantial Evidence for Plato's Island Atlantis in the Souss-Massa plain in today's South-Morocco*, Germany: asalas.org, 2008 updated 2012
https://web.archive.org/web/20190325094903/http://asalas.com/doku.php

Hübner, Michael, and Hübner, Sebastian, *New Evidence for a Large Prehistoric Settlement in a Caldera-Like Geomorphological Structure in Southwest Morocco*, Germany: asalas.org, 2012
https://web.archive.org/web/20190325094903/http://asalas.com/doku.php

O'Connell, Tony, *Atlantipedia: An A–Z Guide to the Search for Plato's Atlantis*, (a well-organized website for researching all things Atlantis)
https://atlantipedia.ie

Plato, *Critias*, translated by Benjamin Jowett, New York: Scribner's Sons, 1871

Plato, *Timaeus*, translated by Benjamin Jowett, New York: Scribner's Sons, 1871

ABOUT THE AUTHOR

Richard Gartee is an award-winning novelist who has also authored seven college textbooks, eight novels, six collections of poetry, a biography, and the history of the Hippodrome Theatre.

A complete list of his available titles, upcoming events, and forthcoming books is available at **www.gartee.com** where you can also sign up to receive updates on his newest publications as they become available.

Also, please take a moment to leave a short review on Amazon and/or other booksellers' websites. Reviews help to sell books, and sales help an author to keep writing. You can readily find links to online booksellers' websites by visiting www.gartee.com and clicking on the book cover image.

www.ingramcontent.com/pod-product-compliance
Lightning Source LLC
Chambersburg PA
CBHW030804210726
48290CB00002B/426